A Fallen Hero Rises

Book One: Sword of Kassandra Series

M Joseph Murphy

A Fallen Hero Rises

Copyright © 2014 Council of Peacocks Press
All rights reserved.
Editors: L.A. Johannesson, Christie Stratos, & Mary Jae Blakney
ISBN 978-0-9919503-4-8

Cover design by M Joseph Murphy
M Joseph Murphy's Official Website: mjosephmurphy.info

First electronic Edition: December 2013
First Paperback Edition: June 2014

Praise for *M Joseph Murphy*

"You dive into this world and feel for once someone has not re-told the same story with just a different colouring."

- CHRISTOPH FISCHER,
author of *The Three Nations Trilogy*.

"The Council of Peacocks has it all: epic battles, conspiracy theories, romance, and a great story line. The first page will suck you into a complex and unpredictable, page-turning plot."

- TIFFANY HUSON

"This is precisely the kind of book I enjoy reading. It hits all the buttons: Epic battles, …moments of self-discovery, …tales of heroes and villains, and of course there's loads of angst ridden teenagers with badass paranormal/psychokinesis abilities."

- TRAVIS LUEDKE,
Author of *The Nightlife Series*

Works by M Joseph Murphy

ACTIVATION SERIES
Council of Peacocks
Beyond the Black Sea
Terra Incognita (Coming 2015)

SWORD OF KASSANDRA SERIES
A Fallen Hero Rises
Demons of DunDegore (Coming Sept 2014)

Dedication

This book is dedicated to my mother, Sylvia Murphy. She passed away six months before my first book, Council of Peacocks, was published. She was a gifted painter and musician, granting me the freedom to pursue my own art. I owe her everything.

"He who makes a beast of himself gets rid of the pain of being a man."

- Samuel Johnson

"He who fights monsters should see to it that he himself does not become a monster."

- Friedrich Nietzsche

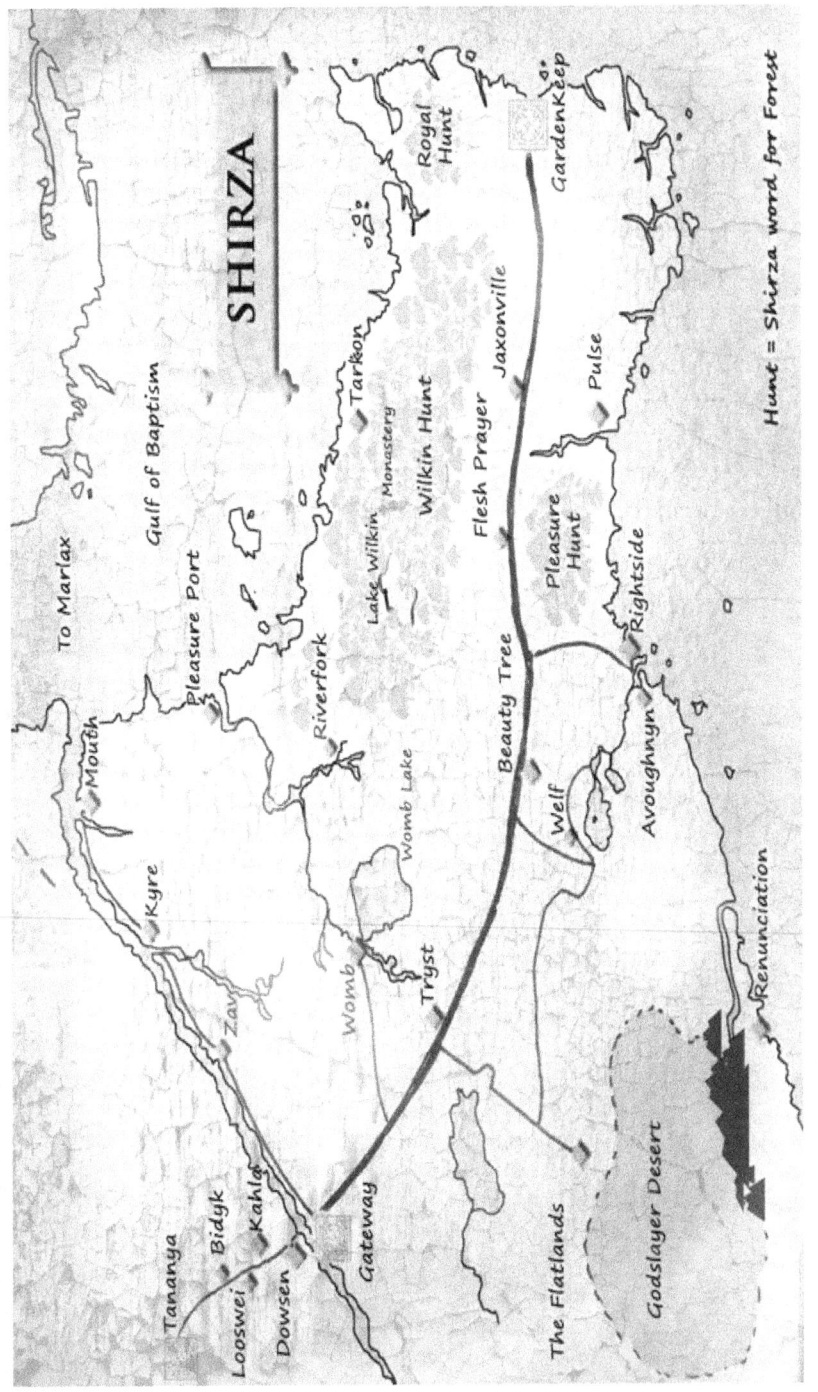

SHIRZA

Hunt = Shirza word for Forest

Dramatis Personae

PROTAGONISTS

Tadgh Dooley — Pronounced Tig (like "tiger" without the "er"). Eighteen years old. High school student from Cleveland, Ohio. Possesses ability to make his wishes come true...at a price. With each wish, he damages the reality field. After the death of his lover, made a deal with a demon named Bes. Lands at the monastery of the Brotherhood of Tyche, wounded near death and amnesiac.

The Sage — Mysterious wise man from the city of GardenKeep. Real name unknown. Consultant to fieldbender guild of Karaj Robat. Possesses magical abilities including elemental control over fire.

THE BROTHERHOOD OF TYCHE

Instructor Mal — Age unknown. Head of the monastery in Shirza. Leader of the Brotherhood

Menphis Bannmerci — Up-and-coming member of the Brotherhood. Assigned as Tadgh's mentor. From the small town of Tarkon in the country of Shirza.

Shonndira Bannmerci — Normally called Shonn. Cousin to Menphis (their fathers are brothers). Servant who works in the kitchens of the monastery. A fod sel-onde with powers of premonition.

Prelate Leif — Lead investigator/spy. Works directly with Instructor Mal to gather information

Prelate Fin — Primary healer in the infirmary

Mirelda — Head of the monastery's kitchen. Shonn's boss.

FIELDBENDER GUILD OF KARAJ ROBAT

Latimier	Head of the fieldbender guild at Karaj Robat.
Eschandel	Member of inner circle at Karaj Robat. Former hunter of fod sel-onde. Recognizes how dangerous Tadgh is and wants him killed.
Siron	Member of the inner circle at Karaj Robat. Skeptic of the damage Tadgh is causing.
Mikhel	Young initiate stationed in DunDegore. Sent to Karaj Robat to inform Karaj Robat about the Sword of Kassandra.
Arem	Kvartermester in charge of the soldiers hunting Tadgh
Ceolbeorht	Minor fieldbender. One of the soldiers hunting Tadgh. Brother to Arem.

ARMIES OF DISPAYRE

General Vyken	Member of the royal family. Stealing artifacts for unknown reason.
Oshu	Fieldbender working with General Vyken
Desdemona	Assistant to General Vyken. An illuminati. Advanced martial arts.
Ein	Assistant to General Vyken. A dem straki. Magical abilities similar to fieldbenders.

MINOR CHARACTERS

Barnes	Assistant to the Sage
Pwella	Barnes lady friend. Works in the kitchen of Lord Vyken's fortress
Gnocko Fnesh	A frie stav from the subterranean country of Trelium, north of the Badlands. Contract-ed by the Sage to investigate General Vyken.
Eiodeesh Mai'Var	Work partner to Gnocko. Trofast warrior raised by a Sirian adopted father.

Chapter One

In the fieldbender guild of Karaj Robat, the Sage closed his eyes in silent prayer. 'Some things you can't come back from. Let's hope this is not one of them.'

His red leather boots stepped quickly over white marble floors as he headed towards the council chamber. Square columns lined the open-air corridor. A cool breeze from the storm raging outside ruffled his high-collared military cape. It did little to cool his temperament. Acolytes in white robes bowed their heads in respect as he passed. He ignored them all, clenching and unclenching his fists, eyes straight ahead. This was no time to pretend he cared about decorum.

Guards flanked either side of the chamber entrance. They stood at attention, hands resting on the hilts of their swords. Both wore ceremonial armor embroidered with the crest of Karaj Robat: a crow superimposed on a red mountain.

The Sage did not slow down as he approached. One guard held up a hand, blocking his path.

"No entry," the guard said. "Fieldbenders only."

The Sage raised one eyebrow and glanced at the other guard.

"Sorry, sir," the second guard said. "He's new. Baubi, stop being an idjit. Let him pass."

The first guard, Baubi, shook his head. "Sorry, Jaymes. I'm not risking my job based on your recommendation. Why would I let this stranger in? I don't even know his name."

Jaymes, the second guard, coughed and went pale. "He's not a stranger. This is the Sage. He's been a consultant to the fieldbenders since before you were born."

Baubi tightened his grip on the hilt. "Stop making fun of how young I am. Besides, the Sage is a position, not a name."

The Sage cleared his throat. "As amusing as you clowns are, I have places to be. I'm expected inside. No one here knows my true name. Names have power. Everyone calls me the Sage. Now are you going to step aside or do I have to push you?"

Baubi started to draw his sword. Jaymes grabbed his arm to stop him.

The Sage's eyes flashed red with an internal flame.

"Please go in, sir," Jaymes said. He quickly opened the twin doors to the chamber. As the doors shut behind him, the Sage heard the two guards continue to bicker.

The meeting had already begun. The council chamber was a large, round room. Tall, gilded columns encircled the room. Between the columns, hundreds of fieldbenders spoke to each other in hushed tones. Most were initiates dressed in white robes. Many blinked rapidly while others nervously glanced at the shadows.

'They look nervous,' the Sage thought. 'That's a good sign. It means they're taking this seriously.'

He pushed through the crowd to reach the white marble table at the center of the room. Like the chamber, it was round. Seven robed men were already seated around the table. These were the leaders of the guild, the ones who had summoned him to the meeting. Two of the chairs around the table were empty. The Sage sat in one and turned to listen to the debate.

"Eschandel, it's just not possible." The speaker, a middle-aged man in green-trimmed silver robes, looked down his nose at a man with slender features in black robes.

"Stop saying that, Sirion." Eschandel slammed his fist against the table. His ice-blue eyes darted from person to person around the table. "For the third time, it is flamin' possible because it's flamin' happened. Sit there and deny it until the moons fall from the sky. It changes nothing. Last night, fifteen Seers had the same vision. A blaze of light flew through space. It slammed into the dimensional prison. Now there's a crack in the Void."

"I think what Sirion is saying is that, perhaps, the Seers are mistaken." This cool voice came from a white-haired man in sky-blue robes. Though much older than the first two speakers, his eyes were sharp and clear. "We need more than their word before we panic."

Eschandel took a deep breath. "As I was about to say before Sirion stuck his head in the sand…again…we have more proof. I present Bender Mikhel from DunDegore. His report should shut you up."

The white-haired man cleared his throat.

"Sorry, Latimer." Eschandel hung his head and rubbed the back of his neck. "His report should help clarify things."

The white-haired man, Latimer, smiled and nodded to show his support.

The Sage turned as a new figure stepped forward. Like the majority of the crowd, this man wore the white robes of an initiate; however, his robes were dirty, the hem caked with mud. He had obviously been traveling.

"I'm Mikhel," the man said. "I can't speak of the Void directly but my guild has reason to believe it is damaged. It's the only explanation for what we found. Something fell out of the Void."

For a moment, there was silence.

Then the room erupted into curses and shouts of disbelief.

Latimer lifted a hand and everyone hushed.

"Please," Eschandel said, "continue."

Mikhel wiped sweat from the edge of his neck as he looked around the room. "I'm part of the research team from DunDegore. As you know, we've explored the ruins for decades. The old Behersker city goes down for miles. We've only uncovered the first 50 levels. Usually we find trinkets – tools, dishware, data disks. Yesterday we found something else."

"Spit it out already," Sirion said. "We don't need an archeology lesson."

"Yes, sir." Mikhel's ears turned red. He glanced at Latimer but, unable to look the leader of the guild in the eye, he focused on Eschandel. "We found a sword. At first, we assumed it was a sculpture, perhaps part of a statue we had yet to discover. No one's ever found a Behersker weapon. There's considerable doubt they actually had conventional weapons. But it proved to be anything but ornamental. The blade was translucent yet harder than any metal, even darkstone. The hilt was opaque and appeared to be crafted from onyx. It's also impervious to damage. We tested it against fire, electricity, acid and blunt force. No effect. When we tested its reaction to fieldbending we began to realize exactly what we'd found. It seemed to eat every spell we threw it at. The archeologists asked me to examine the sword because of my area of expertise. Starfall."

"By the Oak." Latimer covered his mouth with trembling fingers, eyes no longer clear. He glanced at Eschandel. The younger fieldbender nodded and closed his eyes.

"From the look on your face, sir, I see you understand." This time Mikhel was able to look Latimer in the eyes. "The sword has inscriptions visible only when exposed to Akashic energy. The script wasn't Behersker. It was Sirian. The sword has a name."

"The Sword of Kassandra," Latimer said.

Mikhel nodded.

The room became deadly silent as if everyone had forgotten how to breathe.

Sirion shook his head. "Preposterous. The Sword of Kassandra is locked in the Void."

"Correction," Eschandel said. "It *was* locked away. It's not anymore. If you want more evidence let me introduce you to Leinda Farthing. She's our ambassador to the geognosts. She studied with Defksquar some years ago, which makes her the best expert available. I'll let her explain why she's here."

A woman dressed in deer-hide pantaloons and an unbleached tunic stepped out from the crowd. Her long brown hair was pulled back in a tight ponytail. A tribal tattoo decorated the length of her neck: a dragon.

"The head of my guild sent me here to deliver a warning," she said. "I'm sure you all know we specialize in manipulations of foramen and the magnetic subweb of our planet. We are highly attuned to inter-dimensional activity. Two days ago there was activity like we've never felt before. After hours of investigation we discovered the cause. Something came into our world. Think of it like a meteor that smashed through the walls of our dimension instead of crashing down through our atmosphere. Whatever it was, wherever it came from, it didn't close the portal it created. As long as it remains open, other things may enter our world."

"And what say you, Sage?" Latimer stared down at his hands.

The Sage cleared his throat. "I say Sirion needs female companionship more regularly. There is nothing more annoying than someone who claims to be a skeptic but is truly a fascist. Whatever happened, I felt it too. Two days ago. It was similar to the opening of a foramen but more…raw. Dangerous. I have no idea what caused it and, as you know, I despise not knowing. We all knew there was a possibility the Void wouldn't hold forever. If there is any chance it's compromised we have to alert the Great Castles. You should send envoys to the Valgt'til and the Redgraves."

"I tend to agree." Latimer placed his hands, palm down, on the table. "At worst, we appear over-prepared for battle. But if we say nothing and there is a crack in the Void, well, we can't take that risk."

Sirion grumbled. "I'll have you know I get female companionship regularly."

Eschandel chuckled, a wide grin on his face.

"Hardly the most pressing issue at hand," Latimer said. "Sirion, I'll send you back to DunDegore with our friend Mikhel. Help verify it's truly the Sword of Kassandra. Your skepticism will come in handy. If it is, we need to safeguard it. Something that powerful in the wrong hands could be disastrous."

"You mean the Quadumvirate, I suppose."

Latimer stood and looked around the crowd. "We need to move quickly but keep this quiet. By any oath you hold sacred, this news cannot leave this room. Trust no one. The Quadumvirate has spies everywhere. I'll head to Castle Grygar myself. Eschandel, I'll leave you in charge in my absence." He turned to a middle-aged man in red robes, "Bahrza, I'll send you to Castle Redgrave. Your connections in the court will get us a quick audience with the royal family."

The Sage raised his hand before speaking. "It would probably be in our best interest to notify the Nizarians as well."

Latimer nodded. "That's assuming they're not behind this. Gods only know what that race is capable of. I have someone I trust who will deliver the message. From this moment on, be on alert. The Sword of Kassandra may be the least of our worries. There are far worse things imprisoned in the Void. If it's cracked, Dispayre could break free."

The Sage bit his inner cheek. "And that means war."

Chapter Two

I stare down at the warm blood dripping from my hands. The room spins. Blood is splattered everywhere: walls, floor, ceiling. Five bodies lay at my feet. One looks up at me, eyes full of love and sadness.

"What have I done?" My voice is a whisper as I drop to my knees. My mind is blank. I don't remember how I came to this point.

Then there's laughter. Two voices laughing at the same time: one high-pitched like a young girl, the other a deep resonance, like a tiger laughing. My eyes refuse to see it. Someone's there but my eyes will not focus. All I see is glowing eyes and lips covered in fresh blood.

And teeth.

"I will smash you into puddles of bone," the laughing voice says.

I scream. I have to get away.

I push myself up to run but before I get to my feet, the world folds like paper. Darkness swallows all the light, all the sound.

And I fall.

* * *

Tadgh Dooley's eyes shot open.

"What the hell?" he said as he bolted up and glanced around. His surroundings were unfamiliar but the room was clean and smelled of disinfectant. Four beds covered in white sheets were spaced equally apart. "Something's wrong. This isn't Lutheran Hospital back in Cleveland."

He glanced out the windows at the line of trees in the distance. They were taller than any tree he had ever seen. Muffled grunts and knocking sounds echoed in the distance.

Then the pain hit him.

Panicked, he inspected his hands. Splints anchored his fingers. Gauze bandages spotted with blood covered the rest of his hands. He touched his hands to his face. It, too, was bandaged. The strips completely encircled his head. He looked down at his chest. He was topless but several parts of his arms and chest were also gauzed and bandaged.

He heard a soothing voice and turned to face it. A man walked towards him wearing brown leather pants under a white tunic. He also had a bright orange sash tied around his waist like a belt.

"I'm sorry," Tadgh said. "I don't understand you. Do you speak English? Can you tell me where I am?"

The man placed a hand on Tadgh's shoulder and gently pushed him back down into bed. Tadgh looked at the stranger more closely. He appeared to be in his early twenties with brown hair and the tanned skin of someone who worked outside. His eyes, however, made Tadgh uncomfortable. They were an odd shade of hazel with a weird swirl in the iris like he wore custom contacts.

"Where am I?" Blinking rapidly, Tadgh sat up. The man pushed him back again. He spoke to Tadgh a second time with the same smooth tones. A second man entered the room. He wore an almost identical outfit but he did not have the orange sash at the waist. "I said, where am I? Who are you people? What the hell is going on?"

The man with the sash took a step back and crossed his arms. He shook his head and spoke over his shoulder to the other man. The second man chuckled and touched his head. Tadgh got the impression they were questioning his sanity. The first man sighed and placed his palm against Tadgh's forehead as if to check his temperature. At the touch, Tadgh's pain dissipated. For a moment he felt weightless and relaxed. Then everything went black again.

✳✳✳

"There goes another one."

Shonn Bannmerci sat on the stone railing of the veranda watching the sky. His cousin, Menphis, looked up in time to see the third Pharocai of the day as the Nizarian flying ship disappeared behind a cloud. At 6'3", Menphis was slightly taller than his cousin. His upper body muscles were also more refined from the past three years' training with the Brotherhood. He wore the normal uniform of a Prelate of his level: dark brown leather pants, an orange sash at his waist and an armless white tunic.

Shonn was scrawnier with muscles built from toiling in the garden rather than weapon training. He wore unbleached cotton pants and a matching tunic. Both men had similar facial features: thin eyebrows, full lips, high cheekbones. They were obviously related, even though Shonn's hair was shoulder-length and straw colored while Menphis' was short-cropped and reddish-orange.

Menphis lowered his head and returned his attention to his exercises. In the practice yard nearby, Prelate Leif led a group of twenty acolytes through combat training. When he finished, it would be time for Menphis to take his own set of acolytes through training.

"Where you do you think they're going?" Shonn waited for the Pharocai to reappear. He shielded his eyes from the mid-day sun. It was high in the sky, casting only small shadows.

"You know what I think?" Menphis began slow sweeping movements with his arms and hands, several graceful poses linked together by seamless transitions. "I think you're avoiding your duties. I also think you should care less about the coming and goings of the Nizarians. Focus on the land at your feet, not the birds in the sky."

"Did you seriously just quote scripture to me?" Shonn's voice was full of mock scorn.

Menphis sighed and stopped his exercises. "I know why you came with me, Shonn. And I think you made the right decision." He glanced around to make sure no one was within earshot. "The Brothers are more tolerant of fod selonde than the people back home. But I'm not here to escape the world. I'm here because I actually believe in the Brotherhood. Being an Elmire Ahk means I'm supposed to quote scripture. It's kind of our thing."

"Can you at least tell me what's going on with the man that fell?"

Two days ago, an injured man fell from the sky creating a large impact crater at the edge of the monastery. The brothers had been alerted by a sizzling sound, like lightning dancing on water, followed by an earth-shattering thud. Menphis and a few of the other Prelates had carried him to the infirmary.

"Are you sure you want to talk about this?"

"We have to talk about it." Shonn turned away from his cousin. He watched the wind playing in the leaves of the trees surrounding the monastery. "I had one of my premonitions. Something bad is going to happen and it's because of him. And Instructor Mal is actually trying to heal him. I think Prelate Finn has moved into the infirmary just to monitor him."

"The Brotherhood of Tyche is a sacred place for any traveler." Menphis took one last deep breath and then rose out of his stance. "We take in many people others would turn away. That's why you're here, remember? Besides, he's just a boy. Younger than you, I think. It's hard to say for sure because of what was done to his face."

"What do you mean?"

"You didn't see him." Menphis sat beside his cousin on the stone railing. His eyes stayed on the acolytes as they went through their training exercises. "Instructor Mal kept everyone away because it was horrible. Remember that time back home when Viktor Steafans was crushed at the dock? This was worse. When we found him, his face was obliterated by claw marks. All you could see was eyes and raw flesh. I didn't recognize the claw pattern but the marks were deep. I doubt it was any local creature. Whatever attacked him was strong and wanted him dead. Similar wounds were all over his body. On top of that, his hands were mangled. All his fingers were broken. Same with one of his legs. There was also this smell. Prelate Leif said it was ozone. Whatever brought the boy here had the same effect on the air as a lightning strike."

In the pavilion, Prelate Leif finished his training and released his acolytes. They all bowed to their mentor and headed down to the lake for bathing.

"Has Instructor Mal told you anything else about how he thinks our fallen friend ended up here?"

"You seem to think the Instructor tells me everything." Menphis waved back at Prelate Leif who was signaling the courtyard was free. "I'm lucky if I get to speak to him once a week. When we do talk it's always about training or scripture. All he's told me is what I've already told you. He felt it coming. When we stood over the body he told us he'd felt something tear apart the reality field just before the sound."

"Like what fieldbenders do?"

"No." He bowed to a group of three acolytes from his group. They were starting to gather in the pavilion. "Instructor Mal said this wasn't fieldbending. It was an abomination."

"I heard Prelate Dohnald talking to Prelate Finn this morning. He seems to think the boy is a demon. Do you think that's possible?"

"Don't let Instructor Mal hear you say that. I'm serious. Dohnald is convinced he's an expert on demons because he saw a group of fieldbenders summon one a few years ago. I was only a few feet from the boy. If he was a demon I would have sensed it."

"How?"

"If you spent more time listening to me and less time daydreaming, you'd already know that. Sensing auras is one of the first things acolytes learn when they join the Brotherhood. Everyone's aura is unique but there's a vibrational constant. Beings from the same planet vibrate at the same rate. Beings from other planets, like the Nizarians, vibrate differently. Apparently, demons and graunskyeg vibrate in such an unnatural pattern it would make me physically ill. I would sense a demon from a hundred feet away."

"So how was his aura?"

Menphis frowned and turned to look at the infirmary. "It was odd but Instructor Mal assured us he wasn't a demon. Have you been able to remember anything else about your vision?"

"I hate when you call them that," Shonn said. "And no. Nothing else. I have no idea what I saw. It's all blurry. Just images. Bodies lying in the sand. Someone attacking the monastery. I saw that man in there. At least I think it was him. I don't know what to do. I saw the faces of the dead. They're people I know. People I like."

Menphis nodded. "I said as much to Instructor Mal. He knows about your abilities. Now that we know, he's doubled the guards. Maybe we can do something about it this time."

"I don't think it works that way. It never has before. Whenever I see something it always comes true. We can't stop it. Someone or something is coming for that man and people are going to die. Soon."

"Then maybe you should do what I told you to do yesterday. You remember, the first time we had this conversation?"

"I'm not suicidal."

Menphis slapped his cousin lightly on the shoulder. "You know it's the right thing to do, Shonn."

"I absolutely do not know that," Shonn said. "This is the exact opposite of the right thing. The right thing would look at your idea and wag its judgmental finger at it. Where's the sense in trying to stand next to the man someone is trying to kill?"

"Stop being so dramatic," Menphis said. "You're starting to sound like your mother."

Shonn stood and pointed a finger at Menphis. Then he clenched the same hand into a fist and turned to look back out at the courtyard. "If you weren't stronger and faster than me I would so kick your butt."

"Shivering here," Menphis said, a smile on his lips. "Look, I never said become his best friend. I just hate waiting around for something to happen. Let's take some initiative instead of waiting for the bad guys to strike. You sense things. He's at the center of what you're sensing. It's logical to get closer to him. Talk to him. Maybe, if you get him to open up a little, you'll be able to see more of what is coming. Maybe then we can do something to stop it."

Shonn grunted derisively.

"Look." Menphis put his arm around his cousin's shoulder. "I know it hasn't worked before. When your dad died."

Shonn looked into his cousin's eyes. They shared a moment of silence. Then Shonn turned back to look out into the courtyard.

"I remember how guilty you felt," Menphis said. "You used to just stare at the roof, sometimes for hours, and it was like you were seeing it all again. I can't know what it's like to see the things you see. But Shonn, you didn't push your dad off that roof. You know that. Even though you saw it happen before it really happened, you didn't *make* it happen."

"Tell that to my mom." He wiped tears from his eyes with the heel of his hand. "She still can't look me in the face. At least not for long. Ten years later and she still blames me."

"Well, your mom's an idiot. No offense. Look, you were just a kid the first time it happened. You're older now. Maybe this time you can actually do some good. You've never been able to control it before, but what if you could? Just imagine what you could do if you could make this work for you instead of against you."

Shonn opened his mouth to speak. He stopped, swallowing the words he had intended to say. He rubbed his lips and glanced around, making sure no one was nearby.

"You have no idea how…futile it is," he said. "Seeing the future. Bad things happen in my head. Then bad things happen in front of my eyes. And I can't do a damn thing to stop it. I think it might drive me crazy someday. The last two nights I've barely slept. I close my eyes and I hear their screams. I see their bodies, smell their blood. I don't want to get closer…to the stranger or the visions. The only thing keeping me sane is knowing the images eventually fade, even if it's only until the next night. I'm sorry, Menphis. I just can't do this."

Menphis walked to the other end of the veranda. He folded his hands and closed his eyes.

"You're pretty good at controlling your temper." Shonn spoke with a new lightness in his voice. "When we were kids you were the biggest hothead in the neighborhood."

Menphis smiled. "I wouldn't be much of a Brother if I couldn't control my base emotions," Menphis said. "You know he's barely said a word. Instructor Mal and Prelate Finn have been trying to heal him. I've seen Instructor Mal extend his aura and heal a shattered leg without breaking a sweat. Nothing works on the boy."

"Maybe it is fieldbending," Shonn said. "Or it could be another injury. Remember when that acolyte was struck in the throat and couldn't speak for a month? Sometimes people go silly when they're hit in the head. Maybe he'll never wake up."

"Geesh," Menphis said with a smirk. "If only we had a psychic on hand that could find out for sure."

Shonn picked up the nearest thing he could find, an empty water bucket, and threw it at Menphis.

Menphis laughed and knocked it aside casually, beating it away with his hand.

"What did Instructor Mal say about the attack?" Shonn said.

Menphis stopped smiling. "He said be patient. That's all he ever says. Of course he can say that. He's working his way towards immortality. It's pretty easy to be patient when you're going to live forever. He says we're ready for any attack and I tend to agree with him. I mean, you'd have to be insane to attack a monastery filled with Elmire Ahk."

"Crazy," Shonn said. "Or powerful. Maybe both."

"Thank you," Menphis said. "You're proving my point. We need to know what we're up against. Tell you what, just get close to him. Physically. You don't even have to talk to him. Just pretend to do some gardening near the infirmary. Maybe you'll pick something up and maybe you won't. Either way it's worth a try."

Shonn sighed and stood up. "I'll think about it. You should go. Your acolytes are waiting for you and I should get back to the kitchen. Mirelda is expecting me."

Before Menphis could say anything else, Shonn was gone, walking away from the veranda.

Chapter Three

"You're late." Mirelda stood, back to the door, kneading dough as Shonn walked into the kitchen. As always, she wore the brown and green jumpsuit that marked her as Elmire Ahk of the order of SeeGal. Though well into her sixties, working all day in the kitchens kept her physically fit. "Perhaps you think these vegetables are going to peel themselves."

"Sorry." Shonn rushed to the island in the middle of the kitchen. He tied an apron around his waist and washed his hands in the water basin. "I was with my cousin."

"Of course you were. You're always with your cousin." She raised her eyebrow and folded her arms across her chest. "You know what I think? I've been too light on your duties."

Shonn was trapped. He knew if he said his roster was full she'd claim he was simply lax in his duties. If he said he needed more work she would gladly assign it. So he simply hung his head and waited.

"Smart boy." She turned around and returned to the dough.

Mirelda kept him buried with chores for the rest of the day. First, he peeled vegetables for hours. After that, he collected wild mushrooms and herbs from the woods near Lake Wilkin. By the time he returned, it was dinner. After the meal, Shonn and the eleven other help staff washed dishes and cleaned the dining room. By then, it was time for bed.

He retreated to his quarters, one of several 4 x 12 rooms in the building across from the kitchen. He took off his sandals and left them by the door. Then he slipped out of his tunic and pants, dropping them into a hamper filled with similar clothes. Staff members were required to bathe and change clothes every day. One never knew when traveling dignitaries would visit Instructor Mal asking for help with diplomatic negotiations.

He sat on his bed and massaged the tension from his feet. From the room to his left he heard the rumble of deep snores. That was Charr, all 250 pounds of him. He envied the big guy's ability to fall into a deep sleep so quickly. As usual, the room to the right was quiet. It belonged to Becy, an introverted man from GardenKeep. He read by candlelight each night.

"You'll both be dead soon." Tears formed in his eyes as he looked left and right. He dropped his head into his hands until the tears stopped. He walked to the window, pushing aside the curtains for a view of the night. A light burned in the infirmary.

***

The next morning after breakfast, Shonn sat in the courtyard staring at the infirmary. At one end of the courtyard, acolytes performed calisthenics under the watchful eye of Prelate Dohnald. At the other end, Menphis sparred with two other Prelates. He fought with preternatural speed, twisting and jabbing his quarterstaff. It was all too fast for Shonn's eyes to follow, but the other Prelates managed to dodge or block each attack.

"You ever get jealous of them?"

Shonn recognized the voice, so he didn't need to turn around. "You're welcome to enlist, Charr."

"Yeah, right. I'm too old. They rarely accept initiates over sixteen." He rested his hands on his belly and shook his head. "Especially one in my shape. So, do you?"

Shonn glanced quickly at Charr and clenched his teeth. "Sometimes. I wish I was as strong as them. Even the weakest acolyte could kick my butt. But they train all day and meditate all night. That's not a life I want."

Charr slapped Shonn's back. "We work all day *and* work all night. How's that any better? I tell you this much. I don't want to spend the rest of my life a servant."

'But you will,' Shonn thought. He closed his eyes and stared at the ground. With a sigh, he stood and opened his eyes. "Excuse me. I have some gardening to do."

"Um, what? Since when do you volunteer for gardening?"

Shonn walked up the steps and left the courtyard. The infirmary rose before him. He stopped cold. The stranger sat on a bench outside the infirmary.

'That's him?' Shonn stared at the stranger. His face and chest were covered in fresh bandages. He also wore unbleached cotton pants identical to Shonn's.

Shonn looked back over his shoulder at Menphis, hoping for a sign of support. His cousin was too focused on training to even notice him. With a sigh, Shonn walked up the stone steps of the infirmary. He hoped the stranger would turn to look up at him, but there was no movement.

Shonn cleared his throat. "Hello. I'm Shonn. I was hoping I could ask you a few questions."

Slowly the stranger turned to look at him. He said nothing.

"Do you understand me?" Shonn knelt beside the stranger until their eyes were at the same level. "Do you speak Sirian? I can't speak any other languages, but if you can't speak, maybe you could write it and I could have it translated or…"

The stranger turned back to stare at the sky. It was hard to read his expression through all those bandages, but Shonn could see his eyes clearly: deep-black eyes that quivered with a quiet fear and uncertainty.

"Do you know where you are?" Shonn leaned in closer and put a supportive hand on the stranger's knee.

The stranger mumbled something, a series of guttural clicking sounds. It was like nothing Shonn had ever heard before but it had the cadence of language. The stranger spoke for quite awhile and, though he couldn't understand him, Shonn let him speak. As far as he knew, it was the first time the wounded man had said anything.

When the stranger stopped, Shonn shook his head. "I really wish I could understand you. That might save my friends' lives."

Then the stranger said something else.

Shonn went numb. It was like a bell rang somewhere in his head: a single, piercing sound that, for a moment, stopped the entire world. He tried to stand, but his knees felt watery. Every movement seemed to be in slow motion.

As quickly as it started, it was over. The world rushed back on him. His ears filled with the sound of wind in the trees, birds in the distance and the acolytes training in the courtyard.

"What the hell was that?" Shonn said.

Then the stranger said: "Holy crap. I can understand you now."

Chapter Four

Earlier that morning, Tadgh woke up from the same nightmare. This time he stopped himself before he cried out. He settled back into bed and stared out the window until the man with the orange sash brought him breakfast on a tray. There was a pasty, oatmeal-like dish that tasted like cinnamon with a slight after-taste of smoked oysters. He drank a small glass filled with a purple juice. It looked like grape juice but tasted like lemons. They also gave him a grapefruit-like fruit on the plate. It was, by far, his favorite. Its skin was edible and its meat tasted like honey and watermelon.

The monk spoke to him, but Tadgh could not understand a word. He simply smiled and nodded. Then he remembered his smile was hidden behind the bandages around his head. Eventually, the monk left him alone to eat. Later, another monk removed the breakfast dishes. There was more incomprehensible muttering.

'I could really use some subtitles,' he thought.

Later, the monk with the orange sash returned with another man dressed like him. They lay their hands on him and chanted. Tadgh had no idea what they were doing, but it seemed to work. The pain in his hands and chest dissipated. When they finished, they lifted him outside and left him on a bench. His left leg was in a cast, making it difficult to walk on his own.

For the first time, he saw the source of the sounds he'd heard yesterday.

'Apparently I landed in a kung fu movie.' Dozens of teenage boys stood in rows within an octagonal courtyard. All wore white, sleeveless robes. They punched and kicked the air, grunting with each thrust. An older man wearing the same robe with an orange sash at the waist shouted orders at them. Occasionally, he stopped in front of one and corrected his form. Farther away, a group of three men fought with staves.

'How the hell are they moving so fast? That's not even possible. Then again, neither is amnesia, but I seem to have it. I know it eventually happens to someone on every TV show in history. A trauma erases their memory, pushing it so far down the victim can't recall anything. I know it's ridiculous. All the experts say real amnesia is pretty rare and almost never the result of a simple blow to the head.'

He remembered most things. 'I know my name. Tadgh Dooley. I'm 17 years old. The idiots in school always teased me as a kid. Called me "Tie Drooley." It was a big joke to them. They'd tie me to fences, bike racks, street lamps. Anything they could think of. I changed schools three times. Never helped.'

'I remember my parents, too. My mom, Jolanta, works at the marina. My dad, Ian, is a manager at Sherwin-Williams. We live in Cleveland, 13204 Euclid Ave. I can see my bedroom. Light blue walls, dark hardwood floors, white curtains, white sheets on the bed.'

And he remembered pain.

He stared at his bandaged hands. 'How did I get here? I've no idea where I am, but this place just doesn't feel…right. The sun's too big. Maybe I'm near the equator, but I'm pretty sure the sun doesn't change color anywhere on Earth.'

The sky above was cloudless. Turquoise blue. The sun was significantly more reddish than he'd ever seen. Occasionally, birds flew past his line of sight. They were unlike any kind he'd seen before.

'It's almost like I'm on another planet. But how is that even possible? Was I kidnapped by aliens or something?'

Again he had a flash of a pain. A memory. But no other memories came. No visuals, no sounds: just a dark empty moment of pain and fear.

Then he saw something that made his heart beat a little faster. One of the most beautiful men he'd ever seen in his life walked directly towards him. Though not as muscular as the monk-types, he still seemed perfectly constructed. His tousled blond hair was roughly cut and damp with sweat from the early morning heat. Something stirred inside Tadgh. His pulsed quickened and he turned away.

'I remember this, too,' he thought. Last summer watching boys at the beach wearing swim trunks, splashing in the waves. They all went to his school but he didn't know any of them. More to the point, none of them knew him. They were on the volleyball team. He was on the yearbook committee. They all had girlfriends. He wanted a boyfriend.

Another flash of pain: something scraping across his face, someone laughing. He shook the memory away and turned back to the approaching man. Although he appeared to be older than Tadgh, his blue eyes seemed open and vulnerable. That and his easy smile and smooth face gave him a boyish innocence mingled with a body that was solidly masculine.

'Like Farm Boy from Princess Bride,' he thought. Tadgh's eyes traced the gentle slope of his hairless cheek down the smooth neck to his chest. Then he looked away.

'What the hell am I doing? I have no idea what these people will do to me if they find out I am…' He blinked rapidly and kept his eyes on the ground.

The man moved closer to him. He spoke in the same rhythm of syllables and tones as the monks. A quiet rage built up inside Tadgh mingled with a not-so-quiet yearning. He avoided looking into those eyes.

The blonde man knelt at his feet, his voice soft and pleading. Tadgh couldn't help himself. He stared into those eyes and something inside him melted. All the confusion over his lack of memory faded. The only thing in existence that mattered was this beautiful, nameless man. He wanted to touch his cheeks and kiss those lips.

"God, I wish I could talk to you," he said.

The world stopped. The air grew heavy, making it impossible to draw in breath. Something swallowed up the sound of the wind in the trees and the distant call of birds. The man looked shocked, as if he'd felt the moment too.

The man spoke. "What the hell was that?"

"Holy crap," Tadgh said. "I can understand you now."

"Really?" The man removed his hand but did not move away. "How? Did you do that?"

"Did I do what?"

"There was a...never mind. We can talk about that later. My name is Shonndira Bannmerci. I'm from the town of Tarkon north of here. What's your name?"

"Tadgh," he responded. His voice felt weak. It was hard to concentrate with those blue eyes so close to his face. "I'm just happy to finally be able to communicate with someone. My name's Tadgh Dooley. I'm from Cleveland. Where am I?"

Shonn smiled. "Tig Dooley. Nice to meet you. I've never heard of this Cleveland. Is that in Norshire?"

Tadgh shook his head. "Isn't Norshire somewhere in England?"

Shonn shook his head slowly. The smile started to fade a little from his face. "I've also never heard of this England. Can you tell me the last thing you remember?"

"How the hell have you never heard of England? I mean, they pretty much owned the whole planet at one point." Tadgh looked up at the sky, at the odd-colored sun.

Shonn followed his eyes up and exhaled. "It's not completely unheard of. People coming from other worlds. They say sometimes they slip through a foramen."

"What's a foramen?"

Shonn sat on the bench beside Tadgh. "I'm not an expert, but it's supposed to be a weak spot in the reality field. Sometimes people and animals from other planets stumble into foramen. Geognosts can use them to travel quickly around the world. They know how to use them better than any fieldbender. Are you some sort of geognost? Is that how you crashed at the monastery?"

"What do you mean, crashed? I don't know what a geognost is but I don't think I'm one. I have no idea how I got here." Panic rose in Tadgh. Shonn placed a comforting hand on his shoulder and, for a moment, the fear retreated.

"Whatever happened, you're safe now." Shonn removed his hand. "The Brothers found you in pretty bad shape. You were covered in blood, torn up by claw marks. Do you remember what happened?"

Pain. Tadgh touched his head. "No. My memory is foggy. I can't remember things. I've been trying to, but it's all one big empty nothing."

"Damn." Shonn hit the bench with the heel of his hand. "I was hoping you could tell me something so I could stop…"

"Stop what?"

Shonn shook his head and stood. "Never mind. It was a long shot, anyway."

"Did I hear talking?" The monk with the orange sash appeared from inside the infirmary.

"Yes, you did, Prelate Finn." Shonn said.

"Weird." Tadgh said. "I can understand him now, too. Thanks for the food. I wanted to thank you before, but…you know."

"This is a good sign," Prelate Finn said. He came and knelt to look Tadgh in the eye. "I was worried there might be brain damage. If you've finally regained the ability to speak it's probable that any damage was temporary."

"I don't think he ever lost the ability to speak, Prelate," Shonn said. "I don't think he speaks our language."

"Do you think he's from Norshire?" Prelate Finn looked into Tadgh's eyes. "The eye color would be right, but the irises are very unusual."

"I don't think he's from Maghe Sihre at all," Shonn said. "It's possible he fell through a foramen from another world."

Prelate Finn narrowed his eyes, studying Tadgh. "Shonn, why don't you run and get Instructor Mal. He'll want to know about this." Then, inhaling sharply, he stood. "I'll take our friend inside. Now that we can talk, I'd like to run a few tests."

Shonn bowed his head in acknowledgement. "Of course. I'll be back soon."

Tadgh watched him go and turned to Prelate Finn. "Can someone please tell me where the hell I am?"

Chapter Five

Instructor Mal stumbled, nearly falling into his desk.

"Instructor!" Prelate Leif rushed to the side of the leader of the monastery and grabbed his arm.

The Instructor held up a hand, palm outward, signaling he was okay. Then, he pushed past his pride and accepted help. Reluctantly, he let Leif guide him to a bench at the edge of the room.

"Suddenly, I feel every one of my 65 years." Instructor Mal looked at his hands. They were shaking.

"Nonsense, Instructor. You don't look a day older than me."

"Looks can be deceiving." Instructor Mal frowned and pinched his lower lip. "I don't know what happened. For just a moment it felt like the entire reality field unhinged itself."

"Was it a graunskyeg?" Leif's eyes shone with excitement.

Instructor Mal smiled. "You're far too eager to meet monsters. Be careful what you wish for. This was worse than a graunskyeg. More unnatural. Something tore through my willpower like tissue paper. I'm not sure what it was. I've never felt anything like it before. I will meditate on it."

"I felt nothing."

"You're still young. Stay with us another 30 years and your senses will improve. Now, where were we?"

"My report from Tarkon." Leif moved to sit on the floor in front of Mal.

"Yes. You were just discussing some rumor about a Lord from GardenKeep building an army." The Brotherhood of Tyche worked primarily as mediators and arbitrators in diplomatic circles. From time to time they also worked as gatherers of information. Often, the right piece of intelligence revealed at the right time made all the difference in negotiation. "What does Tarkon city council say?"

"They dismiss the rumors. Very formally."

"Of course."

"It's a safe tactic." Prelate Leif nodded. "My hunch is they know something. They may be in on it."

Instructor Mal waved his hand, dismissing the thought. "More likely they don't know enough to act on it. Admitting that makes them look weak. Who's your source?"

"His name's Stefan, a dock worker. He's seen numerous ships come in and out of port carrying questionable goods. I thought he might be exaggerating, so I checked his aura. He at least believes he's telling the truth."

"What else did he say about this Lord you mentioned? Anything that could identify him?"

Prelate Leif looked away. "I shouldn't have used that word. Stefan described what the man wore. It was expensive darkstone armor. He mentioned the man's entire entourage wore similar outfits. The amount of money and protection suggests he's royal. I managed a quick peek at some shipping manifests. Something odd is being brought out of GardenKeep and heading north. Lord or not, officially he's a collector of Behersker relics." Leif hesitated, holding his breath for a moment. "There was something else. Possibly unrelated. There's another set of rumblings in Tarkon. Darker ones. Rumors of something happening in Oakthorne, far to the north. There's talk of the war spilling over to Celtica."

"You think this man is working for the Trofast." Instructor Mal exhaled slowly.

Leif frowned and shook his head. "I've no proof."

"Any sign of a Trofast in town?"

Leif sighed. "It's just a hunch. The pieces of this puzzle don't fit. Something else is going on there. It doesn't make sense."

Instructor Mal glanced at his hands. They no longer shook. "Go back to Tarkon. Stay until you get specific details on this man and his army. I have my suspicions, but I'd rather not voice them until I have more reason to be concerned. Find out what is leaving GardenKeep on those ships. I know you have duties with your acolytes. I will make sure that Prelate Dohnald sees to them."

Prelate Leif stood, bowed to his leader, and left the room.

Alone again, Instructor Mal rubbed the back of his head. Whatever he'd felt a moment before, it still had his head ringing.

'I have a hunch, too,' he thought. 'Whatever is going on in Tarkon is part of something much larger. A change is coming. We must be ready.'

***

Miles to the south, in the port city of GardenKeep, the Sage dropped his glass of wine.

He looked down, watching it fall. The world seemed to flow in slow motion: red liquid spurted from the lead crystal. Then the world rushed forward again. He faltered, putting a hand on the window sill to steady himself.

"Sir!" His twenty-year-old servant, Barnes, rushed to pick up the broken glass. "Are you okay? It looked like you were having a seizure. My father used to get them sometimes. Course, you'll remember that on account of he worked for you back in the…"

"Stop talking." The Sage rubbed his temples and closed his eyes. "I need a moment."

Barnes picked up the rest of the glass and left the room. The Sage waited until his servant left, then collapsed in a chair by the window.

'That was unnerving,' he thought. 'I haven't felt power like that since I came here. It was similar to the way djinn alter reality, but there are no djinn on Maghe Sihre. It's why I came here so long ago. Three hundred years in relative peace. It can't be a coincidence. In the last few days something cracked the Void and something else altered reality. What will I do if the djinn are here?'

Barnes returned with a fresh glass of wine. The Sage reached for it and drank it all in one gulp.

"You felt something, didn't you? Another crack in the Void?"

The Sage shook his head. "No. Another mystery. I'm surrounded by mysteries these days. Speaking of, you were about to tell me you'd learned something about the robberies."

"Yes," Barnes said. He dropped to his knees and applied a white powder to the wine that had spilled onto the carpet. He continued to speak as the powder sizzled and absorbed the wine. "Three more break-ins last night. One at the Museum of Culture, one at the capitol building, and a third at the home of Lord Benion. That makes twenty in the last month if you believe the newspapers. Word on the street is there's been nearly double that. Some council members choose not to report their losses."

"Politicians." The Sage stared out the open window at the streets below. "They'd watch the world burn around them rather than admit incompetence. A sign of weakness could hurt their chances for re-election. What did they take?"

Barnes nodded. "As before, many things were stolen – gold, jewels, etc. – but you don't have to look too closely to see the pattern."

"More relics?"

"They don't call you the Sage for nothing." Barnes sat in a wooden chair across the table from his employer. "They stole a Behersker relic each time. It doesn't make any sense. Those things are nearly impossible to pawn. They're not a power source. You can't even melt them down to sell for scrap."

"Anyone dumb enough to display stolen Behersker relics in their homes would quickly gain the attention of the authorities."

"Exactly." Barnes rubbed his forehead. "It makes no sense. They have no street value. Maybe they're being shipped to a collector up north. But someone is exerting a lot of effort to steal random old junk."

"Behersker relics are ancient technology, not junk. I suspect this is not random at all." Below, two blond children played a game with colorful hoops and ribbons in front of a baker. A gentle breeze carried the scent of fresh-baked bread. "At first glance a puzzle never makes sense. You just have to look at the pieces in the right way. Take Mrs. Zelma, for example."

"The woman that runs the bakery? What about her?"

"She'll be dead within a year." The Sage kept his eyes on the children. "Her husband will kill her. I can't tell you the exact date, but it will happen. Mrs. Zelma is having an affair with the father of those children down there. When her husband was younger, he fell ill with the fyftha virus. His father came to me for help. The boy nearly died but the treatment was successful. Unfortunately, it left him sterile. Mrs. Zelma knows this but she still wants a child. You can tell by the way she holds her stomach every time she watches children playing. Based on my observations, she's two months pregnant with a child that will look a little bit too much like those children down there. Secrets like that don't stay hidden for long. Her husband is trusting, but he's not an idiot. He won't believe his sterility's been cured. He also has a severe addiction to Darkwood mushrooms. When he finds out, he will kill her."

"Should we tell her?"

The Sage wiped his eyes and turned away from the window. "Tell her what? Stop messing around on your husband? She's going to do what she wants to do. She thinks she's being careful, but anyone who knows what to look for can see it's too late. I've been around for a while now. I've seen this sort of thing many times."

Barnes went to the window and looked down at the children. "Dad always said he felt sorry for you in a way. He said it must be horrible to know things like you do. To see patterns. I'd never want to know the future. Look at those kids. Do you ever wish you were still like them? So innocent."

The Sage let his eyes fall. He stared at nothing. "I had my childhood stolen. I've never been innocent."

Barnes cleared his throat and changed the subject. "Who do you think is behind these robberies?"

The Sage grunted and glanced back at Barnes. "That's a mystery. And I hate mysteries. Tell me you've found out something useful about Lord Vyken."

Barnes returned to his seat. "Well, at least in that investigation there's some good news. It's amazing what people talk about down at the pub after a few drinks. Lord Vyken has moved into the old fort beyond the city walls. They say he's building an army. And by 'they' I mean the people he's hired to feed that army. I met a lovely young woman with very eager thighs who says there are at least three hundred men gathered there."

"How exactly are her thighs eager?"

Barnes blushed. "If you have to ask, you need to get out of this house more often. Tell me, sir, with everything happening with the Void, why are we still looking into Lord Vyken?"

"I'm not sure." The Sage hesitated for a moment, staring at his empty wine glass. "As I said, sometimes things are not as random as they appear. As a member of the royal family of GardenKeep, Lord Vyken is well within his rights. He can gather a personal security force at his family estate. If anyone questioned the size of his force, he could mention fear over the recent robberies." The Sage leaned back. A thought formed in his mind. "Oh dear. I'm starting to see a pattern here. Could I bother you to see this woman again, the one with the eager thighs?"

Barnes grinned, his eyes bright and wicked. "You're a slave driver, but I'll see what I can do."

***

In Karaj Robat, miles to the north, Eschandel fell to his knees. A sharp pain shot through his spine; every nerve in his body screamed. He looked down at his hands and watched them spasm uncontrollably. He focused his will on his fingers, forcing them to stop. After several stuttering attempts, he stood on weak legs. He spun in a slow circle. Every fieldbender around him was also on the floor. Most were recovering more slowly than he.

"What in the world…?"

Eschandel glanced over at the person who spoke. Cyrus, one of his oldest friends, rose to his feet. He wore silver-trimmed white robes. He kept his gray hair short, giving severity to his rough features.

Eschandel wiped the dirt on his hands against his robes. "It felt like someone took a chunk of the reality field and threw it into the Void. I've never felt something so repugnant."

"You don't think…?" Cyrus' eyes went wide.

Eschandel felt his stomach roil as his whole body went cold. "Send word to the Seers. We need to know if the crack in the Void is any larger."

Cyrus flinched. "Surely this can't be related. Whatever caused the crack in the Void didn't affect us last time. We had to rely on the Seers and the geognosts."

"And that's what worries me." Eschandel scratched his neck and wiped the sweat from his forehead. "This was stronger. And there was an intelligence behind it."

"Someone's doing this on purpose? Do you think the Quadumvirate has some new type of magic?"

"No. It felt like…" Eschandel lowered his voice to a whisper and leaned close to his comrade. "It felt like a fod sel-onde."

Cyrus started to laugh but stopped when he saw the look on Eschandel's face. "Whatever that was, it knocked twenty trained fieldbenders nearly unconscious. I don't want to think about how powerful a fod sel-onde would have to be to do that."

"I know what a fod sel-onde feels like." Eschandel shivered. "I used to hunt them, remember? Those abominations break all the laws of physics. You may be right. This might be completely unrelated to the crack in the Void. But if I'm right, when we check with the Seers, we'll learn the crack is larger now. Get to them immediately. If the crack is larger, we need to turn their attention away from the Sword of Kassandra and track down this fod sel-onde. I'll meet with Kvartermester Arem and arrange for a tracking team."

Cyrus turned to leave but hesitated. "If there's a fod sel-onde out there powerful enough to break the Void, what else can it do?"

Eschandel nodded. "Exactly. We need to destroy it immediately. We can't afford to let this abomination live."

Chapter Six

Tadgh sat on the edge of his bed in the infirmary and watched a man approach. He was dressed differently than the others. His robes were orange, his sash red. He was also significantly older than anyone else Tadgh had seen in the monastery. His arms were thick with muscle. There was a steely resolve in his face that frightened Tadgh.

Tadgh looked up at Prelate Finn. "Is that your leader?"

"That's not really the word we would use, but yes, I guess you could say that." Finn held a palm against Tadgh's chest. A ripple of energy went through Tadgh's body. After a moment, Finn removed his hand. "Hmm. Your blood pressure is fine. Heart rate is a little fast, but that's been normal for you. When he comes in you should address him as Instructor Mal. Instructor is his title just as my title is Prelate. Do you have a title?"

"Um, mister, I guess. My name is Mr. Tadgh Dooley, but where I'm from almost every man is a mister. Unless you're a doctor…or a soldier. Or nurse. Or professor. I've never actually thought about how many titles we have."

Tadgh stopped rambling when the Instructor entered the room. The Instructor's eyes never left Tadgh. Something about that stare reminded Tadgh of x-rays. He felt exposed on a cellular level.

Instructor Mal handed a small sheet of paper to Prelate Finn. "Please gather these supplies for Prelate Leif. He's heading north on an important mission. Time is of the essence."

Prelate Finn took the piece of paper, leaving Tadgh alone in the infirmary with Instructor Mal. Tagdh suddenly found it hard to swallow. Or breathe.

"You're nervous." A brief smile crossed Instructor Mal's lips. Almost immediately it slid away. When he looked at Tadgh, it was like he could see right down into his soul. "I hear you are suddenly able to speak perfect Sirian. That is...unbelievably fortunate. I suppose you don't know how that happened?"

Tadgh shook his head, unable to speak.

"Do you remember how you came here? Where you came from?"

Tadgh bit his lips, shrugged his shoulders, and shook his head.

Instructor Mal nodded and folded his hands. "Well, let's start with what you do know. Do you remember your name?"

"Yes," Tadgh answered. "Of course I remember my name. It's Tadgh Dooley."

The Instructors eyes narrowed. "That is an...unusual name. How did you come by this name?"

"I have evil parents." Tadgh meant it as a joke but, after seeing how the Instructor tensed, he decided it was not the time for humor. "I mean, they weren't evil as in blood sacrifices and baby-killing orgies. Just...it's kind of a weird name for a kid in America. My father's Irish and he thought it would be great to give me a real Irish name. It's spelled T-A-D-G-H but it's pronounced just like tiger without the -er. My dad's kind of behind the times. Anyway, I'm sorry I'm rambling a bit but it's just great to finally be able to communicate with..."

Instructor Mal held up a hand, stopping Tadgh mid-sentence. "How exactly did you come to learn our language?"

Tadgh lowered his eyes.

"I mean you no harm, son, but I need to know if you're a threat to the people I care about." The Instructor took a step forward and grabbed Tadgh by the chin. The tight grip forced him to look up into the Instructor's eyes. "So, I will ask you again. How did you come to learn our language? Be specific."

Tadgh felt nauseous. "I don't know. I swear I have no idea what happened. I was talking with that guy, Shonn, and got so frustrated. I could see he was trying to talk to me and

I really wanted to understand. It was all a jumble of sounds. I got angry. And I remember wishing I could speak to him."

"And then you could." Instructor Mal let his hand slip away. He looked over Tadgh's shoulder with the same x-ray vision. A moment later he grabbed Tadgh by the forearm. A pulse of energy shot through Tadgh's body. It was similar to the one Prelate Finn had sent, but stronger. A moment later, Instructor Mal drew his hand back quickly. He shook it as if trying to shake something sticky and wet from his fingers. "Merciful Tyche. You're a fod sel-onde."

"What does that mean?"

Instructor Mal looked back at him and crossed his arms. "Before I tell you what a fod sel-onde is I need you to tell me what you remember. Where are you from? What led you to come to here?"

"It's not like I have real amnesia or anything." Tadgh looked up into Instructor Mal's eyes briefly, then turned to stare at the floor. "I remember my name, my family, my school. I keep trying to go back to the last thing I remember, but it's not there. I can tell I'm blocking something, but I don't know what. Can you tell me where I am?"

"You're at a monastery of the Brotherhood of Tyche." Instructor Mal uncrossed his arms and sat on the bed beside Tadgh. "We're southeast of Lake Wilkin. The city of Tarkon is a few days' ride north of here. To the south is Flesh Prayer. Do these names mean anything to you?" He waited until Tadgh shook his head before continuing. "Maybe you've heard of GardenKeep. It's the largest city in Shirza. From the look on your face I'm guessing you've never even heard of Shirza. You're from somewhere else, aren't you? You're not from Maghe Sihre."

The last sentence was said as a statement, not a question.

"I'm not sure," Tadgh said. "I mean, I know that I've never heard any of those names before. I guess I kind of already knew I wasn't on Earth anymore. That's where I'm from, Earth. Cleveland, to be specific. It's in Ohio. United

States of America? Now I know I have to be on another planet. Everyone on Earth knows America. So you're telling me this really isn't Earth? That somehow I've…. Oh my God. I really was kidnapped by aliens."

Instructor Mal narrowed his eyes. "Are people from your world often kidnapped by these aliens you speak of?"

"God, no," Tadgh said. "I mean, I didn't think so, but…. Crap. I have no idea how I got here. How did you find me?"

"You made it pretty easy," Instructor Mal said. For a moment, the smile reappeared on his face. "You fell from the sky. Based on the impact crater, I'd say you fell at least a mile and slammed right into the dirt. Oh, I know it sounds impossible. That kind of fall would have killed a regular Sirian. From the expression on your face I'm guessing it should have killed someone from your world as well. But it didn't kill you. Curious."

"Not really the word I would use." Tadgh touched his chest and stared at his broken leg.

"Well, it's even more curious because of your name. In the common Sirian tongue, Tig is another word for Fallen. As in something that has dropped from the heavens. That seems a little too coincidental. And I don't believe in coincidences." For several long minutes, Instructor Mal said nothing. He simply sat there looking at Tadgh. Eventually, he nodded. "I have a way to help you recover your memories."

"Are you going to hypnotize me?" Tadgh felt even more vulnerable than before.

Instructor Mal raised an eyebrow. "I'm not sure what this word means, hypnotize. However you learned our language, it seems it was an imperfect method. Maybe you have words for things that we don't have. What I can do is slip my energy field into your mind. That should help remove the blocks."

"Is it safe?"

"Yes. Of course." Instructor Mal put a hand on Tadgh's shoulder. "I'm an Elmire Ahk, not a fieldbender. We don't seek power for power's sake. Everyone at this monastery is focused on gaining complete control over our own mind, body, and spirit. Doing so helps us realize we are all connected. Harming you would harm me as well. There will be pain."

Tadgh nodded and let his shoulders slump. "What should I do? Count backwards from a hundred or something?"

"Hmm, curious. That actually might help. Yes, it could distract your conscious mind enough to let my energy field reach the subconscious. Perhaps later you can tell me more about this hypnosis you spoke about. Close your eyes and try this counting backwards thing. Start from one hundred. If this works, you'll feel something very quickly. The memory of the event that brought you here is blocked. So think of a day before that, a special day when something extraordinary happened. Something impossible to forget. We can establish a past for you and move forward.

"That's easy," Tadgh said with a smile. "The first day Colin touched me."

***

I'm sitting in Spanish class. It's just after March break. Carrie, my girlfriend, is still in Florida with her family. My friend Dan is showing me some book he bought off eBay. He claims it's a real copy of the Necronomicon, but I know he is full of crap. There's no such thing. But it has pictures and the artwork is pretty cool, so I play along.

"Congratulations."

I turn around and my brain freezes. It's Colin. He's wearing that blue t-shirt I like and he's got his hands in the front pockets of his jeans. He looks down at me with those deep green eyes and I kind of forget to breathe. He puts his hand on my left shoulder and gives it a slight squeeze. My mouth is dry. I say nothing until Dan clears his throat.

"Congratulations for what?" I say.

"You and Carrie." Colin smiles, but I notice his left eye twitches. "I heard you're dating. I'm glad."

My face goes red. I know he's lying. He's not happy for me at all. I can see it in his face. We've locked eyes so many times, had so many silent moments where we'd just stare at each other. I know he wants me. At least I think I know it. I mean, what if I'm wrong? What if everything we shared is only in my head? What if I make a move and Colin is repulsed? He could run and tell his friend, Carrie, the whole school.

I mutter something in thanks and Colin walks away. Strangely, Dan giggles and closes the book. Class starts and I force myself to forget Colin.

That night I get a text from Colin. He wants to meet me in the park behind the Kiwanis club. I'm nervous. Maybe it's a set up. But what if it isn't? What if he really wants...something?

We meet up after 9:00 p.m. I walk over to him and my stomach is all knotted up. I'm terrified, but he just smiles at me. When I finally reach him he doesn't say anything. He just grabs me by the back of the head and draws me towards him. We kiss. The world spins around me. My body feels lighter than air. I can no longer tell where my body ends and Colin's begins. Time stops and the moment seems to last forever.

He walks me home. We hold hands.

***

"That's a good start," Instructor Mal said. "I can feel your mind opening. Take it forward a little. What's the next thing you remember?"

***

Monday night. I'm out with Carrie at this youth group meeting at her church. We watch this movie after: giant scorpions march down a street, spearing people through the chest. Somehow this relates to the Rapture. Carrie is holding my hand but I barely feel it. All I can think of is Colin and the kiss. Carrie squeezes my hand and I'm looking into her eyes, touching her and thinking of someone else. I feel all greasy inside.

I walk Carrie home. Then I text Colin. He sends me a topless pic. He's in his bathroom just getting out of the shower. His hair is wet and tousled. There's a burgundy towel wrapped around his waist. I stop walking because I can't trust my knees anymore. He is just so beautiful. He wants to be with me. I used to think it was all nonsense, this 'the heart wants what the heart wants' thing. I thought people were just weak willed or something. But as soon as I saw that picture, as soon as that feeling came over me, I knew I was done.

I go over to his place. He sneaks outside and we make out behind his garage. His hands are under my shirt touching my nipples and…

***

"Okay, I think we can skip this part," Instructor Mal said, clearing his throat. "Unless this boy pushed you through a foramen I'm fairly certain that has nothing to do with how you got here. What's the next thing you remember?"

***

My friend Dan is beaten pretty badly and ended up in the hospital. Some idiots from the football team. He came out. That means he told people he was gay. I mean, it's the 21st century and all, but there were a few idiots from the football team. Almost everyone is okay with it, but…. It makes the local news, but Dan refuses to name names. I think I get why. He just wants to go back to the way it used to be. To pretend it never happened. To forget.

Things get worse from here on.

Carrie borrows my phone to update her Facebook. It's lunchtime and we're out on the bleachers because the weather is nice. I can't believe I am so stupid! Anyway, she sees a conversation between me and Colin. Before I can stop her, she smashes my phone and starts screaming at me. I tell her to keep her voice down, saying it's not what it looks like. Other people hear us. She runs away and I'm stuck there, everyone stares at me as I pick up the pieces of my phone.

A few hours later Colin pulls me into an empty classroom. He's so angry. Carrie waited for him after Biology and confronted him in the hallway. He feels betrayed, like I did it on purpose or something. He says he thinks we should not be seen together for a while. But I tell him I can't do that. I reach for him. He pulls away at first, but I can tell he doesn't want to. I kiss him until we hear footsteps. I don't realize I'm crying until he brushes tears away from my cheeks.

By the end of the week, Dan's back in school. He's covered in bruises and his left arm is in a cast. It terrifies me to be seen with him, but how can I not support him? Most people are supportive. A few point at us, whispering behind our back, when they see us together. At the end of the day, I go to my locker to drop off my books and I see it. "Faggot." Someone spray-painted it across my locker. I can't help it. I start to cry a little bit. And I am so angry. Embarrassed and upset but mostly furious. And I remember thinking I would sell my soul just to get even with them. I wished I had a way to get back at them.

***

Instructor Mal sighed. "Oh dear."

"Look, can we stop being so judgmental? I can't help being gay." Tadgh shivered, suddenly freezing inside.

"My reaction is not based on to whom you're attracted. Your world must be a peaceful place if that is an issue of any significance. Here we have greater concerns. Unfortunately, I see a pattern. I think I know what your power is."

"What power?" Tadgh rubbed his arms trying to bring some heat to his body.

"No one knows why it happens, not even the Nizarians with all their advanced science." Instructor Mal pinched the bridge of his nose. "Every once in a while a person is born with an ability not normal for their species. Some believe this is part of our evolution. Others believe it is a corruption in the genetic programming of the Beherskers who made us all. Still others believe that millennia of fieldbending have weakened the reality field, causing grave fault lines in the biological makeup of other species. Their phylogenetic potential. All we know for sure is that these fod sel-ondes can be powerful and dangerous."

"But what is a fod sel-onde? Is it like a mutant or something?"

"Hmm. Perhaps that is a good word. Technically, fod sel-onde translates to 'birth evil'. Most people here, on Maghe Sihre, view them as abominations. There's an entire branch of fieldbenders devoted to tracking down fod sel-onde and killing them. Don't worry, you're safe here. At least as safe as anyone like you could be. The Brotherhood of Tyche views fod sel-onde differently. We don't believe anything created by the gods is born evil. The real questions is, are we safe from you?"

"How could I be dangerous?"

The Instructor exhaled slowly. Then he locked eyes with Tadgh. "As I said, I see a pattern. Twice you asked for something selfish and impossible. The first time you asked for revenge. The second time you asked to be able to speak our language. Can you not see the danger?"

Tadgh laughed. For a moment. "You're serious. You actually think I'm able to have my wishes come true? Why isn't that a good power?"

"Mortals should not have the power of gods, Tadgh."

"That sounds like a cop-out. If I could make my wishes come true, I would just wish myself back…"

Instructor Mal placed a hand over Tadgh's mouth. "Don't even think about finishing that sentence."

Instantly, all thought stopped in his mind. Everything became deathly still, peaceful.

Tadgh nodded in understanding.

Instructor Mal removed his hand. "Everyone thinks they understand reality. Whether or not we're right or wrong is a question we'll learn in the next life. However, there are certain tenets most religions have in common with science. The world as we know it is constructed of various energy fields that shape and influence what we see as reality. One of these is the combined perceptions and expectations of the mortals that live on a planet. A global subconscious, if you will. Individually, most mortals are not powerful enough to change reality. But if enough people come together and want there to be a change, change will happen.

"Despite the propaganda, most fod sel-ondes are not dangerous. One powerful enough to grant his or her own wishes is a different story. Moments ago, when you wished to be able to speak our language, a wave of disruption went through the reality field. It was like nothing I'd ever felt before. At the time I didn't know what it was. It nearly knocked me unconscious. For now, the real problem is that if I felt it, others would have felt it as well. Can you think of what lengths some might go to get a weapon as powerful as you?"

"I'm not a weapon."

"I assure you others will see you as a weapon first and a person second. I would advise you to never use your power again. Every country, every person of power on Maghe Sihre has someone on their payroll who can sense changes in the reality field. Elmire Ahk, fieldbenders, geognosts, demstraki. Different names for people trained to manipulate energy fields. Each time you use your ability it is like shooting a signal to every one of them. That is a force I cannot protect you from."

Tadgh put his bandaged hand to his head. "I just want to go home."

"There are easier ways to travel between the worlds," Instructor Mal stood and straightened his robes. "I'd recommend going to the geognosts in Karaj Robat. They are the experts. However, there's also a major guild of fieldbenders there. It would be too risky. There's a man in GardenKeep knowledgeable in many things. He is called the Sage. If there's a way to get you home, he will know it. I'll have one of our prelates, Menphis, travel with you. The journey will take nearly two weeks."

"Two weeks? How far away is this city?"

"Not far as the birds fly. Tyche demands we travel by foot, so there are no Nizarian cycles here. It will take you almost a full day to get out of the hunt. After that the journey will be along the highway. You'll find inns to sleep in every night as soon as you hit the highway. Give me a few days to arrange for a few supplies and some money to fund the journey."

Tadgh looked down at his wounds. "I don't really see how I'm going to be able to walk for two hours let alone two weeks."

"It's true that some of your wounds have proven resistant to healing but we can have your broken bones fixed today. The people at this monastery are among the best healers on the planet. It was very fortunate for to land her. "

Instructor Mal turned to leave. Then he stopped and turned back to Tadgh.

"Now that I've opened your mind, the memories should start coming back to you slowly. With luck, all your memories will be back by the time you meet the Sage."

Chapter Seven

Out of habit, Tadgh glanced at his wrist. His watch, like all his own clothing, was gone. He folded his hands behind his head and stared at the ceiling. He wanted to sleep but, with the bandages around his head, it was impossible to get comfortable. Normally he slept on his stomach. The cast on his leg and the wounds on his chest forced him to lie on his back. Every movement made him feel even more uncomfortable.

'I know I should find this place relaxing, but it's just too quiet here.' He was a city boy; he missed the hum of the furnace, the roar of the occasional car. Here there was nothing but the whirling of an unidentifiable insect and the leaves rustling in the wind. A cool breeze blew through the open windows of the infirmary. The air was cleaner than anything back on Earth.

Instructor Mal's words from the morning repeated constantly in his mind. 'Am I really a fod sel-onde? Do I really have the ability to make my wishes come true? I've always wanted to be a superhero. What kid doesn't? But it's not so cool if every time I use it I alert a group of people who want me dead.'

They wanted to kill him just for being what he was. However, in a strange way, he was used to that. After all, that's how all this began.

***

I'm in the hospital. I blink. Everything seems slow. My eyes trace the line of a tube inserted in my arm back to the bag of liquid hanging above me. I have no idea what they're putting into me. My mother stands by the window, crying. My father screams at someone in the hallway. I think it's the police this time. Earlier, a reporter from some CNN magazine snuck in and asked me questions. I don't remember what I said, but Dad's not happy.

"Mom, go home," I say.

She doesn't look at me. She just waves her hand as if to deflect the thought.

"I promise I'm not going anywhere. You heard Dr. Goertz. I'm stable now. No danger. Just go home and get some rest."

"There won't be any rest at home, Tadgh. There are reporters all over our street. Everyone wants a sound bite. They want to hear us talk about…" She glances back at me but only for a moment. Hand on chin, fingers covering her lips, she falls silent. I drift into a daze listening to the background noises outside my room. The whoosh of the floor buffer, conversations from down the hall, the sound of a TV next door. Father is no longer screaming.

When my mom speaks again her voice is barely a whisper. "It's not right what they did to you. But I hope you realize you've chosen a very hard life for yourself."

"I didn't choose this." My throat tightens up, making it hard for the words to come out. I clench my fists as much as I can. "Who would ever choose this? All I want is to be normal."

"Then try harder." My mother turns away from the window and faces the back wall. I can hear her sniffling as if trying to stop tears from flowing. "If it wasn't for the woman that scared them off, those boys would have killed you. I know I'm supposed to be supportive, but you could have died. Just like your friend."

"Not yet." I close my eyes. "Please. I can't deal with that yet."

"You think I can?" She reaches for her purse and pulls out a small, orange bottle: a new prescription. She dry swallows two pills and, after replacing the bottle zips the purse closed. "Maybe you're right. I should go home and get some sleep. Call me if you need anything. And don't talk to any more reporters."

I bury my head in the pillow. I don't trust myself to speak. When I look up again, I'm alone.

The drugs I'm on don't really take away the pain. I feel this heavy pressure pushing down on the broken parts of me. I have sutures and gauze all over my body: the places they had to stitch back together.

I slip into sleep and I'm back on the ground again. They are above me, stomping on me. Heavy boots kick in my ribs. I remember the sound of my bones breaking. They laugh each time I cry out. I know each of them from school. Now they look like strangers. Colin is only a few feet away from me. He's not moving. Someone spits in my face and asks if I like it. The worst memory is what they do with the baseball bat.

I wake up and push the dream away. I don't want to think about it. It's too much. The doctors say I'm very fortunate; there's no permanent damage. I don't feel so lucky. Colin is dead. I know I should feel sad, but all I feel is helpless. A rage builds up inside of me. I run it over and over in my mind: I want to hurt them, slowly. I want to make them suffer.

"I wish there was a way to make them feel what I feel."

From the window, a cat meows.

It's such an unexpected thing that all my anger disappears. 'How the hell did a cat get in my room? I'm on the sixth floor.'

I look over at the open window and see a cat crouching there. Something's not quite right. Its eyes are too bright, the fur unnaturally orange. The way it purrs terrifies me. I can't move. Every part of my body goes numb except for my eyes. I watch as it jumps off the window sill and lands on the bed. Slowly, it crawls up my chest. The whole time it approaches, its eyes are locked on me. The room gets darker, smaller. It feels like the walls are collapsing in on me. Now its purr sounds more like laughter. The cat stands on my throat. Hard to breathe. It puts a paw on my lips and forces my mouth open. Then, its lips move and it speaks to me, not like a cat but like a human.

"Wish granted," it says. "We'll talk of payment later."

It spits something into my open mouth. I choke. I feel it growing, spreading over my teeth and my tongue. I try to spit it out. The cat just closes my lips and stares into my eyes. I try to scream. My vocal chords are numb. Whatever it spit into my mouth spreads through my entire body. Muscle and bone structures change. My legs and arms grow larger, shattering the casts. I flex my arms and legs. Suddenly they are healed and pain-free. Before I can celebrate, I realize my body hasn't stopped changing. Orange fur, the same color as the cat's, sprouts from every inch of my body. I look down at my hands. Each finger now ends in a thick, black claw.

The cat leaps off me and suddenly I can move again. I throw myself out of bed and land on the floor with a thud. I stumble to the mirror in the bathroom.

When I see my face, I scream.

I hear the door to my hospital room open. Turning towards the sound, I see two police officers in uniform, the ones stationed for my protection. They look at me and draw their guns. I raise my hand, telling them not to shoot, but they're scared. I can't blame them. They fire their weapons so many times I can't count. The bullets slice through me, so hot. The blunt force knocks me back.

Then the bullets are pushed back out of my flesh. They drop to the bathroom floor; the sound of bullets bouncing on tile is the only thing I hear. Before the sound dies away, my body repairs the damage, leaving no sign of injury on my body.

The police officers stare at me, shock written on their faces. Before they can fire again, I push past them. I hit one man so hard he slams against the opposite wall, cracking the drywall. I hear someone scream, but I don't wait around to see who it is. I run towards the first exit sign I see. I race down the stairs wearing only my hospital gown, but I feel warm. My fur insulates me. I realize I'm taking the stairs really quickly. My body seems stronger now. Faster.

When I hit the second landing, I hear sounds from behind me. They are following. I have to be faster. I jump down the next flight and land easily, painlessly. I'm not thinking: just moving on instinct. I jump down the next several flights. Finally I'm outside.

It's evening. A quick look reminds me where I am: Lutheran Hospital. The parking lot in front of me is lit by lamps. Beyond that is Riverview Towers.

"Hide. Head for the trees." My voice sounds weird, deep and demonic. I run across the parking lot and stop at the edge of West 25th Street. The traffic is steady but I know I can't wait for the light. I hear the bang of a door slamming open and someone calls out from behind me. Without thinking, I jump. For a moment it feels like I'm flying. Cool wind blows through my fur. I move so quickly the world blurs around me. Then I'm on the other side of the street.

"Holy crap," I say. I realize I jumped 10' high and over 40' across. Before I can think about that too much, another bullet slams into my chest. I look up at the nearby apartment building and jump again. My hands, now paws, grasp the railing on the fifth floor and I pull myself up. They are shooting at me again so I keep jumping up until I'm on the roof of the building.

It's dark but my eyes adjust. I can see better now in the dark than I could before, but it's different. Everything has a greenish tinge to it. I remember that cats are semi-colorblind, but my sight is far from the strangest part of the night. I rush to the other side of the building. I see the water and the trees from here. I also hear the sound of sirens behind me.

I look over the edge, wondering if I could make the jump down from here. Even if my body can handle it, my head and my fear of heights cannot. Instead, I jump down to the first balcony and drop, floor by floor, until I'm on the third floor. Then I jump to the ground and start running. I pass through the back parking lot, my bare feet, now also paws, are surprisingly insensitive to the hard concrete.

I am halfway through the fields of the Ohio City Farm before I hear shots again. Thankfully, they miss. Although the wounds healed, being shot was the worst pain of my life.

On the other side of the farm, I jump across the traffic of Franklin Ave. and tumble less than gracefully through the underbrush. I land on my feet and jump up into the foliage of a nearby tree. My animal instinct tells me to run, but I hold firm. Men with guns are searching for me, but a part of me knows they will wait for backup. They will not chase the monster into the darkness.

Time passes. Clinging to the bark of the tree is easy with my strong arms and sharp claws. Below me several police officers shine flashlights into the darkness. The light shines near me repeatedly. I have no idea how they don't see me. Maybe whatever has happened to me lets me blend into the shadows better. Eventually, they give up the search and leave. After the sound of their voices fade, I relax. I stare down at my furry hands, too numb to think. Eventually I drift into sleep.

I wake to the sound of feet hitting pavement. My eyes flash open and I fall out of the tree. Just before I hit the ground, my feet are underneath me. I land in a perfect squat and watch as two men in tracksuits jog by. They are wearing headphones, oblivious to me.

I shiver. A quick glance down reveals I'm a man again. Without fur to keep me warm, the winter air cuts into me. I glance over my shoulder at my bare behind and duck down further.

"Such a shy boy," a voice says.

The cat from the hospital slinks out of the shadowy underbrush. Even though it is daylight, its eyes still glow brightly.

"What the hell are you?" I take a step back. "What have you done to me?"

The cat coos and comes closer to me. "What I am is a helper. What I've done is help you. You wanted revenge. I've given you the means. What more do you need know?"

"I turned into a flippin' were-cat last night. I think I need to know more about that."

"You're probably right," the cat said. "Knowing what you are, knowing what you can do will expedite the next step. Still, this may not be the best place for that conversation."

"Well, we can't exactly hang out at a Starbucks," I say. "Naked people talking to cats tend to stand out."

The cat tilts his head to one side. "Fine. Is that better?"

The air around my skin goes warm and moist for a moment. When I look down, I am wearing jeans and a warm bomber jacket over a light grey sweater.

"How did you do that?"

"The question you should be asking yourself is *why* I did it. Follow me. There's a utility shed this way. We can talk inside."

He doesn't wait for me. He heads off along the edge of the water. I run after him, keeping to the woods. After what happened at the hospital, I have no idea if anyone is looking for me. Although it's early, I don't want to chance running into any other runners. Minutes later we arrive at a 6' tall chain link fence. The cat walks to the fence and jumps over it.

I get to the fence and look for a way in. The cat looks back and me and sighs.

"Switch," he says.

I look back at him blankly.

The cat sits and crosses his front paws. "Please tell me I did not choose an idiot as my avatar. Switch to your feline form. All it takes is a thought."

"I don't under…" But then I do understand. It's like this switch goes off in my mind and suddenly my bones and muscles are changing again. Fur shoots out over my body and I feel so much stronger. It takes less than a minute. Once I'm in feline form, I jump over the fence easily. My cat guide stands and leads me through an open door into a small tool shed. Once we are both inside, the door closes behind us.

"Much better," the cat says. "I could tell you my name is Bes, but I'm sure you've never heard of me. Suffice it to say that, in my time, I was worshipped as a deity. My area of expertise was the protection of women, young children and warriors."

"I am none of the above," I say.

"Oh, but you are." Bes lifts his chin. "Perhaps not before, but you are now. You just needed the right tools. Now you have them. In this form you are stronger, faster, and more agile than humanly possible. You also have another perk." The cat turns its head and stares at a bundle of three-foot long rebar. One of the shafts jumps clear. It flies through the air and slams into my gut. I look down. I can see it cutting into me. I look behind me; it has gone out the other side.

"Don't pass out, now," Bes says. "Showing is always more effective than having me say it. Simple weapons like this cannot kill you. I would, however, stay away from anything silver. That metal has an unfortunate affect on shapeshifters. Are you going to leave that in you?"

I look down at the shaft. It causes me very little pain and I realize I'm losing only minimal blood. With both hands, I grab the base of the rebar right where it enters me and pull it out. It comes slowly. The sound is…disturbing…but the pain is more like a paper cut than a mortal wound. When it's free of my body I let it clank to the floor. A small splatter of blood pools out over the middle section. I look down at my body and the hole in my abdomen. It is already healing.

"As I said, nifty." The cat jumps up onto a table covered in tools, putting it closer to eye level with me. "Now, as with most things in life, these gifts do not come for free. There is a price, but it's one I think you'll be willing to pay."

"What do you want from me?" I glance down at my hands. They are covered in a thin layer of blood.

"The typical. You kill, I take their souls. Not literally their souls, of course, because that's impossible. I want their life energy. And for that, I give you one last gift. Lay your hands on a man or woman and they will submit their will to yours. They will do anything for you. Ask them to give you their life energy. You can't steal it. They have to give it. Your body will store the energy until I come back to claim it. Once you've killed the men who killed your love, I will return. I'll claim the energy you've collected and take back these gifts I've given you. A simple 'quid pro quo,' as it were. Now, do you think you can live up to your end of the bargain? Can you actually kill these boys?"

My lips spread in a slow smile.

**

Tadgh woke from the dream covered in sweat. He looked down at his hands. There was no sign of claws or blood. Only shaking fingers.

Chapter Eight

Prelate Leif sat at an outdoor café drinking hot tea. He watched the woman in darkstone armor over the top of his cup. She stood on the opposite side of the city square beside the door to a bookstore. Housewives filled the market doing their daily shopping while their husbands worked in the lumber mills at the edge of town. Each wore drab, functional dresses, their hair hidden by white scarves. Most were slightly plump, the benefit of an easy life filled with sufficient food and freedom from violence.

A lean, cold woman stood outside the bookstore, the threat of violence in her eyes. She wore slick, expensive-looking darkstone armor and carried a thick short sword at her hip.

"What kind of bookstore needs an armed guard?" He whispered the words to himself and drank the rest of his tea. He wore a simple, unbleached cotton shirt and deep green cotton pants. 'Good thing I followed Instructor Mal's directives. My Elmire Ahk uniform would have marked me as a member of the Brotherhood of Tyche. At least dressed as a mill worker I'll be slightly more inconspicuous.'

A heavy, balding man in mottled pink and white robes walked up to the woman. After a quick exchange of words, she reached behind and pushed open the door to the bookstore. The man bowed his head slightly and slipped inside.

Leif stood and left a few coins on the table to pay for the tea. He moved casually across the square. He stopped at the occasional booth to peruse their goods: smoked fish, golden jewelry from Norshire, exotic spices from the New World. Then, he walked past the woman in the darkstone armor. He kept his eyes on the ground and moved quickly to give the illusion he was in a hurry to get somewhere. When he was several blocks away he doubled back.

He'd been coming to Tarkon for years on supply runs. He knew these streets; he knew these people. Aside from the city's police force, the woman was the only person he'd seen with the look of someone who lives by the sword.

Tarkon, like Pleasure Port to the northwest and GardenKeep to the southeast, was a major shipping port. It traded mostly in lumber and furs from Wilkin Hunt. This was a young city, only a few hundred years old. Most cities in Shirza had been founded shortly after the War of Independence, when the people of Maghe Sihre broke free from the tyranny of the Great Castles. The major religion of the area was the worship of Fricka. Her religious order, the Sisterhood of the Flesh, was the largest branch of Elmire Ahk in the country. Her followers saw all beauty and acts of love as expressions of divinity. Wondrous buildings of stone and marble were at the center of Shirza civilization. Glass and crystal sculptures adorned city squares surrounded by fountains of clear, drinkable water.

Unlike most cities in Shirza, Tarkon had no stone structures. Founded by members of the new religion, the Pheonides, its architecture was one of necessity. It favored wood, mostly for practical reasons. The city sat at the edge of the largest Hunt in the country; Wilkin Hunt was over 400 miles long and 150 miles wide at its widest. Most of Shirza was highly developed farmland; however, the continent needed lumber for construction. There were specific economic advantages to keeping the woods wild and free.

Leif stepped off the main streets. Using a series of alleyways, he headed back to the bookstore. The practical design of Tarkon worked to his advantage. Most of the commercial area was set up in rows of long rectangles. While the outer walls were thick, interior walls were just thick enough to dampen sound between stores.

The bookstore shared a side wall with the stonemasons' guild. When he noticed the out-of-place darkstone armor, Prelate Leif walked in the front door of the guild. He muddled the guildmaster's mind and stole the keys to the building from him. He also convinced the guildmaster to go home for the day. Now Leif slipped through the back door.

He found himself in a storage room filled with metal filing cabinets. Using the strength and grace from his training, he jumped to the top one of the cabinets and landed silently. He closed his eyes and focused his breathing until he gained control of his aura. When he opened his eyes, he looked at the ceiling. He touched one of the nails that secured the wooden planks. With a squeak, the nail shot upwards, flying free of the wood.

Wiping sweat from his forehead, he closed his eyes again.

'This will take hours. But I can't risk moving quickly. The noise would alert whoever's in the bookstore.'

Seven nails later, the first board came loose. Hands trembling with the mental exertion, he placed the board beside him. He sat on the cabinet and wiped sweat from his forehead. The strain on his aura had drained him.

'With any luck, I can remove the second board and be in the attic by afternoon siesta.' He had time, so he closed his eyes and slept.

When he woke, light filtered through the window above the door. He took this to mean the sun was close to being directly overhead. Midday: he was on time. He stood and began on the next board. After every nail shot into the attic, he quietly lowered the second plank to the floor. He grabbed the thick crossbeam and easily pulled himself into the dark attic.

Functionality also meant shared roofs and attics. There was no insulation. It never got cold enough in the south to justify it. On hands and knees he crawled along the crossbeams. He moved slowly, expertly spreading out the weight of his body to move silently. Below he heard voices muffled by the thick wood.

He pulled a machine from his pocket: a small metal spool with tiny green lights moving in concentric circles on one end. He'd never seen anything like it before yesterday.

Instructor Mal had given it to him to help with his mission. It was Nizarian technology but, to him, it was no different than fieldbending. It allowed you to turn any material into a one-way mirror. Instructor Mal had placed it over a table to demonstrate. Immediately the table had become transparent from one side while still appearing opaque from the other.

Leif went to where the voices were strongest and placed the device beneath him. As soon as the concentric lights hit the wood, there was a momentary hum. Then the device went silent and a three foot square section of the wood became as clear as glass. Suddenly, the words were no longer muffled. Leif heard everything clearly.

"How?" Leif slapped a hand over his mouth to stop the sound before he gave himself away. Below him was the overweight man in the pink and white mottled robes. That was not what scared him.

It was the Trofast, a member of the oldest native race on Maghe Sihre. Most were allied with the armies of Dispayre. Physically, they were the largest of the races. This one stood two heads taller than an average Sirian. He wore an elaborate set of armor with rings and pieces of red fabric over darkstone plate. His slick, oily black hair contrasted against his mottled mauve skin. To Leif, it seemed unnatural for flesh to be that color.

"Your excuses bore me, Oshu," the Trofast said. Arms crossed over his chest, he sagged against the wall. His deep voice rattled in the room below. "The Quadumvirate gave you one task. Something is weakening the Void. Find the source. We need to find it and make it work faster. If you're not capable of finding it, perhaps you will serve us better as an Umbral Knight."

"Come now, Ein," a new voice said. The speaker was out of sight, not beneath the transparent section. "Threatening the poor bender won't help us find the source any faster."

"Of course, Lord Vyken," the Trofast, Ein, said.

Oshu wiped sweat from his palm on his robes. "I'll find the source. It's just taking longer than expected. You have to understand. Something that powerful leaves ripples on the reality field, but they're hard to track."

"Again with the excuses." Ein pointed at Oshu. His fingers started to crackle with orange and purple energy.

'Fantastic,' Leif thought. 'He's not just a Trofast. He's a flipping demstraki.' The demstraki were a breakaway sect of fieldbenders. They used the Damatamen plant, an herb with mauve-colored leaves and flowers, to enhance their ability to manipulate the reality field. 'What the hell is going on here? And why are they talking about the Void?'

"I said, enough, Ein." Lord Vyken, the previously unseen speaker, walked into view: a middle-aged Sirian with graying hair. He wore a loose, white tunic with rolled up sleeves. "Throwing your magic in our faces makes you look petty. Oshu knows you're serious. He also knows continued incompetence will have…consequences."

Ein grunted, a heavy unnerving sound.

"I'll find the source by week's end." Oshu wiped sweat from his forehead with the back of his hand. "If you'll give me leave to kill a few people, there's a blood spell I could try."

"Kill no one." Lord Vyken stabbed his index finger into Oshu's chest. "The whole idea of a secret invasion is that we stay secret. Myan will destroy you if you ruin this. Unexplained deaths bring suspicion. Our forces will be at full strength by the end of next month. The artifact will be in our hands shortly after that. Only then do we make our move. Understood?"

Oshu lowered his head. "Perfectly. I know the source is somewhere in Shirza, my lord."

"Shirza is a big country." Ein uncrossed his arms and clenched his fists.

"I know!" Oshu bared his teeth and punched the wall beside him.

Ein raised an eyebrow.

Oshu sighed. "I mean, I'm aware of its size. I also have the vibration of the source. If it so much as twinges again I can pinpoint its location immediately to within 100 paces. I'll find the source. Maybe you should be worried about the bloody graunskyeg living up to their end of the bargain."

Prelate Leif went pale. 'Graunskyeg? They're working with the living dead? What the hell have I stumbled into?'

"Perhaps we should ask them directly," Lord Vyken said. "Oshu, leave us. Head back to your quarters for now. Be back an hour after sunset. On your way out, please send Desdemona inside for a moment."

"Yes, my lord." Oshu bowed slightly towards both Lord Vyken and Ein before leaving.

Once Oshu was out of earshot, Ein leaned close to Lord Vyken. "Is he really the best you could find?"

Smiling, Lord Vyken put a hand on Ein's shoulder. "I know he doesn't look like much, but he's stronger than he seems. I knew his father, an excellent soldier. Oshu passed the Examination of the Rock. He would have risen to the rank of Minor Bender if I hadn't stolen him away first. Whatever rivalry exists between demstraki and benders is of no concern to me. We have a common goal here. Stay focused."

Ein's eye twitched. He looked like he wanted to say something further but chose silence instead.

The woman who had been guarding the door appeared. "I shouldn't leave my post for too long, my lord. This city is not safe."

Lord Vyken smiled. "Are all Illuminati as suspicious as you?"

"It makes us good at our job," she said. Away from the sun, her darkstone armor seemed to gleam even brighter. "I'm telling you, this city is too quiet. Something's wrong. Earlier today, I saw a stranger in the market. He did a very good job at being inconspicuous."

"Our location is secure, Desdemona," Ein said. "I've set wards up around the doors and windows. No one is getting in here and no one is spying on us. Your religion makes you paranoid."

Desdemona barely looked at the demstraki. "Stop calling it a religion. My lord, what did you want from me?"

"It's possible our good friend Oshu may be leaving us soon," Lord Vyken said. "We may need to restrain him and send him north. Will you be able to do that for me?"

"Of course," Desdemona said. "I know three different ways to sneak into that tower of his. Give the word and I'll take him in his sleep. Or kill him, whatever pleases you."

Lord Vyken shook his head. "Take him alive, by all means. He's worth more that way. I'll let you know if and when it's necessary to move."

"Yes, sir." Desdemona saluted by touching her forehead and left the room. A moment later, Lord Vyken motioned to Ein. The demstraki left the room as well. Once he was alone, Lord Vyken sat behind a desk and read from a stack of reports.

Prelate Leif moved the one-way mirror device directly above Lord Vyken's reading position. He studied the reports as well as he could from this distance. Though he could read the words, the context was lost on him. He had no way of knowing what archeological reports from the island of DunDegore had to do with progress in the copper mines of Surransin. There were multiple reports on troop movements near Castle Falls and a Norshire Salvager named Sir Overyl.

'What the hell is going on?' Prelate Leif pulled a small notebook and pencil from his pocket. He scribbled down notes as quickly as possible. 'This is all beyond me. I hope Instructor Mal can make sense of this.'

Hours passed and the room grew dark. Lord Vyken touched the base of the Nizarian lamp. His desk lit up, revealing maps and reports on spies within the Great Castles.

Leif stopped writing. A sudden coldness drifted in from below, a sensation unlike anything he had ever felt before. Looking around at the attic's shadows, he realized it was far later than expected. The sun was long since down.

Below, Ein and Oshu walked back into the room.

Lord Vyken looked up from the reports. "He's here?"

Oshu nodded. "Be grateful you cannot feel his presence. Vile creatures."

"Wait until you are in the presence of an Umbral Knight," Ein said. "Now that is a sensation." His eyes danced from shadow to shadow. He seemed to be looking for something. A moment later, the subject of his searching was visible. Shadows bled down the walls like thick oil seeping from the corners. Then the shadows dripped upwards. They splashed the ceiling with impenetrable darkness, dimming Leif's view of the room. The drips intensified until a steady flow of oily liquid streamed between floor and ceiling. From the midst of this darkness, a face appeared near the wall.

'By all that's holy,' Prelate Leif thought. 'What is that?'

Oshu shook his head. "Must you be so dramatic, Teric?"

"I could always use the front door," the figure in shadow replied. "Of course, townspeople tend to get a little nervous when they see my kind. Don't tell me shadow traveling unnerves you, fieldbender?"

Oshu grunted and turned away.

"Where are the others?" Lord Vyken asked.

"Unable to attend, my lord." Teric's face smiled under the wavering shadow. "My kind have ways to communicate. When you speak to me, it is like you are speaking to the others. What news do you have?"

"Most campaigns progress on schedule," Lord Vyken motioned towards the stacks of reports before him. "There's been some resistance in Surransin, but nothing we can't handle. My main concern is the unknown force cracking the Void open. If the force continues at this rate, the Void will be breachable within a month."

"Curious." Teric's face rippled in the shadow like stone under water. "Could Dispayre be working from the other side?"

"Unlikely," Ein said. "The Void was designed to rob him of his will and intellect. He should be comatose. A few more of these cracks, however, and he'll start to wake."

Lord Vyken closed his eyes and pinched the bridge of his nose. "It's too fast. We're not ready for this. The truth is we have no idea what is causing the cracks. Oshu is looking into it for me. He assures me he's making progress. But that's not why you're here. The cracking of the Void means certain parts of the plan must be moved forward significantly. How soon can the graunskyeg converge on DunDegore?"

"They need at least a year," Teric said. "I have already created my allotted share. Finding subjects is easier for me because I'm close to civilization. The others live in more remote areas. Two near Vaasa to the far north, one in King's Cliff on the edge of the Badlands. A fourth is across the Celtica Sea in Lareth. If we take too many too quickly we risk alerting the local authorities. Wasting resources on a useless battle near our homes is the last thing we need."

"We may not have a year," Oshu said.

"Exactly," Lord Vyken said. "Please let the others know things have changed. The Void has cracked twice this week. If the intensity decreases you may get your full year. If the intensity increases, the Void could be open in six months. Perhaps it would be best to…"

Suddenly, Teric raised his hand: a solid mass of ivory-cool flesh emerging from the liquid shadow. "We are not alone."

"Nonsense," Ein said. "My wards…"

"Are over windows and doors," Teric said. "I can feel them. Still, they didn't prevent me from getting in here, did they? My guess is you forgot about the attic."

Teric raised his eyes and looked directly at Prelate Leif.

"Damn," Leif said. He grabbed the Nizarian device and shut down the two-way mirror, but it was too late. Before he could place it in his pocket there were icy hands around his throat. The air turned cold and slick around him as he was pulled into the shadows. Just as quickly, he was thrown into the light. He found himself on all fours in the room below, directly in front of Lord Vyken.

"Impossible!" Ein said. "There was no way into the attic. I checked."

"Obviously you didn't check enough," Lord Vyken said. "What have you heard, spy?"

Prelate Leif quickly contained his fear. He lifted his head to look squarely at Lord Vyken. He wanted a clear look at the man's face. If he made it out of this alive, there was a chance he could identify the man later.

Ein shot a bolt of yellow energy from his outstretched hand. It slashed into Leif's shoulder. Blood gushed from the wound. He screamed in pain but quickly regained control of himself.

"Who sent you, little bug?" Teric said. "Your blood is so pure. Sickening, really. I would take you for an Elmire Ahk. Which false god do you worship?"

"What kind of creature are you?" Prelate Leif studied Teric's face.

Teric grabbed Leif's chin. "You have been very sheltered if you do not recognize my kind."

"We should kill him," Oshu said.

"Not until we know who sent him," Lord Vyken said. "Take him to your tower. You have a place for questioning there, correct?"

"Of course," Oshu said. "Do we risk dragging him through the streets? What if he's seen too much?"

Lord Vyken bit his thumbnail. "Take him after the bars close. Anyone that sees him will assume he's drunk. He looks on the verge of unconsciousness now. Ein, blast him in the head. That should…"

Prelate Leif moved. Faster than the others expected, he slid between Ein's legs. Then, focusing all the strength of his body into his fists, he punched the demstraki's knee. The force that had driven nails from the wood shattered Ein's leg. The demstraki fell.

Before Leif could stand, Oshu shot a bolt of purple energy at him. It hit square in his back, driving him forcefully forward. His head bounced off the wood, nose shattered and vision blurred.

"Throw him to me," Teric said. "I can smell his blood."

"Back off," Lord Vyken said. "We need him alive."

While Ein moaned in pain, Oshu walked forward and grabbed Prelate Leif by the hair. "Don't do that again. I'm being nice to you, but my patience has limits. Have you ever felt the rage of a fieldbender?"

Prelate Leif tried to focus. He shot his arm out but it stopped in midair. Then every bone in his hand snapped. He screamed as the pain overcame all rational thought.

"I said, behave," Oshu said. "If he is Elmire Ahk, he's a dangerous prisoner. We should bind his hands and feet."

'Thanks for reminding me,' Leif thought.

With his good hand he reached into his pocket for the pencil. He focused the entire power of his aura. Faster than the eye could follow, he threw the pencil at Oshu. It stabbed the fieldbender in the eye. Even before Oshu started to scream, Leif jumped to his feet. He ran towards the front door. He did not get far before icy cold hands grabbed him by the throat again.

"Such a strong toy you are," Teric said. Leaning forward, he sniffed Leif's neck. "Your fear makes you tasty. Please continue to struggle. It makes this more fun."

"No!" Leif called upon his training and summoned the spirit of Tyche. There was no visible sign of the deity's presence except for Teric's response. The cool marble-like arms started to steam. Rot and disease spread out over the flesh. Then it was Teric's turn to scream.

"Cheating Elmire Ahk!" Teric pulled his hands away and jumped into the shadows. He reappeared at the back of the bookstore. "It won't save you. I don't have to be near you to kill you."

'Let's not put that to the test,' Prelate Leif thought. Before Teric made another move, Leif ran for the door. He slammed through the front door, racing past the guard before she could draw her sword. All around him the market was alive, filled with people gathered for drink and song.

'I have to get back to the monastery. But I'm a long way from home.' He ran to the edge of town, cradling his shattered hand in his other arm. He kept to the lit areas. He could not trust what monster would appear from the shadows.

Chapter Nine

Tadgh sat on the bench outside the infirmary trying to forget about last night's dream. A blur of movement turned his attention to the woods: tall coniferous trees with large, unfamiliar leaves. At the edge of the trees, a woman stood, half-hidden in shadow. She wore a blue dress, her long dark hair hanging to her shoulders. From this distance, her facial features were difficult to distinguish.

"How are you?" He turned to find Shonn standing beside him. He smiled as their eyes met.

Tadgh turned away, blushing. "Who's that?" Just like the first time they met, his body felt numb.

Shonn looked around the woods. "Who's who?"

"That woman." Tadgh turned back to the woods. She was gone. "Weird. I saw a woman in the woods. I didn't think there were any women at the monastery."

"There are a few." Shonn shrugged. "It might have been Mirelda, our head cook. She's often in the woods, talking to trees or something. Don't ask. It's just something followers of the Oak Lord do. You didn't answer my question. How are you?"

Tadgh sighed. "I honestly have no idea. Prelate Finn and a bunch of other monks prayed over me…or something. They finally healed my leg, so I'm not an invalid anymore. But they can't seem to fix whatever is wrong with my face. So I'm stuck with these damn bandages for a while."

Shonn sat on the bench beside Tadgh. "I think I have something that will distract you from that. I'm heading into the hunt. Want to come with me?"

"I'm not much of a hunter."

Shonn laughed. "Hunt means a place of trees. Northerners call them forests. The one all around us is called Wilkin Hunt. It's the largest in all of Shirza. So will you come with me?"

"I don't know," Tadgh said. "My leg is still a little tender."

"Exercise is exactly what your leg needs." Shonn placed his hand on Tadgh's knee. "Prelate Finn needs a few things from the lake. It's an easy walk, but long. I know I'm not the best company, but…"

"Yes you are," Tadgh said too quickly. He looked into Shonn's eyes.

Shonn smiled, his eyes sparkled.

Tadgh swallowed and looked away. "I mean, sure I'll come with you. Do you think Prelate Finn will mind me wandering off?"

"If we're back before supper they won't even notice you're gone. Besides, you've been here for days and you haven't even seen the whole monastery yet. I can show you what it looks like from the outside. On the other side of the lake there's a cliff. From the top you can see for miles around. I'd like to show you." Standing, Shonn reached out a hand and helped Tadgh to his feet.

The brief contact sent an electric shock through Tadgh's body. For a moment, he held the other man's hand even after he was on his feet. Shonn returned the stare but took his hand back.

"This way," Shonn said.

Tadgh followed him, smiling under his bandages.

They spent the day wandering through the woods. Tadgh was happy to discover that his leg was, in fact, completely healed. The more he walked the stronger he felt. Occasionally, Shonn would kneel down to clip some flower or fungus. He added everything to a wooden basket he carried. Shonn talked about his childhood and his cousin. He also answered Tadgh's questions about local culture and traditions. For Tadgh, it didn't matter what Shonn was actually saying. All that mattered was that he was talking to him.

By the time the sun was high above them, they reached the lake. Shonn spent several minutes scraping green moss from rocks into glass containers.

"That's disgusting," Tadgh said. "Do I want to know what that is?"

Shonn laughed. "It's called argrave. The brothers use this in their healing salves. This kind of thing is beyond me. So I've told you all about my childhood. What was it like for you growing up?"

Tadgh felt the smile on his face slip a little. "Fine, I guess. I mean, I can't complain. My parents made decent money. We had a pretty big house in the city. Do you guys have cities here?"

"Of course we have cities. What? Did you think we all live in the woods?"

"How would I know? You have monks that can heal broken bones by chanting. We don't have that where I'm from. Anyway, life was okay but…" He took a deep breath. He wasn't sure how much he could share with Shonn. Saying too much could destroy their friendship, whatever kind of friendship it was they were building. He stared at the ground, surprised as the words tumbled out of his mouth. "I always knew I was different than other boys. I knew if they found out the truth about me, they, I don't know…I guess I kept people at a distance. Even the ones that wanted to be my friends. They never really got to know the real me, which kept me kind of safe but also completely…"

"Alone?"

Tadgh looked up. Shonn had stopped the scraping and was staring at him.

He nodded in response.

Shonn started scraping again. "I felt the same way. Do you know what they do with fod sel-ondes in Tarkon? Hell, almost everywhere on this planet. They stage a phony trial and then execute us. No one is ever found innocent."

"Wait. You're a fod sel-onde? Instructor Mal said I was one too."

"Really?" Shonn stared at Tadgh for a moment. When Tadgh nodded, Shonn laughed. "Maybe that's why I feel…. Anyway, be careful who you tell you're a fod sel-onde. The fieldbending guilds have convinced everyone we're a threat. They think we can destroy the reality field or blow up the world. They don't actually go into detail about why or how. They just say we have to be killed. Do you have any idea what that feels like? Fod sel-onde are used to frighten children…like rampaging Rheiballough or Lord Dispayre."

"What's a Rheiballough?"

"Giant horned beast native to the Badlands. They say they're the size of a small house."

"Sounds charming. Who is Lord Dispayre?"

Shonn laughed. "Wow. Now there's a question I've never heard anyone ask. He's the boogie man. Well, if you believe the talk, he's responsible for everything that goes wrong in the world. I don't believe that. I think we're capable of many wrong things ourselves. To make a very long story short, he's the dark god worshipped by the Trofast. He was sent into a Hell dimension after Starfall, imprisoned by the very force of the reality field."

"I'm sensing a lot of backstory there. So, what happens if he gets free?"

"The usual." Shonn shrugged. "Death, destruction, screaming babies. Talking goats. No one believes it. It's just a story meant to control people. It has nothing to do with you and me. Come on. I have what I need. If your leg can handle it, let's get to the top of this cliff. You'll never believe the view."

The climb took almost an hour. Thick vegetation grew up through jagged rocks. There was always something to hold on to. Tadgh found the climb easy. For some reason, he was stronger than he expected. Maybe gravity was lighter on this planet.

'Or maybe I'm still a cat-demon,' he thought. He pushed his fears aside and focused on the climb. When they reached the top, Tadgh stood at the edge of a rocky ledge.

They looked to the east out over the treetops at the monastery in the distance.

The first thing he noticed was the towered square at the heart of the monastery. Tadgh had not been there yet, but he knew it was where the Brothers gathered for prayer. Steep stairs led to the inner temple. At each of its four corners, a slender pinecone-shaped tower rose high in the air, each carved from gray stone. In the center of the four towers, a fifth one jutted up higher and more slender than the others. Two sets of exquisite outer walls surrounded the inner temple. The lowest part of the wall was horizontally-rippled sandstone. Above that was a walkway lined with square pillars. A third level was stone shingles that rippled like frozen water. Between the walls and the center towers stood a series of interconnected square galleries, all open air and filled with rich vegetation.

"Holy crap," Tadgh said.

"What exactly is sacred about feces?" Shonn said. "Is that a cultural thing on your planet?"

Tadgh rolled his eyes. "No, it's just a saying." He couldn't take his eyes off the monastery. "This is unbelievable."

Shonn smiled. "I told you it was beautiful."

"That's not what I mean. Of course it's beautiful, but I've seen this before. This temple looks exactly like a place back on Earth. We call it Angkor Wat. I've never been there, but I've seen enough pictures. I didn't see the resemblance before."

"Really?" Shonn set his basket down and stood beside Tadgh. "The Brotherhood of Tyche has many temples just like this around the continent. What is this place, Angkor Wat?"

"I don't really know." Tadgh blinked rapidly and bit his lip. "Some sort of temple city in Cambodia. I've never been that interested in history or architecture before. Suddenly, I really wish I had. How is this possible? I mean, it feels like I'm dreaming. It's the same bloody design. The only difference is that Angkor Wat is in ruins and this place is perfectly maintained. I bet this is what Angkor Wat looked like hundreds of years ago."

"Maybe our worlds have more in common than we thought." Shonn stuck his hands in his pants pockets and moved closer to Tadgh. "We have this legend about an ancient race called the Beherskers. I'm not an expert in history or architecture, either, but here's what I know. There are dozens of ruins all over the world. Some say they used to be Beherskers cities. They disappeared millennia ago, but they were supposed to have incredible powers. According to legend, they created fieldbending and had machines that could travel between the stars. It's also said they created most of the other races on Maghe Sihre. Beherskers created cities that spanned almost the entire continent and built the great Castles to the north. And then one day they just disappeared. They took to the skies in search of other worlds to explore. Maybe they found your world. It would also help explain how your body looks so much like a Sirian body."

Tadgh turned his face away from the monastery. His face was only inches from Shonn. He stared down at the other man's lips.

Shonn inhaled and, as if realizing how close he was, took a step back. Tadgh reached out and touched Shonn's face. For a moment, the entire world stopped. Even the wind in the trees seemed to disappear. The two of them looked into each other's eyes. The only movement in the world was the rise and fall of their chests. Suddenly, Tadgh was reminded of Colin, the way the other boy's lips felt on his. He removed his hand.

"I'm sorry," he said. It felt like his heart was going to break. "I don't know what came over me."

Shonn pressed closer, his hand resting on Tadgh's lower back. He stared into Tadgh's eyes. Tadgh was paralyzed. All thoughts of Colin disappeared. He could think of nothing in the world except the blue eyes that saw directly into his soul.

There were no more words and no more thought for several hours.

Chapter Ten

"How much trouble are you in?" Beneath his bandages, Tadgh could not stop smiling.

Shonn laughed. "Mirelda will skin me alive. I'll probably be on outhouse duty for the rest of the month. But it was worth it. The only thing that would have made today better was if I could see your face."

"I wish you could see my face, too," Tadgh said.

Immediately after the words left his mouth he knew he'd made a mistake. He felt the world go still for a moment but it was not as powerful as before. The ripples were there but not as jarring.

Shonn flinched. "Did you feel that?"

"It was nothing." Tadgh looked at the ground. "I hope. I should let you go. Will I see you tomorrow?"

Again Shonn laughed, a sound like gold covered in honey. "You probably won't want to see me tomorrow. After I clean out the outhouses I'll probably have to stand 30' away from any civilized person. But I'll try to come to you."

Heat rushed through Tadgh's body. He wanted to focus on how he felt about Shonn, but he was too worried about what he'd just done. He remembered Instructor Mal's warnings about the use of his power. Was his face really healed now? And if it was, how many people had felt him use the ability?

Shonn ran off towards the kitchen and Tadgh headed back to the infirmary, his mind moving a mile a minute. When he got there, Prelate Finn was just shutting things down for the night.

"There you are," Finn said. "Did you have fun in the woods?"

"How the hell did you know?" Tadgh felt immediately guilty. "Dear God, if you monks are psychic, how much did you…. Oh. You mean going for the walk. Yes. That was fun. Educational."

Prelate Finn stared at Tadgh, blinked, then shook his head. "How's the leg? Do you still feel any stiffness?"

"No," Tadgh said. "It's as good as new. But I think there's another problem. Did Instructor Mal tell you what he thinks I am?"

Prelate Finn nodded and sat on the edge of one of the unoccupied beds. "He believes you are fod sel-onde. Did something happen?"

"I'm afraid so. Can you remove the bandages over my head? I think I accidentally healed myself."

"Are you sure?" Prelate Finn picked up a pair of thin scissors and walked over to Tadgh. "Your face was covered in deep gashes. We stopped the bleeding but there was extensive damage. If you're wrong, are you prepared to see what you look like?"

"I don't think you'll see any damage," Tadgh said.

Prelate Finn exhaled slowly. "Understood. Hop up on the bed and I'll get those bandages off. Let's see what you've done."

The process was agonizingly slow. The bandages were heavier than Tadgh had expected. When the last piece was unraveled, Prelate Finn stepped back and handed Tadgh a mirror. He saw a young man with lightly tanned skin and smooth cheekbones. His chin was rounded with a slight hint of a cleft. He had a snubbed nose and small, thin lips. Free of the bandages, his black eyes sparkled even more against the contrast of his thick eyelashes and even thicker eyebrows. Shaggy brown hair hung over his ears and forehead.

"Not even a hint of a scar," Prelate Finn said. "That is some ability you have. If only we could use it properly."

"I shouldn't have used it on myself." Tadgh sighed and handed the mirror back to Prelate Finn. "Instructor Mal said it was dangerous, that I could damage the reality field. He said there are fieldbenders out there who would kill me for what I am. How could I have been so stupid?"

"The deed is done. Hating yourself will not undo it. For now, I see no harm. All I see is a young man who has regained his face. I've left some food by your bed. Get something to eat and then call it a night. We can talk more about this in the morning."

After Prelate Finn left, Tadgh ate a meal of dried meats and bread. Then he slipped beneath the covers of his bed. It had been an eventful day. He was very tired. Exhausted, he quickly fell into a dream.

***

There he is: James Fitzpatrick. He's one of the boys that attacked me. He's a year younger than me but he doesn't look it. He's like a mass of solid muscle stuffed into his letterman jacket. His blond hair is tucked loosely under a black knit cap. He glances up at the gently falling snow and smiles.

I want him dead.

After my meeting with Bes, I track him from the one place I know he and my other attackers will be: school. I jump to the roof and wait. I'm not looking for James specifically; he's just the first one I see. He leaves with his girlfriend, arm-in-arm, laughing. Why isn't he in jail? When they are far enough away I jump down and switch back to human form to be less conspicuous. I follow them to his girlfriend's house. They do not look behind them, not even once.

I'm in feline form now, crouched behind a row of shrubbery across the street from the girlfriend's house. I've been waiting for him to come back out for hours in the cold, but I don't mind. Night is a new world to my new senses. Everything is shades of green and yellow. The smells are more vibrant, full. Even from 100' away I can smell the sweat and cologne on James. My hearing is so acute, I've heard their whole evening play out from across the street.

They have supper with her family. When supper ends, they play video games until the girl's parents head to bed. After that I hear them pant and moan from the living room couch.

James hums as he walks home. I can barely control my rage. I remember how he sneered at me as he kicked in my ribs, how he laughed as Colin died. I catch myself growling and stop. I don't want to give away my position.

Twice he stops mid-step and looks behind him. He turns slowly, searching the shadows. For some reason he cannot see me. When he reaches his house, he slips around to the side entrance and fumbles through his pockets for keys. He drops them and looks behind him. He is panting, his eyes darting from shadow to shadow. I crouch behind a car and wait. Somewhere nearby, a dog howls into the night. It feels me: a hunter moving through the herd.

James finds his keys. He jams them into the lock as he looks over his shoulder. He runs inside, slamming the door behind him. I stand and walk slowly to the back door.

I hear two sets of footsteps inside. James talks with an older woman. I assume it is his mother. Then the talk turns to shouts. James stomps upstairs. I slip around the house, looking for a way in. I find one: a window looking into the kitchen. I see a woman in a white blouse and black slacks: a waitress uniform. She has short-cropped blond hair and looks to be in her mid-thirties. I watch her look at the ceiling with tears in her eyes. When she goes into the basement, I go back to the side door. It is locked. I grab the knob and squeeze, tearing it like paper. Within moments the knob is gone. After that, the door swings open silently. I stand in the doorway. Snow falls on the threshold.

'So easy,' I think. I smile as I step inside.

I unplug the refrigerator and lift it easily across the kitchen. Silently, I lay it sideways in front of the basement door, barricading his mother down there. I do not want to be disturbed.

Upstairs, I hear a door swing open on hinges that need to be oiled. A moment later, I hear another door close and the hum of a bathroom fan start. I jump up the flight of stairs, a single silent movement. I head towards the only room with an open door and a light on. I scan the room, my nose telling me it is James'. Dirty clothes are piled around a white hamper. School books sit untouched on a cluttered desk. Hearing the fan shut off, I slip into his closet. I leave the door open. I watch as he comes back into the room and lies on his bed. He's wearing a white t-shirt and plaid boxer shorts. He's so close I could take him by force. But according to Bes, there is another way.

He puts on headphones and closes his eyes. I step from the closet and creep forward. From downstairs I hear the basement door bang against the refrigerator. James hears nothing through his headphones. I reach my claws out and touch his cheek. His eyes flash open, his mouth twitching, ready to scream. I look into his eyes. All I can think of is the open stare of Colin's dead face.

"You owe me," I say. "Give me your life."

James smiles, a look of ecstasy in his eyes and on his lips. He moans. "Anything for you," he says.

I feel energy unlike anything I've felt before. It slides past my fur and into my bones. It fills me up. When I look down again, the light begins to fade in his eyes.

But it's not enough.

I slash open his throat. There is so much blood. It sprays over the room and sinks into my fur. But James does not scream. He looks up at me with love in his eyes. As he dies, I can feel his life energy seeping into me. It makes me stronger, but I know it will not last. I'm just a vessel. Once I finish killing them all, Bes will take the souls as payment. But in that moment, it does not matter. I watch the light go out in his eyes and I am happy.

***

A scream cut through the night.

Tadgh opened his eyes and sat up in bed. 'Did I imagine that?'

Now he heard nothing but the comforting night sounds he'd become accustomed to: wind in the trees, insects. He looked down and saw his white tunic plastered to his chest with sweat. He slipped it off over his head and let the cool night air dry his skin.

'Was that a memory?' He draped the damp shirt over the end of his bed and went to the window. 'Maybe it was my own scream. Is that what woke me?'

Looking out over the dark monastery, he saw nothing but shadows.

"Something's wrong. It's too quiet." He crept out the front door, his bare feet padding quietly against the wood floor. His black hair blew gently in the wind. It carried with it a new scent. "Is that blood?"

Then there was another scream, louder and longer than the first. Tadgh ran back into the infirmary and crouched behind the door. He focused. His hearing became more acute. Now he could hear swords slashing through flesh and bodies falling to the dirt.

"Shonn." Without thinking, he ran from the infirmary and headed towards the servants' quarters. No matter what the danger, he could not let another man he cared for die. He saw the first bodies in the training pavilion. The smell of blood was thick now. He scanned the bodies, looking for familiar faces. They were all strangers.

He sniffed the air. 'That's him. Shonn. He's nearby and frightened. For the record, smelling people is incredibly creepy.'

Goosebumps peppered his skin as the night suddenly felt colder.

'That wasn't just a dream. Did that really happen? Did I really kill James like that?'

Pushing the thought away, he followed Shonn's scent. Though he couldn't see any sign of combat, the sound of battle grew louder. He came across several more bodies bleeding into the dirt at the entrance to the servants' quarters.

"Hang on, Shonn," he said. "I'm coming for you."

Chapter Eleven

Menphis was walking the paved pathway back to his room when he felt the disturbance.

'What is that?' Holding a hand across his stomach, he searched the shadows of the monastery. Nothing he saw supported the way he felt. 'It's like a sound just at the edge of my hearing. I can feel it in my chest. Boom. Boom. Boom. Something out there is…off.'

He stepped off the path into one of the many courtyards of the monastery. He turned in a slow circle, watching the doorways and paths. Nothing moved except the wind in the trees.

"I have to get higher." Nearby, a set of steep stairs led to one of the towers. He took the stairs two at a time. His strong legs brought him quickly to the top. Then he saw it.

In the distance, a shape ran out of the woods. A dozen figures, obscured by the night, pursued close behind. He caught sight of metal shining in the moonlight. The pursuers were armed.

'I don't know who that is, but they're in trouble.' He jumped from the 30' tall tower. Landing in a roll, he ran towards the person being chased. 'No time to raise the alarm. The others will catch him before the Brothers could get here.'

Tyche was the god of traveling. The Elmire Ahk who honored him learned to move quickly. Menphis, like all Prelates, could move much faster than the average Sirian. He was within arm's reach of the fleeing figure in under a minute. He saw the figure's face, recognizing him immediately.

"Prelate Leif!" He shouted the name as his comrade stumbled and fell into him.

Prelate Leif looked up into his eyes, face paled and bloodied from several wounds. A large gash opened his forehead and he cradled one of his arms. What happened? Who did this?"

Leif shook his head. "No time. Run."

Menphis threw Leif over his shoulder and ran towards the infirmary. Before he'd run very far something slammed into his back, sending him flying. He cried out and watched as Leif's body flew through the air. He collided with a pillar along a nearby building.

Shaking off the pain, Menphis stood. Then nausea and vertigo weakened him again. Only this time, he saw the source. A creature with inhumanly pale skin emerged from the shadows. Although it appeared Sirian, everything about it screamed of the unnatural. It seemed to glide across the ground, rather than walk.

"It's been a while since I've seen a man move that quickly." The creature turned to Prelate Leif, who was trying to get to his feet. "Your friend was a fool to think he could evade a graunskyeg, leaving a bloody trail like that. I can taste his blood on my tongue. There is nowhere on this planet I could not find him now."

Something blurred through the night, faster than even Menphis' eyes could follow. It slammed into the creature, sending it flying back towards the woods. The creature slammed into the thick trunk of an old tree. The blur slowed and became a person: Instructor Mal. In his hand was a quarterstaff, the traditional training weapon of the Brotherhood of Tyche.

"Sir," Menphis said, "is that really a graunskyeg?"

Instructor Mal pointed at Leif. "Get him out of here."

With a nod, Menphis ran to pick up Leif. After verifying his friend was still breathing, he gathered Leif into his arms, more gently this time. As he headed towards the infirmary, other Prelates ran the other way, coming to join Instructor Mal in front of the monastery.

'I can't focus on them. I have to get Leif to the infirmary. He's not dying on my watch.'

Behind him, the sounds of fighting grew louder.

***

Shonn lay in bed, smiling up at the ceiling. Surprisingly, Mirelda had not skinned him alive. She had actually said he was back sooner than she expected. Instead of punishment, she had assigned him with washing down the tables in the dining area. He was happy for the time alone. He needed time to think.

'That was amazing. I barely know him, but what happened today with Tadgh made me feel so alive. It's like I've been asleep my whole life. There's something about those eyes. And the sadness in his voice. I can't explain it. It's mesmerizing. All I want to do is go to him. The infirmary isn't far. He's probably still up, and even if he's not...'

Shonn cried out. Pain jabbed through his skull. Every inch of his body screamed at him to run.

"It's happening." He sat up and got dressed. He opened his door and looked outside. "Everything is quiet but it won't be for long." He looked up at the moons in the sky; both were waning, thin sliver crescents in the dark sky.

'It's just like I saw it. I have to tell Menphis. Being by his side is the safest place for me because I have the worst ability of all time. Why can't I be like those fod sel-onde with useful abilities like being super strong or being able to shoot energy from my hands? Being psychic is useless against a sword.'

Staying close to the wall, Shonn headed towards the Prelate quarters. He constantly looked around him for signs of danger. A rush of movement behind him made him look up. Three figures dressed in armor ran along the roofs. Shonn ducked behind a pillar and held his breath.

'If I stay, they'll find me,' he thought. 'If I move, they'll see me. What do I do?' He glanced around the pillar. One of the armored figures jumped from the roof and landed in the courtyard with a thud. It was a woman, black hair in a tight ponytail. She wore darkstone armor and held a thick short sword in her hands. She walked to Shonn's door and opened it. Finding the room empty, she moved to the next one: Charr's. A moment later, there was a hushed gurgle and the woman reemerged. She shook blood from her blade and moved to the next door.

'Damn it.' Shonn turned away, swallowing the scream in his throat. 'It's too late to help Charr now. I have to get to Menphis. And Tadgh. Guess I'll have to chance moving.'

More figures jumped off the roof and began opening every door.

Shonn ran.

***

Tadgh clenched his fists, his nails digging into his palms. 'This is insane. I have to get out of here. But I can't leave without Shonn.'

A man in dark leather armor dropped out of the sky right in front of him. Before Tadgh could react, the man stabbed him. A short sword stabbed into his bared chest and poked out the other side.

Tadgh looked up into the eyes of his attacker. His eyes slid down to the sword embedded in his chest. Every movement felt slow and hyper-real. Then he realized something.

"There's no blood." Quickly, he looked back up at his attacker and saw the same realization move across his face.

With a grunt, his assailant pulled out the sword and slashed at Tadgh's neck. Moving more on instinct than skill, Tadgh spun away from the attack and jumped. When he looked back, he saw that he'd jumped more than twenty feet away.

Two more swordsmen jumped off the roof. All three of them raced towards him. Tadgh thought back to the dreams and what Bes had said. 'It should be easy. Just a thought and I'll be in feline form.'

Something clicked in his mind and the transformation began. Thick orange fur sprouted from his skin. His hands grew larger, the nails extending into thick claws.

The attackers stopped approaching.

One swordsman turned to the others. "What the hell is that thing?"

"Run for Desdemona," another said. "My sword didn't work on it."

"Your sword didn't work because you don't know how to use it," the third man said. He ran at Tadgh, sword high. Tadgh easily dodged the attack. With each passing second, he grew faster, more agile. The sword slashed and stabbed at him. He avoided each blow. Despite himself, he smiled. The swordsman saw the smile and fear flashed through his eyes.

Tadgh reached out and grabbed the man by the throat and said one word: "Stop."

Suddenly the swordsman froze, stiff as a statue. Tadgh smiled again. 'I can feel you in there. You're fighting me but you're going to lose.'

An instant later the man smiled back at him with adoration.

"What kind of monster are you?"

Tadgh turned towards the remaining swordsman. "I have no idea. But I don't think you should attack me again." He looked back into the adoring eyes of the man he'd enchanted. "Protect me."

His puppet nodded and drew a dagger from his belt. He hurtled it at his former comrade. The blade struck him in the eye. The swordsman screamed and clutched at the dagger's hilt.

Tadgh shivered. 'I did that. Dear God, that man is blind now because of me. Maybe I am a monster. Though a part of me is terrified, another part is exhilarated. It feels nice, for once, not to be the victim.'

He turned to the man he enchanted. "What's your name?"

"Asbaund." The puppet walked over to his still-screaming comrade and pulled the dagger out. In the same movement, he drove the dagger down again, severing the vocal cords. Screams turned to wet gurgles.

"Totally disgusting," Tadgh said. "Why are you here? Why are you killing people?"

"We're pursuing someone." Asbaund wiped his dagger against the dying man's leather armor then sheathed it. "A spy. He heard some information he shouldn't have. We need to make sure he doesn't talk. Our orders are to kill everyone who might be involved. We could have killed him in the woods but Teric said we needed to see who he was working for. And now we're here."

"What kind of information?"

Something slammed into Tadgh's head. He flew through the air and landed in the dirt several feet away. Vision blurred, he shook his head clear. A woman stood beside Asbaund. Two other swordsmen stood behind her.

"Just like I told you, Desdemona," one man said. "A monster. Asbaund said it's immune to weapons. What is it? Some sort of demon?"

"Whatever it is, I hurt it." Desdemona sheathed her sword. "If I can hurt it, I can kill it. I'll take care of this thing. Go see to Oshu and Teric. Make sure the spy is killed. Nothing's more important."

"What did you do to me?" Tadgh pushed himself to his feet as she approached.

"Oh," she said. "The creature speaks. What I did was kick you in the head. I'm going to do it a few more times and see what happens."

"Excuse me if I don't stick around for that." Tadgh jumped as high and wide as he could. He landed at the base of a tower and glanced down at the courtyard. What he saw wasn't encouraging. "That's so not fair."

Desdemona floated up through the air.

"You can fly?"

"I'm not really in a mood for talking." Inch by inch, she moved slowly towards him. "Are you going to stand still or what?"

Tadgh jumped again, landing on the other side of the roof.

Desdemona followed.

∗∗∗

Menphis reached the infirmary and found it empty.

"Prelate Finn?" He lowered Leif into the first empty bed and looked around. The place was deserted. Even the stranger was gone. "Damn. Hold on, Leif. Healing is not really my specialty but I'll see what I can do."

Menphis ran to a cabinet and pulled out bandages and cloths. He washed his hands and dipped a cloth in alcohol. Leif moaned in pain as Menphis cleaned the wounds on his colleague's face.

"The wounds on your face look worse than they really are. I need to see how bad your injuries are. Hold on. Try not to move." With a pair of scissors, he cut Leif's shirt away to see the worst of the injuries. He prodded dark bruises on Leif's torso. "Looks like you've got some broken ribs. Based on your aura you've also got some internal bleeding and a punctured lung. I can get you stabilized but you're going to need Finn to reverse these injuries."

Leif grabbed Menphis' hand. "Please. Get Instructor Mal. I have to tell him. It's bigger than we thought. He has to know in case I don't make it."

"That type of talk is not helping." Menphis pulled his hand back. He wiped down Leif's chest with alcohol, looking for signs of cuts. "Slow your breathing and your circulation. Can you do that for me? Just like in training. Slow your heart rate and focus on healing yourself. I've seen you in worse shape than this in combat training. Remember that time Dendrik smashed your head into a wall."

"This isn't training, Menphis." Leif coughed. A trickle of blood stained his lips. "I think that thing out there is a graunskyeg. A real one. It feels so wrong. I saw it do impossible things. But that's not the worst part, Menphis. I heard what they're planning."

"Shh." Menphis put a hand on Leif's chest, gently pushing him down to his back. "Stop talking now. The movement isn't helping. I'm going to try to stop the bleeding and set your ribs. You focus on your punctured lung. It's going to hurt. Are you ready?"

Leif's eyes blazed with frustration for a moment. Then his face went placid and he nodded.

"Try not to scream." Menphis looked out the window. The sound of battle grew louder now. "I don't want to give away our position if we can help it."

Closing his eyes, Menphis found his center. He extended his aura down through his hands and into Leif's body. His senses left the physical world and focused on the energetic. Cells pulsed and tissue mended. Then Menphis' energy coated Leif's ribs, pushing and prodding them back to their original position. Leif covered his mouth with his forearm to muffle the cries of pain.

Minutes passed. Eventually, Menphis opened his eyes and, exhausted, fell to his knees.

"This is why I hate healing," he said "It drains my aura so much it'll take days for me to recover."

A strange voice spoke from the doorway. "Sadly for you, you don't have days. Step away from the spy and I'll make your death quick."

Adrenaline pushed Menphis to his feet. Crouched in combat position, his eyes fell on an overweight man wearing light-colored robes. In the darkness it was hard to distinguish his facial features, but all he needed was position.

"That's not going to happen," Menphis said. "I didn't just save his life so you could kill him."

"Careful," Leif said. "He's a fieldbender. His name's Oshu."

"And that's why we need you dead," Oshu said. "You know too much. What else did you hear? Never mind. You'll never get the chance to tell anyone. I know you Elmire Ahk have a few tricks up your sleeves. Believe me when I say it is nothing compared to fieldbending. I can kill you from across the room."

"Then why haven't you?" Menphis moved between Oshu and Leif.

Oshu sneered, his teeth bright in the dark. "Your friend blinded me. I owe him a slow death." He raised his hands. They crackled with orange and purple energy.

Menphis prepared to jump out of the way. Then something unexpected happened.

Chapter Twelve

Shonn saw his cousin run towards the infirmary carrying someone over his shoulder. Keeping one eye on the roof, he followed as quickly as he could.

'I feel completely vulnerable,' he thought. 'I have no weapon. Even if I did, I have no combat training. If these invaders find me, I'll be dead in seconds.'

He stopped at the edge of the pavilion. It was a quick run to the infirmary. He was about to make a run for it when something moved through the night. By moonlight, Shonn saw an overweight man in pink robes move into the infirmary. A sharp pain jabbed in Shonn's head: a memory of his precognition.

'The fieldbender,' he thought. 'I remember seeing him kill Becy in my dream. I don't remember this part, though. If I don't do something, he could kill Menphis. But what can I do? Menphis is the fighter.'

An idea formed in his mind. It was a truly terrible idea but it was the only thing he could think of.

Screaming as loud as possible, he ran straight at the fieldbender.

***

Menphis heard his cousin scream.

"What?" Oshu turned to look behind him for an instant. It was all the opening Menphis needed.

He sprung from his crouched position and punched his left hand into the fieldbender's throat. His right hand slammed, open palm, into the bender's ribcage. Oshu flew out the door of the infirmary, landing on this back in the dirt.

Before he could recover, Shonn repeatedly kicked the balding man in the head.

"Enough." Menphis pulled Shonn away. "He's out cold."

"How can you tell?"

"I can read auras, remember? Is this it? The attack you saw coming?"

Shonn nodded. "Do you have any idea who these people are? I don't recognize their armor."

"No." Menphis turned towards the sound of the battle. "But they didn't come here for the stranger. It's Leif they want. We have other things to worry about. There's a graunskyeg here."

"Bull. There's no such thing as graunskyegs."

"I'd be happy to bring you over to the creature so you can tell the creature it doesn't exist. I saw it, Shonn. I've never felt anything so abhorrent."

Shonn glanced back at the infirmary. "Where's Tadgh?"

"Who?" Menphis wiped the sweat from his forehead. "You mean the stranger? I don't know."

"He wasn't in the infirmary?"

Menphis shook his head. "Why do you care so much? Two days ago I couldn't convince you to talk to him. We have more important things to think about right now."

"There's nothing more important than Tadgh." Shonn's eyes went wide. He blushed and turned away.

Menphis stared at Shonn, then shook his head. "I don't know what that's supposed to mean, but he wasn't in the infirmary. Prelate Leif, however, is in there and injured. I need you to stay with him. I'll throw this fieldbender in the cellars on the off chance he wakes up. Then I have to head back to the main gate. Instructor Mal and the others are trying to fight off the graunskyeg."

"I can do that. Listen." Shonn grabbed Menphis' arm. "If you see Tadgh, make sure he's okay. Can you do that for me?"

Menphis looked down at Shonn's hand on his arm. "When this is over you're going to tell me why the stranger is suddenly so important to you. For now, I have to focus on the monastery. Go to Leif and stay hidden. Be safe."

***

Desdemona floated through the air and landed on the roof not far from Tadgh. "Really getting tired of this, demon. You can jump. Good for you. I can levitate. There's nowhere you can go that I can't follow. So why don't you do us both a favor and stop running?"

Tadgh was panting, exhausted. 'She's right. Running isn't doing any good. This feels just like Superman 2. How the hell can I fight this crazy Kryptonian chick?' He crouched down on all fours and tried to catch his breath. 'I could just wish her away. What's the worst that could happen?'

Something landed next to him on the roof. He was so shocked he nearly jumped away. A strong, familiar hand gripped his shoulder. He looked up into Instructor Mal's face. Relief flooded him.

"Don't even think about it," the Instructor said.

"What?" Eyes wide, Tadgh took a step back. "I wasn't going to do anything."

"Yes, you were. When this is over, we'll have another conversation about the dangers of using your abilities. Until then, use your other strengths."

"But she's a freaking flying warrior!" Tadgh screamed. "What can I do against someone like that?"

Instructor Mal raised one eyebrow.

Tadgh realized Instructor Mal was completely unperturbed by his feline form. The invaders had called him a monster. Instructor Mal still saw him as Tadgh. "What do you see in me?" he asked.

"I need to get back," Instructor Mal said. "You have to fight this one alone." Then he jumped away, landing more than thirty feet away.

Tadgh rolled his eyes. "This is worse than Crouching Tiger Hidden Dragon. Is there anyone here that can't fly?"

Something slammed into his chest. He looked down in time to see it was Desdemona's boot. She had kicked so hard he flew off the roof towards the training pavilion. He flipped and landed easily on his feet. He jumped backwards, narrowly escaping a pile-driver attack.

Desdemona walked in a circle around Tadgh. "Whatever you are, you sure can move. That was a nice trick. So are you done running yet?"

Tadgh thought back to what Instructor Mal had said.

"Yep, guess so. Bring it, bitch."

***

"What the hell is that?" Looking out the window of the infirmary, Shonn saw the furry creature tumble off the roof.

"You remember I'm stuck in the bed, right?" Prelate Leif turned towards him. "I can't see anything from here. Is it the graunskyeg?"

"I have no idea." He'd never seen anything like it. He knew he should be terrified of it, but for some reason it felt familiar. "Until today, I thought graunskyeg were just stories to scare children. This looks like a man but larger. It's covered in orange fur."

"Did you say fur?"

Shonn nodded. "That's what it looks like."

Prelate Leif tried to sit up in bed but the effort proved too much. He collapsed with a grunt. "Damn. Nearly dying sucks. The graunskyeg didn't have fur before but I've heard they can shape-shift. What's it doing? Is it attacking us?"

"No." Shonn fought to understand the flow of his feelings. "It's attacking the invaders. I'm confused. Do you know who these people are? Why are they after you?"

"I can't say much. I'm under orders from Instructor Mal. Does it look like anyone's headed this way?"

"Not that I can see." Shonn studied the furry creature. Something inside him clicked. "No. That's not possible. How?"

Shonn ran out the door towards Tadgh.

***

"Ready to fight?" Desdemona stretched her arms as she approached Tadgh.

"Better," Tadgh said. "I'm ready to win. Take your best shot."

Desdemona swung her leg at Tadgh so quickly he couldn't move out of the way. Her boot connected with the side of his head, bringing him to his knees. Before he could get back up she slammed her armored knee into his nose. He heard something snap and his head flew backwards.

"I knew I could kill you," she said. "Anything that bleeds can be killed.

Tadgh screamed as something stabbed into his back. He looked down at his chest. The sword's tip pierced him. Blood dripped from him, darkening the dirt. He fought to breathe. Panic rose in him, but he pushed it down. He thought back to Instructor Mal's words.

Use what you have.

Desdemona pulled out the sword and stabbed him again.

Tadgh screamed in pain. His whole body spasmed. The pain broke his concentration. He started to shift back to human form.

'Just a few more seconds,' he thought.

"Any last words, demon?" Desdemona grabbed him by the hair. She pulled his face up, forcing him to look at her. Her eyes were lit with glee and triumph.

"Yes," Tadgh said. "Thank you for being stupid."

Desdemona's eyes wrinkled with confusion for a moment. Then Tadgh reached out and touched her face. Her will was much stronger than Asbaund's but she still succumbed to his power. She stared at him with love, not bloodlust.

"What can I do for you, master?" Her voice was soft, almost a purr.

"You can start by getting this damned sword out of me."

"Of course." She pulled the blade out quickly. Tadgh screamed in pain again.

"Tadgh?"

He looked over and saw Shonn running towards him. He held up a hand, wanting Shonn to stay back. The thought of Shonn seeing him like this, half-way human, half something else, made him nauseous. He looked past Shonn. Several Elmire Ahk had gathered around as well. Everyone stared at him. He slipped all the way back to human form.

"Let me help," Shonn threw one of Tadgh's arms around his shoulders to help support him. Tadgh tried to push him away, but his limbs were too weak. Shonn touched Tadgh's cheek. "I knew it was you. I don't know how, but I just knew. Your face is completely healed. How…?"

"Later."

"Is this your fod sel-onde ability? You're a shape-shifter?"

Tadgh shook his head. "That's another long story. Are you okay?"

Shonn smiled, then took his hand off Tadgh's cheek. "I'm fine, but my cousin went to fight with Instructor Mal. I know it's hard to believe but he says there is a graunskyeg here."

"I have no idea what that is."

Desdemona answered, a look of complete devotion frozen on her face. "A graunskyeg is a creature of the Void, a monster that exists somewhere between life and death. The weak ones eat the raw flesh of the living, cannibals. The strong ones can survive by only drinking blood."

Tadgh stared at Shonn, mouth open in shock. "You're kidding. A vampire? There's a freakin' vampire nearby? I am really starting to hate your planet. No offense."

Shonn laughed. "None taken. So what are we going to do?"

Tadgh pushed himself away from Shonn and turned to Desdemona. "You're a person of some authority with this group, correct?"

She nodded.

"Good. I want you to call a retreat. Say you accomplished whatever you need to or that there's no way you can get the job done. I don't care. Make up any lie that will convince the others to leave. Can you do that for me?"

"Anything for you." Desdemona's voice purred with the hint of sexual hunger. Tadgh shivered in revulsion: not at her offer but by what he had done to her. She ran back through the monastery towards the sounds of battle.

When she was gone, Tadgh felt his knees weaken and his head start to swim. Shonn caught him before he hit the ground. Then, there was only darkness.

Chapter Thirteen

In the city of DunDegore, five people stood in a room with an impossible object. The Sage stood beside Elmontrazar, perhaps the most respected fieldbender on Maghe Sihre. Beside him stood Mikhel, the young fieldbender who had brought word of the Sword of Kassandra to the council in Karaj Robat. His clothing was no longer covered in dust from the road. His brown hair was washed, his pale face free of dirt. Across from them, staring down at the artifact, was Torch Karehn, head of the local Church of Pheonides. Sirion paced back and forth in the distance.

"So is it real?" The Sage stared at the crystalline sword through the Nizarian energy field. It was nearly five feet long and over eight inches across at the widest point. The blade was translucent with an opaque hilt.

"We know it's real," Sirion said. The sleeves of his silver robe were rolled up, an accommodation for the unseasonably warm day. "What we don't know is what it is."

"With all due respect, Sirion, I don't think he was talking to you." Elmontrazar said. "I was there when the Sword of Kassandra was created, after all."

Elmontrazar was Valgt'til, the second oldest race on Maghe Sihre and former servants to the Beherskers. Their physical appearance made them quite distinguishable from the other races on Maghe Sihre. Their faces were longer and thinner than Sirians with slanted eyes and large, pointed ears. Elmontrazar had snow-white hair and slate-gray skin. He wore a Nizarian battle suit constructed from gray bioplastics, a material as flexible as cotton, yet more resilient than steel. The one-piece unit was similar in style to a leather jumpsuit but included advanced homeostatic generators. He extended his hand over the energy field, tracing the glyphs etched into the blade.

"Yes, we're all aware of how old you are." Sirion crossed his arms, refusing to look Elmontrazar in the eyes.

"Well, hells bells. I barely know how old I am nowadays." Elmontrazar winked at Mikhel. "But I do know this sword. It's been many years since I've seen it, but this is the Sword of Kassandra. I remember when Orpthus created this for Tempertin. That man was a wonder."

"Who, sir?" Mikhel said. "Tempertin?"

Elmontrazar shook his head and brushed strands of white hair away from his face. "I meant Orpthus. Don't get me wrong. Tempertin was a strong, powerful man, but Orpthus inspired me to be a better fieldbender. He manipulated the reality field with such finesse that you couldn't feel a whisper of distortion standing right next to him. I've had centuries of practice since then. Still, an instrument like this is beyond me. Are we sure it's secure here?"

"Of course not," Torch Karehn said. Deep wrinkles spread out over her face and hands. She wore a pant suit: red pants with an orange blazer over a white blouse. She touched the gold necklace at her neck: a wide-winged bird taking flight. It was the symbol of the Church of the Phoenix Lord. "I told you we need to get that thing off this island before word leaks out. This is no place for a blood bath. There are five grade schools within a block of this museum. What do you think will happen to those children if the Quadumvirate learn it's here?"

"The Quadumvirate won't find out." Mikhel clenched his fist and the energy field around the Sword darkened. In a matter of seconds, impenetrable darkness concealed the sword.

"Someone always talks." Torch Karehn fingered the golden bird figure on her necklace. "We cannot trust the locals to keep quiet. Eventually the Quadumvirate will find someone who has a price. Maybe someone with a drug problem or a sick child. Do we have any idea how many people have seen this thing?"

"How could we know that?" Sirion said. "The archeologists had no way of knowing what it really was. It's been on display for weeks now. Hundreds of people could have seen it."

"Exactly!" Torch Karehn put her hands on her hips. "Hundreds of people, many of them not even locals. And you expect them to keep quiet about a discovery like this? Even if they don't know what it is…."

Mikhel interrupted. "They don't. I can guarantee that much. Outside of the people in this room, only five members of my fieldbender guild have been told about the Sword of Kassandra."

Torch Karehn straightened her shoulders and glared at Mikhel. "Even so, people saw it. They can describe it. Mikhel, if you managed to figure out what it is, can you honestly say no one else will?"

Mikhel turned away and stared at the ground.

"Perhaps it would be best to move the Sword to a more secure location," the Sage said.

"Hmm," Elmontrazar said. "And what do you think the Great Castles will say if I carry this away to the Nizarians?"

"Oh, I'm sure I can guess their reaction." The Sage walked to a plate glass window that looked out on the city. Below, a market spread out before him. Merchants sold souvenirs under the canopied booths. The area was filled with tourists, despite the rain. "The Redgravians will claim it is theirs by right. Tempertin and Orpthus fought with the Redgravian army during Starfall. Though the Valgt'til have no legitimate claim, I'm sure they'll come up with something. And then there is the Quadumvirate. Karehn's right. They will find out about it. It's only a matter of time. And when they do, they will send an army to retrieve it. Something this powerful is worth risking an international incident."

"Is there nowhere we can send this?" Sirion asked. "No place beyond the reach of the Quadumvirate?"

The Sage leaned his head back against the window behind him. "I know one place it would be relatively safe. But I refuse to send it there."

Elmontrazar raised an eyebrow. "Do you mean...?"

"Not discussing it." The Sage shook his head and sighed. "Do you know how the sword worked? How was Tempertin able to use this and seal the Void?"

"I was a young man then," Elmontrazar said. "I hadn't even passed the Examination of the Rock yet. I was just there to feed the fieldbending. Orpthus used me and a hundred others the same way a Nizarian landrider uses a battery. If we hope to use the Sword, it needs to be studied. Perhaps we could send for Defksquar."

"No!" Both the Sage and Torch Karehn shouted at the same time.

"I know his reputation." Elmontrazar bowed his head. "Truth be told, he deserves most of it. But he is the closest thing we have to Tempertin today. They are from the same planet, after all."

"If I see that man I will kill him," the Sage said. "You know what he's done to me. What he will do. If you involve him, I am out."

Elmontrazar sighed. "Are all your people as pig-headed as you?"

"I don't have a people," the Sage said, turning back to the window. "Not anymore."

Torch Karehn joined the Sage at the window and lowered her voice. "Where exactly is a safe place for something like this? DunDegore is my home. I'm biased. Can you think of any place that isn't someone's home? I don't want to be responsible for the deaths of innocents."

"I understand." The Sage closed his eyes for a moment. When he opened them, just for a moment, he thought he saw a familiar face in the crowds of the city. She wore a blue dress, and despite the distance, seemed to be looking directly at him.

'Echo?' His heart stopped. He blinked several times to clear his eyes. When he looked again, the woman was gone.

Torch Karehn touched his shoulder. "Sage, what is it? You looked like you saw a ghost."

"I did." He shook his head and turned his back to the city.

"So, are we just going to leave it here?" Mikhel looked around the room. "Torch Karehn is right. This museum is at the heart of DunDegore. Thousands of tourists visit every day. Thousands more live on the island to support the tourist industry. I have an idea. There's an Elmire Ahk monastery a few miles north of here. Maybe we could store it there."

Elmontrazar smiled. "Excellent idea. If memory serves, the monastery is run by the Brotherhood of Tyche. It is close enough to keep an eye on, and no one would expect a weapon like this being kept by the diplomats."

"That could work," the Sage said. "I know the Brotherhood. They have another monastery near GardenKeep. They're more than diplomats. They're trained warriors. If anyone's prepared to guard something like this, they are." He turned to Sirion. "Latimer put you in charge. Can you transport the Sword of Kassandra to the monastery?"

Sirion nodded.

"I'll go with you," Torch Karehn said. "The Aerie can survive without me for a day or two. And I know Instructor Symms well. We served on several interfaith committees together. I may be able to smooth the negotiations."

Sirion pulled in a deep breath. "I'll take Mikhel and a few others with me. A small party will raise less attention, but I'll bring some protection just in case."

"I'll meet you at the monastery tomorrow to check on security." The Sage clasped his hands behind his back, a thoughtful expression on his face. "I hope this is enough. I have to tell you, this is all starting to feel a little too familiar for me. I came to Maghe Sihre to escape this kind of nonsense."

"I know what you've been through, my friend. I understand your reticence. But perhaps you are not meant for a tranquil life." Elmontrazar shrugged and turned away from the Sage. "Mikhel, perhaps you can take me to your guild. We'll arrange for constant surveillance of the sword until it's taken to the monastery."

Torch Karehn placed her hand lightly on the Sage's forearm. "When the Redgraves find out we're acting without them, they'll be furious. It's one thing to fight a war against the Quadumvirate. The people will rally against them. But the Redgraves? It's a dangerous decision to alienate the most powerful nation on the planet."

"We have a saying on my homeworld," the Sage said. "Possession is 9/10 of the law. They don't have it. We do. I'm not going to lie to you, Karehn. We've known each other far too long for that. I have a bad feeling about this."

"The Phoenix Lord teaches us that the strongest flame produces the strongest steel." Torch Karehn smiled briefly and touched her necklace again. "You're a good man, Sage. Stay strong."

The Sage put his arm around Karehn. "For better or worse, the Redgrave and the royal families are not here. It's up to us to keep the Sword safe."

"I don't think they would agree with that."

The Sage looked back out over the city. He tried one last time to find a sign of that familiar face he longed to see again. "In the immortal words of Mick Jagger, 'You can't always get what you want.'"

***

Tadgh opened his eyes. He found himself in a small, rectangular, windowless room. The memory of the night before flooded back.

'Where the hell am I?' He went to the door, half expecting it to be locked. The knob turned easily. There was, however, a guard posted on the other side: an Elmire Ahk dressed in Prelate attire complete with orange sash.

"Wait inside," the Prelate said.

"Am I in trouble?" Tadgh swallowed. His mouth was dry.

"Please just wait inside." The Prelate spoke without a trace of fear or anger in his voice, but Tadgh could smell the fear on his skin. When he realized he could smell the fear, he felt nauseous and defeated. He went back inside and lay in bed for hours, staring at the ceiling.

Eventually, there was a knock at the door. He sniffed. The person on the other side of the door smelled familiar. He called out, his voice flush with excitement.

"Shonn?"

"No."

Tadgh bit his lip in disappointment as he realized who he was speaking with. He opened the door.

"You must be Menphis," he said. Although the Elmire Ahk smelled similar to his cousin, they looked almost nothing alike. He was taller with more pronounced muscles. His hair was buzzed short and reddish. Everything about him screamed order and discipline, militancy.

Menphis nodded. "How did you know that? Never mind. The Instructor wants to speak to you in private. Follow me?"

"Is something wrong?"

"Is something...?" Menphis glared at Tadgh. "Are you dense? Of course there's something wrong. Hundreds of people are dead and you're a flaming monster. But for some reason Instructor Mal doesn't want us to kill you. He wants to talk to you. So are you going to come with me, or do I have to bonk you on the head and drag you there?"

Sweat dripped down Tadgh's armpits.

Menphis sighed deeply and scratched his nose. "Look, I don't know what to think about you. Maybe you're not a monster. My cousin seems to like you. I'm not even sure I want to know what's going on between the two of you. But you saved us last night." Menphis looked over his shoulder and waved the guard away. "Come on. Instructor Mal is waiting."

Tadgh followed Menphis through the stone walkways. Cool air blew through his hair as they moved through the pillared paths. Judging by the sun, it was early afternoon. He realized he must have slept longer than he had expected.

"What is the Instructor going to do with me?"

Menphis mumbled something under his breath.

"Pardon?"

"It will be better coming directly from him." Menphis spoke without looking at Tadgh. "It's not really my place."

"Am I in trouble?" Tadgh sped up so he was walking side-by-side with Menphis instead of trailing behind him. "I know we don't know each other, but can you please tell me? Is the Instructor going to kill me?"

Menphis stopped but would not look into Tadgh's eyes. "We don't execute people. We're not animals. And whatever else you are, my cousin assures me you are a person. Can you please stop talking and just follow me?"

They walked the rest of the way in silence. Most signs of last night's conflict had been cleaned up. But no amount of cleaning could remove the dark stains of spilt blood in the dirt. They soon arrived at a metal door – gold and silver – inscribed with abstract geometric shapes. Menphis knocked on the door, each rap of his knuckles causing a hollow reverberation like the ringing of a bell.

"Enter," a voice from within said.

Menphis opened the door and motioned for Tadgh to enter. He did not follow Tadgh inside.

Tadgh found himself in a large room with very little furniture. A desk built from reddish wood sat at the far end. Several low benches lined each wall. Dozens of open windows let in fresh air and light from outside. Hundreds of tall white pillar candles around the room flickered lightly in the breeze. Incense filled the air. The scent reminded him vaguely of jasmine and sandalwood. There was only one person in the room: Instructor Mal. He sat cross-legged in the center of the room, eyes closed with hands pressed in prayer before his chest.

Tadgh closed the door and took several steps forward. Then the stillness stopped him. He looked around at the flames from the candles. Each seemed to rise and lower in concert with Instructor Mal's breath. He even heard his own breath. It was harsh and heavy, threatening to destroy the sanctity of the area. For no reason he could put his finger on, he felt utterly terrified. He wanted to run, to scream, to…

"Sit," Instructor Mal said.

Tadgh yelped.

"Please." The Instructor opened his eyes. Tadgh stared at the man's deep blue eyes and the gentle smile on his lips. All thought of fear disappeared. Tadgh moved forward and sat cross-legged a few feet in front of him.

"Menphis said you wanted to see me."

Instructor Mal held up a hand, motioning Tadgh to stay quiet. The air in the room filled with tension, like the pressure before a storm. The room was completely silent, but the air grew heavier and thicker. Tadgh wanted to scream. Tears fell from his eyes.

"Are you sorry?" Instructor Mal stared into Tadgh's eyes. All the light from the room disappeared. There was only darkness and the Elmire Ahk's eyes.

Tadgh swallowed. "For what?"

Instructor Mal closed his eyes. The room completely disappeared this time. Tadgh was back in James Fitzpatrick's bedroom. Blood dripped slowly from the walls. Nothing else in the room moved. Tadgh saw himself in cat form standing over James' dead body, licking blood from his paws.

Tadgh leaned over and vomited. "Stop," he whispered. "I can't…"

"Are you sorry?" Instructor Mal opened his eyes. This time it was barely a question.

Tadgh wiped his lips and chin clean. It was difficult to do because his hands were shaking so much. "I…I don't know. If that really happened, if it's not just a dream, well, when it happened I felt, I don't know, justified. That bastard killed Colin. He nearly killed me. At the time I just…" Tadgh stopped and looked up at Instructor Mal.

The Elmire Ahk did not respond. He did not even blink.

"When I look at that moment all I see is evil. I don't see justice or vengeance. All I see is evil. I have no idea what's going on. First there's the attack, then there's demons and now I'm on an alien planet talking to Kwai Chang Caine after an attack by a vampire."

"Who is the Kwai Chang Caine? One of your spiritual leaders?"

"Um, no. The lead character on the best TV show ever, Kung Fu." Tadgh sighed and hung his head. "Which you've never seen because this is an alien planet. None of this can be real." Tadgh stared down at his hands. They were still shaking, so he crossed his arms to stop them. "But I know it is. This feels real. I know I turned into that thing last night. I can't pretend I didn't. I…I just don't want to be a monster."

"But you are a monster, aren't you?" Instructor Mal asked the question with a slight smile on his lips.

Tadgh hung his head. He didn't know what to say.

"It is written on your soul," Instructor Mal said. "I recognized it the first time I saw you. You are not a demon, but I can feel the touch of a demon on you. You are not a graunskyeg, but I see in your memories you have fed on another person's soul. It is not about your ability to alter reality or the fact that you can turn into that creature from last night. It is as evident as the color of your hair, the calluses on your palms. Rage turned you into a monster. The demon just helped. You were tempted into evil by forces trained for millennia in how to manipulate the weaknesses of man. I can't help but notice you still have not answered my question."

Anger tickled at the back of Tadgh's mind. "What do you want from me? Would it bring them back? If I say I'm sorry will it absolve me? I think we both know the answer to that."

"Do we?" The smile slid from Instructor Mal's lips. "You can alter reality. Would you use that ability to bring those boys back to life? Would you use it to take away your ability to turn into that creature from last night?"

The rage died in Tadgh. He turned away from Mal's eyes, no longer able to face the accusation in them.

"I…I don't know if I could bring them back," he said. "I don't like that I killed them. Especially like that. But I'm not sad they are dead. How am I supposed to live with that? How do I sleep at night knowing what I am? Do the others know? Shonn and Menphis?"

Instructor Mal said nothing.

"Will you tell them? Shonn is a friend, I think. But he doesn't know what I've done."

"If he does not know your life, he is not a friend." Instructor Mal's voice held a quality that forced Tadgh to look back at him: a stillness in his features and his body. The only parts of him that seemed to move were his eyes and his mouth. "You have feelings for Shonn. That, too, is evident. However, how can you be certain he has feelings for you?"

Tadgh blushed.

"That is not what I mean." Instructor Mal sighed. "You need to consider something. Are you sure you did not force Shonn to have feelings for you?"

The rage came roaring back. "Are you saying I altered reality, that I forced him to like me?"

"Possibly. But you have other abilities. What you did with the soldiers last night, for instance. With a touch you were able to turn people out to kill you into devoted servants. Can you be so sure you did not do the same thing to Shonn?"

"Oh." All the heat left his body. He stared at his hands and thought back. What came first: the touch or the interest from Shonn? "I hadn't thought about it. Damn. How can I know for sure?"

"I have no answer for that. Perhaps the Sage will be able to answer that question when you meet with him. Preparations for the journey are almost complete. Maybe Shonn's feelings for you are genuine, maybe they are not. But I want you to consider something. All Elmire Ahk, no matter what their school or deity, are focused on celebrating the joys of life on this planet. We fight to ensure all Sirians can live their lives in peace and joy. There is something inside you, Tadgh, that makes you more than just a monster. You have potential to do great things if you start making different choices. You remember I told you what your name means in our language?"

Tadgh nodded. "You said it means Fallen."

"Yes. Often a man must fall before he becomes a hero, a force for justice. A soldier of light. However, if the man continues to fall, he becomes something very different. In our faith we believe all things happen for a reason. I can see from your expression you have heard this saying before. The gods move us where we need to be. I believe you were sent here for a reason. I have devoted my life to Tyche many years now. In return for my devotion, occasionally I catch glimpses of something you might call destiny. And the destiny I see for you stops here."

Tadgh could not breathe. If the Instructor attacked, he wasn't sure he could fight back. He wasn't sure he wanted to.

"You misunderstand, child." The Instructor stood and lowered a hand to help Tadgh to his feet. "You do that often, don't you? See the worst in everything. Your destiny stops at this temple because you are meant to join the Brotherhood of Tyche."

"Wh...what?" Tadgh felt his knees grow weak. Thankfully, the Instructor pulled him to his feet, or Tadgh would have fallen on his face.

"I believe those were the exact words Menphis used when I told him you would be joining us. I believe you are still meant to visit the Sage. Only he can provide the answers to your questions about how you came to our planet. But I believe you will come back to the monastery. You are fallen, lost. You need time to find yourself again. I'd already planned for Menphis to take you to GardenKeep. In light of your situation, I'm sending Shonn with you. The Sage has a way of knowing things. Seeing you and Shonn together will probably be enough to determine if his feelings are real. Menphis will start your training on the way to GardenKeep. Take the training seriously. I assure you, he will."

Chapter Fourteen

"Five more?" The Sage massaged his neck to reduce the tension.

"Yes, sir," Barnes said as he poured another glass of wine. "For some reason the robberies have intensified. Every member of city council has been hit now. In fact, it would be easier to count the members of the upper class who have not been hit. Whatever it is that's going on, it's escalating."

"Well, there could be good news to that," the Sage said. "Maybe whatever is happening is nearly over. Maybe the thieves will move on to other targets. And that's where the bad news could be. This could escalate into something completely different. Damn. When it rains it pours, as they say."

"Who actually says that, sir?" Barnes replied. "I've never heard that before."

"Just a saying from back home." The Sage took a drink of wine. "I have a feeling, Barnes. There's some piece of this puzzle I'm not seeing. I know I should investigate further, but I don't have time. Between securing that blasted sword in DunDegore and trying to find the source of the reality disruptions, I'm stretched to my limits. Have you learned anything else from your young woman with the eager thighs?"

"Pwella."

The Sage raised an eyebrow.

Barnes blushed. "Well, um, our relationship may have progressed slightly. She really is a lovely girl. You should meet her."

"I absolutely should not meet her." The Sage traced a finger along the edge of his wine glass. "I am happy for you, Barnes. Truly. I remember when your father met your mother. She was beautiful. Strong. Spirited. They spent the rest of their lives happier than most. I've known you since you were born, just like I knew your father his whole life.

You have never been just a servant to me. I hope you know that."

"Geesh," Barnes said. "No reason to get all mushy because I fancy a maid."

"I think we both know she's not just a barmaid to you anymore. I can see it in your eyes." The Sage thought back to DunDegore, the woman in the blue dress. "I was in love once, in another life. Her name was Echo. I know how it can build you up. Make you a better man. But if it happens at the wrong time, in the wrong place, it can destroy you. We are at the edge of dark times. Remember that when you are with Pwella. Whatever you feel for her, she works for Lord Vyken. Be careful with your words or you may get her into trouble."

"You wouldn't." Barnes went pale. His mouth fell open.

The Sage refused to look at Barnes.

"Oh." Barnes blinked slowly, tears forming in his eyes. "Understood."

The Sage, seeing Barnes' reaction, smacked himself in the forehead. "I'm sorry. I promised myself when I came here I wouldn't be this type of person again. I swore I would be different. With everything bad going on in the world, maybe I can do one good thing. See if you can convince Pwella to transfer to my kitchen. We haven't had a cook on staff since your mother left us. Let's get her away from Lord Vyken before it's too late. I owe it to your parents to look after you."

Barnes smiled and wiped the tears from his eyes. "Well, it's not like we're engaged, sir."

"Let's help her live long enough for you to find out if you want to marry her."

Chapter Fifteen

"This is the worst idea ever," Tadgh said. "Who the hell ever thought it was a good idea to walk on foot to a city two weeks away?"

"How else can you walk if not on foot?" Menphis barely looked at Tadgh as they walked through the woods. The three of them had left the monastery half an hour ago. Tadgh had been complaining since then.

"You can always walk on your hands," Shonn said. "You are a shape-shifter, after all. You could probably swing through the trees or…"

"I'm not Tarzan." Tadgh glanced over and saw the look of confusion on Shonn's face. "And that reference is completely lost on you. Damn. It's hard to be witty if the people around you have no concept of pop culture. Don't you guys have horses or cars or something?"

"Walking is a spiritual activity," Menphis said. "Tyche teaches us that by moving across the planet using the power of our bodies we become one with nature. It helps us maintain our purity."

"I'll trade in some purity for a four-by-four." Tadgh smacked his skin as some mosquito-like insect bit him.

"I'm not sure you have enough purity to trade in," Menphis said. He stopped walking and hung his head for a moment. "That was probably in poor taste. Prelate Leif is a good friend. He and several others are alive because you sent those soldiers away."

Shonn paled. "Most of the serving staff are dead. We would have lost them all if not for Mirelda fighting them off by the kitchen. She paid for it. She'll be in the infirmary for weeks."

"Look, this is going to be a long walk if you spend the entire time complaining," Menphis said. "Instructor Mal put me in charge of your training, Tadgh. Against every ounce of common sense, he wants you to become a Brother of Tyche.

So every time I hear you complain you will drop down immediately and give me twenty pushups."

Tadgh laughed.

Menphis stared at him, unblinking.

"Wait. You can't be serious. I can't even do five pushups."

"You know," Menphis said. "I think that sounded like a complaint. What do you think, Shonn?"

"Definitely a complaint." Shonn nodded solemnly as he wiped the grin from his face. Then he took a piece of fruit resembling an orange-colored banana from his backpack. He was very careful not to look Tadgh in the eyes.

"Oh, come on," Tadgh said. "Not you, too?"

"Is that another complaint?" Menphis asked. "Do you want to do 40 pushups?"

Tadgh sighed. He stood in the middle of the woods now. A quick look around proved he was completely lost. As insane as Menphis sounded, what choice did he really have?

"You know, America doesn't have the draft. I never signed up for this."

"That was definitely another complaint," Shonn said. "Tadgh, you should probably just stop talking."

"I am so going to make you pay for that." Tadgh moved to a relatively cleared section of the woods and dropped to the ground. He started doing pushups. After the tenth one, he realized a difference. He was not out of breath and his muscles were not even close to exhausted. He breezed past twenty quickly. When he hit sixty he sat down, a proud smile plastered to his lips.

"Hmm," Menphis said. "You're not as weak as you look. So, for every complaint you make, 100 pushups."

"Ah come on!" Tadgh jumped to his feet. Menphis walked away. Shonn laughed even harder now.

***

In Karaj Robat, Eschandel stood in the darkened tower of the Seers. He waved his hand slowly across the scrying pool. The inky water swirled and trembled. Colors appeared, only to spin back into blackness. It took nearly a full minute for the pool to settle into a picture: three men walking through the woods. Eschandel flicked his hands over the water. The scrying pool settled on one of the faces: a pale-skinned young man in a white sleeveless robe and loose leather pants. His disheveled brown hair glistened with oil and sweat. His eyes were black, unusual for Sirians on this continent. Most on the continent of Celtica had green, blue or hazel eyes. His lips were thick and lush for a man with soft, deep philtral ridges. There were no visible wrinkles, suggesting he was probably very young. He had no visible whiskers and there was only minimal chest hair visible at the opening of his tunic.

"Is that him?"

Eschandel nodded.

"You're sure he's the one you felt?" A second figure appeared by the scrying pool. She was dressed in high-polished darkstone armor. The black metallic cuirass hung over her entire torso and faded in flexible black leaves like a skirt around her groin and upper legs. The armor bore the crest of Karaj Robat – a red mountain with a black bird superimposed on it. She kept her red hair short to the scalp, giving her face a severity to match the cold steel of her green eyes.

Eschandel touched his lips with a clenched fist. "Yes, Kvartermester Arem. He's the fod sel-onde who shook the reality field. He cracked the Void."

"He looks young." Arem crossed her arms across her chest and frowned in concentration. "No more than 18."

"To be honest, that has me even more scared." Eschandel leaned over the edge of the scrying pool to get a closer look at Tadgh. "If he can do this now, I hate to think of what he could do in a few years."

"How powerful could one of them become?"

Eschandel shook visibly even through his thick robes. "I don't want to find out. I'll place a tracking spell on him. A small one to be discreet. Phoenix Lord preserve us if he feels us coming. Get your team to the ships before the end of day. From what we've heard, they're heading to GardenKeep. If you leave now, you should be there in two weeks.

With a wave of his hand, Eschandel dismissed the scrying pool.

As the image disappeared, Kvartermester Arem nodded and squared her shoulders. "Let us pray a single squad will be enough."

***

Tadgh paused mid-step. A shiver ran through him as a wave of cold pressure settled into his bones. Looking left and right, he searched the forest. Although birds sang in the trees above him, there was no sign of movement. He looked down at his bare arms. Goosebumps covered his skin.

"Something wrong?" Menphis tilted his head to one side and stopped walking.

Tadgh shook his head. "Not sure. We have a saying on Earth, my world. 'It feels like someone just walked over my grave.'"

"That's morbid." Shonn finished eating the fruit that looked like a banana and threw the skin into the woods. "What does it mean?"

"Just a premonition, I guess." Tadgh looked up. Between the leaves and the branches, clouds overhead rolled lazily to the west. Insects buzzed amongst the underbrush.

Shonn looked to his cousin. Menphis shook his head slightly.

Tadgh sighed. "It's probably nothing. What were you saying about the town we're staying in tonight?"

Menphis continued walking. "As I said, it's called Flesh Prayer. It has one of the major shrines to the goddess Fricka. You'll see a large presence of the Sisterhood of the Flesh. I'm only mentioning it because it can be unsettling to those unfamiliar with their practices. The Sisterhood view copulation as a prayer to the divine. To those who worship

Fricka, refusal of sex is seen as a denial of sacrament. Since you're now considered an acolyte of the Brotherhood of Tyche, you should be free from their advances. But don't be surprised if you see certain activity on the streets."

"Seriously?" Tadgh flinched. "Right on the streets? Is the goddess against bedrooms or something?"

Shonn laughed. "Well, this should be fun."

Menphis, trying to hide his smile, lowered his head. "You might want to avoid saying things like that once we get to town. The locals have little tolerance for foreigners trying to impose their own morality on their behavior. Etiquette dictates we respect how others choose to worship."

"You said I would be exempt because I'm an acolyte." Tadgh felt his mouth go dry. "Dear God. Don't tell me I have to take a vow of chastity."

"Now that is a prayer you *would* hear in Flesh Prayer." Shonn shifted his backpack to the other shoulder. "Cousin, we should probably stop for a breather soon. We've been walking for hours now."

"Half an hour more," Menphis said. "If we don't get to Flesh Prayer before nightfall, it will be difficult finding rooms. Also, the last thing we need is to wander into town after the locals have a few pints of beer in them. To answer your question, Tadgh, no. You have not taken a vow of chastity. Although some Brothers do choose to remain chaste, it is not a prerequisite of membership. I only meant you are free of advances because they will see you as a man of religion. They will not try to impress their religion on you, either."

"I can't believe I'm a priest in training," Tadgh said. "My Irish grandmother would be so proud."

They walked in silence until they settled at the edge of a clearing for a short break. Dropping their backpacks, they stopped. Tadgh leaned his back against a tree and ate a piece of dried meat.

"Wait." A thought formed in Tadgh's mind. "You guys have horses here, don't you?"

"Yes," Menphis said. "We also have trees and stones and fish. You find that strange?"

"Well, yeah." Tadgh leaned forward. "Don't you? I mean, I'm from another planet. What's the likelihood that two completely separate planets would evolve to have the same basic ecosystem? I'm not a biologist or physicist or whatever, but…don't you think that sounds a little unlikely?"

"No more unlikely than two separate planets developing sentient life forms that look almost identical." Menphis narrowed his eyes and focused on Tadgh. "Anyone looking at you would assume you were Sirian. There are subtle differences, but nothing you'd catch on first glance." He scratched his lower lip and shrugged. "Maybe it's the work of the Beherskers."

"That's what I said," Shonn said. "You remember, the other day in the woods?"

Tadgh's cheeks flushed. "Yeah, it kind of left an impression on me."

Shonn coughed and blushed as well.

Menphis looked slowly back and forth between the two of them. "What happened in the woods?"

"Um…" Tadgh said.

"It was the monastery," Shonn said a little too quickly. "I took Tadgh to the top of the cliff by Lake Wilkin. When he saw the monastery, he said he recognized it. He said it looked like something from his planet. I told him a bit about the legend of the Beherskers. Maybe when they left Maghe Sihre they went to his planet."

"Oh," Tadgh said. "That part. We have similar stories back home, too. I guess you'd call them legends. There are ancient cities and monuments that don't fit into generally accepted history. Some people say they were built by aliens or Atlanteans. I've never really thought about it much. What can you tell me about them, these Beherskers? What were they like?"

"We know very little," Shonn said. "There are statues of them on the isle of DunDegore. That's the nearest

Behersker ruins. Near being relative. If you walk, it would take a month or two. When we get back from GardenKeep you can ask around. I know Prelate Finn has been there. The Brotherhood has another monastery not far from the ruins. As for what they were like, we know even less. They left millennia ago. All we know for certain is what the other races tell us, the Trofast and the Valgt'til."

Tadgh's mouth dropped open. "Wait. What do you mean, other races? People with other skin colors?"

"No," Menphis squinted at Tadgh, looking at him as if he was a little insane. "How does different skin color make you a different race? The Trofast and the Valgt'til are completely different species. We have no more in common with them genetically than horses have with bears. Does your planet have only one race?"

Tadgh shrugged. "I think so. Although, who the hell knows anymore? Will there be any of these Trofast or Valgt'til in Flesh Prayer?"

"Unlikely," Menphis said. "We would see Valgt'til once in a while in Tarkon. It's a major shipping point just like GardenKeep. I remember the first time I saw one I thought they looked like moving crystal filled with sunlight: beautiful and a little bit terrifying. As for Trofast, they are not exactly popular in the south because of their part in the war."

"There's a war?"

Shonn stretched. "Isn't there always a war?"

Tadgh cocked his head to one side. "Well, I suppose. Who's fighting?"

Menphis yawned. "It's a long story. I'll get you a history book. Just remember not to ask questions like that once you get to town. I'm not sure what Prelate Leif said to him, but Instructor Mal is worried. He told us not to draw attention to ourselves."

"He's probably worried about those soldiers that attacked the monastery." Shonn took a drink of water from a metal flask. "I can't believe there was a blasted graunskyeg."

"Can we talk about that for a minute?" Tadgh asked. "What exactly is a graunskyeg? Desdemona said they're creatures of the Void. Is it another race like the Trofast or Valgt'til?"

Menphis glanced over his shoulder at the shadows. His shoulders grew tense and eyes narrowed. Shonn sat up very straight, his hands gripping the fabric of his shirt.

"No," Menphis said. "Graunskyegs aren't even alive. When I was a kid, we told scary stories around campfires about them. They stalk their prey at night, always hungry, always hunting. Instructor Mal talked about them from time to time in training. I always thought he was teaching us mythology."

"So they are like vampires," Tadgh said. "That's what we call them back home. They feed on blood, and if one bites you, you become a vampire too."

"Dear God," Shonn said. "Your world must be a living hell. You must be overrun with these vampires."

"Not exactly," Tadgh said. "As far as I know, vampires are just stories. So graunskyegs aren't created that way in your stories?"

Menphis shook his head. "Only fieldbending can create a graunskyeg. They start as mindless eating machines. They dig themselves out of their graves in search of food. They leave behind piles of slaughtered bodies. If they feed enough, they turn into a greater monster, one with intelligence and supernatural powers. Wherever that graunskyeg came from, it is either not local or very old. We would have heard of a series of mass killings."

"Well this is a cheery conversation." Shonn pushed himself off the ground. He stood and stretched. "Maybe we should get going. If there is a graunskyeg around, I'd rather not face it in the woods tonight."

"Good idea," Menphis stood as well. "If we hustle we should be in Flesh Prayer within seven hours."

Chapter Sixteen

Five hours later, Tadgh, Shonn and Menphis left the woods of Wilkin Hunt. They spent the next hour trudging through knee-high grasses before finally reaching a road.

"Incredible," Tadgh said. "It looks just like a real highway. I wasn't expecting this."

"What's that supposed to mean?" Shonn smacked Tadgh's arm, a sharp snap with a bit too much strength behind it.

"Ow." Tadgh rubbed his arm. "Watch the abuse."

Shonn smiled. "You can take it. You're invulnerable, remember?"

Tadgh rolled his eyes. "I just assumed, you know, that your level of technology was a bit behind ours. I mean, you live in a monastery in the middle of nowhere with no running water and no electricity. What else could I expect?"

Menphis grunted. "Are there no areas of your world without power?"

"None I've ever been to," Tadgh said. "So you do have cars and stuff? I just assumed you all rode horses."

"There's nothing wrong with riding a horse," Shonn said. "I'm not sure I really understand this word 'car'. It might be like Nizarian technology. They have vehicles that move over land at great speed."

"Who are the Nizarians? Are they another race?"

Menphis stopped. "I think from now on whenever you ask a question I will make you stand on your head. When we get to Flesh Prayer, I'll buy a few books and you can start reading. I'm training you to be a Brother of Tyche, not a history major."

An hour later they arrived at the outskirts of Flesh Prayer.

"Wow," Tadgh said. "This is actually a real city."

"I told you." Shonn hit him in the arm. Again.

"Menphis, tell him to stop."

Shonn stuck out his tongue.

"I'll tell him to stop when you stop acting like a tourist," Menphis said. "Try to look like you're bored with everything like everyone else."

It was hard for Tadgh to do that. Everywhere he looked he saw something new. Elegant marble statues lined the road into town. Many gleamed with gold trim; others were draped in silk-like red fabric. While there were no skyscrapers or tall office buildings, the city still felt massive. Block after block of three-story stone structures lined either side of the road into town. Tadgh smelled the perfume of the bare-chested women laughing in doorways and the sweat of the men juggling in the street. They passed bakeries, vegetable stands, and small booths selling sweets fashioned into suggestive shapes. The further they went into town, the louder it became. Well-dressed men and women on horses rode past them. People crammed the sidewalks, drinking from metal mugs. The smell of alcohol and the sound of laughter filled the air.

"This is like spring break in Mexico," Tadgh said. "Can we go for drinks tonight?"

"Yes!" Shonn said.

"Absolutely not," Menphis said.

"Oh, come on," Shonn said. "I haven't had a drink since I moved to the monastery. What's the worst that can happen?"

Tadgh laughed. "In my world we learn never to say that. As soon as someone says it, something really, really bad happens."

Menphis stopped and leaned in close to Tadgh and Shonn. When he spoke it was a whisper, just loud enough for them to hear over the traffic and crowd. "I'm currently traveling with two fod sel-onde, one of whom is a shape-shifter, the day after we were attacked by a small army and a graunskyeg. Forgive me if I'd rather not take unnecessary chances so the two of you can get drunk."

Shonn stamped his foot like a petulant five-year-old. "You are seriously no fun sometimes."

Menphis rolled his eyes and started walking again. "You can have a drink at the hotel as long as you stop making me feel like I'm babysitting."

Twenty minutes later they arrived at a hotel, the Raimarth Inn. The entrance was a set of large wooden French doors that led to a dark-tiled foyer. While Menphis ordered two rooms for them, Tadgh tried, unsuccessfully, to avoid staring at a man and woman copulating on one of the large red couches in the foyer.

"How are you holding up?" Shonn walked over and put a hand on Tadgh's shoulder.

"This is really awkward," Tadgh said. "Couldn't they at least get a room? I mean, we're in a flippin' hotel."

Shonn cleared his throat. "I seem to remember you were okay being out in the open."

"That was completely different! We were in the middle of the woods and...."

"Am I interrupting?" Menphis returned with two sets of keys. "My cousin and I will stay in one room. Tadgh, your room is right next door to ours."

"Is it too much to hope for running water in this place?" Tadgh lifted his arm and smelled his armpit. "I reek."

Menphis and Shonn looked at each other, faces crinkled with confusion.

"Indoor plumbing," Tadgh said. "On my planet we have water brought in from pipes to our houses and hotels so we can bathe. Our outhouses are also indoors. We call them toilets. Is that not common here?"

"Not common at all," Menphis said. "That sounds like Nizarian technology. This hotel does have some amenities most do not. There are toilets attached to each room if I remember correctly. You'll also find a small basin so you can wash the dirt from your faces. But you'll have to head to the public bathhouse to bathe. Let's head to our rooms now. We can meet in an hour for supper. I could use some time to meditate."

"By meditate he means take a nap," Shonn said. "Don't believe a word of this meditation crap."

Menphis glared at Shonn, then shook his head and headed upstairs.

Tadgh and Shonn shared a smile and followed. The stairs were covered in deep wine-red carpet. They climbed to the third floor and walked down a short corridor lined with electric lights.

"So, you *do* have electricity," Tadgh said.

Shonn glanced at the lights and nodded. "These are Nizarian. This technology is expensive. Most people in Shirza don't have them at home. Most hotels like to have it to attract people from the north traveling on business."

Tadgh stared at the lights: twisted tubes of glass inside decorative sconces. "Suddenly I'd like to know more about these Nizarians. How is their technology so much more advanced than yours?"

"Enough questions," Menphis said. "Ask me tomorrow. When we're on the road and not within earshot of strangers. You really need to stop asking questions like that, like you don't know the most basic things about our planet. At least when we're out in public." He handed Tadgh a brass key attached to a thin metal rectangle etched with a strange symbol. The same symbol was painted on a plaque beside the door. "This one here is your room. We'll see you at the bottom of the stairs in an hour."

Tadgh looked at his wrist. "I don't have a watch. How will I know the time?"

Shonn laughed. "Don't hotels where you're from have clocks in the room?"

"Oh," Tadgh said. "Yes. Yes they do. See you in a bit."

Tadgh unlocked the door to his room. He stepped inside, locking it behind him. For a moment, he felt alone, truly alone for the first time since waking up on this strange planet. Leaning against the door, he slipped to the floor. He took several deep breaths. Tension he wasn't aware he'd felt dripped off his shoulders. Glancing around the room, he found it not terribly different from hotel rooms back home. Against one wall sat a queen-sized bed with a wooden headboard. Matching white night tables stood on either side. Thick yellow shag carpeted the floor. There was one window directly opposite the door. He went to it and pushed aside the curtains to look out on the city. His view was limited by a row of buildings directly across from him. In the streets below, servants unloaded boxes and luggage from the back of a horse-drawn cart.

'What kind of world is this?' Tadgh thought. It was so similar to Earth. How had he managed to find a world with an atmosphere the same as Earth, filled with people who looked human who lived in societies so close to those back home? 'Was it my ability to make wishes come true, or something else?'

Closing the curtains, he lay on the bed. His mind raced with questions until supper.

He washed up in the room's small basin before heading downstairs. Menphis and Shonn were already waiting for him in the lobby. The three of them turned right at the bottom of the stairs and headed towards the back of the hotel.

"I went to a pub just like this once." Tadgh pulled out a chair and sat facing the bar. The floor, walls and ceiling were all dark-stained wood. Flowing green curtains covered the walls, creating the illusion of windows and openness. Fifteen tables were set for dinner. Most people in the area were crowded around the bar ordering drinks. A man wearing only a pair of loose trousers and a round hat played an instrument Tadgh didn't recognize: a small, hollow wooden rectangle with ten metal strings running from end to end. The songs he sang must have been popular. Many people at the bar sang along with him.

Shonn waved a waitress over. "What's wrong, Tadgh? You look pale?"

Tadgh shook his head. "I think I'd be less weirded out if everyone had green skin and dressed in sparkles and silver clothing. This is so close to back home. It just doesn't make sense."

"Another question for the Sage, then," Menphis said. "Let's order some food."

"And a beer!" Shonn said. "Come on. You know we deserve one after that day of walking."

Menphis pursed his lips. "Just one. And I mean it this time." The waitress arrived at the table. Menphis ordered fried meat and salad for each of them.

Shonn leaned in close to Tadgh. "He never means it when he says just one. My cousin isn't so bad once you get to know him. He's just acting this way because he's on official Brother business."

"You're lucky," Tadgh said. I wish I was as close to my cousins as you two. Where I'm from, family isn't all that important. It's sad, really."

"It's the same here," Shonn said. "Well, not everywhere. I hear it's different up north in Norshire and the Great Castles. Most of my cousins back in Tarkon are strangers. I've only seen them at family events. You know, weddings, funerals, that sort of thing. Menphis is more like a brother to me than anything. After my father died…" Shonn stopped talking.

"You don't have to tell me," Tadgh said.

"No, it's okay." Shonn looked over at his cousin.

Menphis sighed as he stood. "I'll go get us some beers."

Shonn waited until his cousin was out of earshot. "It was a very long time ago. I should be over it by now. The first time I realized I was different. I saw my father die in my dreams before it happened. That's my fod sel-onde ability. Sometimes my dreams show me the future. It's the worst thing in the world. I can't explain it, but I knew immediately it wasn't just a dream. That whole day I *knew* he was going to die and I sat back and watched it happen. I told my mother. In the morning when I woke up from the dream, I told her

Dad was going to die. She didn't believe me. But then it happened, exactly like it happened in my dream. My mother never forgave me."

Tadgh reached over and grabbed Shonn's hand.

"Thanks," Shonn looked down at Tadgh's hand on his. "She kicked me out. If it wasn't for Menphis and his family, I don't know what would have happened to me." With his free hand, he wiped a tear from his eye. "I don't know what it is about you. Even before I saw your face, I just had this feeling about you."

Tadgh felt nervous. "Really? From the very beginning?"

"No." Shonn smiled. "Actually, when you first came to the monastery I wanted nothing to do with you. You scared me. But Menphis convinced me to talk to you. And the first time you touched me…"

Tadgh pulled his hand away.

"What is it?" Shonn frowned.

"I can't do this," Tadgh said. He got up from the table.

"Don't." Shonn grabbed him by the forearm.

Tadgh sighed. He felt numb. He could not sit back down, but he couldn't move away. "Look, you have a right to know. I'm sorry but…I may have done something to you."

"You didn't do anything to me," Shonn said. "My feelings are…"

"Not real." Tadgh pulled his arm away. He could not look Shonn in the eyes. "You don't really have feelings for me. I made you feel this way and I'm sorry. You saw what I can do. What I did to those invaders, I think I did the same thing to you. I made you love me."

"Hey now, I never said love."

"Really? Are we going to quibble over semantics? You know what I mean."

"Yes, I know what you mean. And you're wrong." Shonn stood and leaned forward, putting his fists against the table. "You didn't do this to me. How can you think that?"

"Am I interrupting?" Menphis set three pints of beer down on the table. "Again?"

Tadgh stared at Shonn, then looked towards the exit.

Menphis bit the inside of his cheek, then sat down. "Look, I have no idea what's going on between you two. But food's on the way. Tadgh, sit. Whatever is going on can wait until after supper."

***

Tadgh sat at the edge of his bed, hands on knees, shoulders slumped. 'Did I mean what I said to Shonn? Or was it just my guilt speaking? I want to believe Shonn's feelings for me are real, but how can I believe that? With just a touch, I turned Desdemona into my best friend. Is it possible I used my abilities to force Shonn to be in love with me?'

There was a knock at the door. Tadgh raced to the door, hoping it would be Shonn. Instead, Menphis stood in the hallway.

"We need to speak," Menphis said.

Tadgh took in a breath to protest. Then he saw the look of steely determination in the Elmire Ahk's eyes. Exhaling, he stepped aside and let Menphis into the room.

Menphis folded his arms. "I know it's late, Tadgh, but something has been weighing on me. I thought it best to address it when Shonn's not around. Do you have feelings for each other?"

Tadgh closed the door. For a moment, he was not sure how to answer, so he simply stared at the ground. "I want to say yes, even though I can tell from your eyes that you don't approve. The truth is I don't know. I have this ability. I have this ability to manipulate people's emotions. They fall completely under my control like they're possessed. That's how I was able to get Desdemona to call for a retreat."

"What does this have to do with my cousin? Are you saying you used your ability on him?"

"I don't know!" Tadgh slammed his fist against the wall, then walked away. When he looked back, there was a sizable hole in the wall. He put his hands behind his back and turned away. "I don't know. Maybe. Have you ever known him to have feelings for another man before?"

Menphis stared at him, eyes blazing. "No. Although, truth be told, I've never known him to be interested in a woman, either."

Tadgh turned to face Menphis. "Instructor Mal already knows. That's why Shonn's coming with us to GardenKeep. He hopes the Sage can determine if I did something to him."

Nostrils flaring, Menphis moved slowly towards Tadgh until he was only a few inches from him. "You will leave him alone if the Sage determines you've bedazzled him. Do I have your word?"

"Of course," Tadgh said. "I'm not a monster. In exchange, I need a favor. Please don't say bedazzled. It means something completely different where I'm from. It involves sequins and tacky clothing."

Menphis snorted. Then he smiled and shook his head. "You're trying to diffuse the situation with humor. I can appreciate that. But, if I find out you have altered my cousin's emotions on purpose, I will break you."

"And I will let you," Tadgh said. "Whatever Shonn feels, my feelings are real. I am attracted to him. I want to be with him. But not like that. Can we end this for tonight? We walked for over eight hours today."

"Fine," Menphis said. "Get your rest. Tomorrow we walk for ten hours."

"If we weren't renting this place, I would so throw something at you right now. Something heavy. Good night, Menphis."

With a smile, the Elmire Ahk walked past Tadgh. He opened the door and went back to his room.

Tadgh stripped out of his dirty and damp travel clothes and slid into bed. He put his arms behind his head and stared at the ceiling until sleep came.

Chapter Seventeen

"You're sure those were his exact words?" The Sage looked over at his two visitors. He had contracted them earlier in the week to look into Lord Vyken's activities. One was a 3-foot-tall man wearing thick black glasses to shield his eyes. He had the typical light orange skin and bright red hair of his people, the Frie Stav. The other was even stranger, a female Trofast with no ties to the Quadumvirate.

"Exactly." The Frie Stav nodded and took a sip of tea from the strange mug before him. "The fieldbender, I think his name was Oshu, was very specific. 'The warzone will be coming to us soon enough,' he said. 'As soon as the sword is secure, things will progress quickly.' I have no blasted idea what it means, but based on your reaction, I guess you do. What is this cup made out of, anyway? Is it glass?"

The Sage shook his head. "Imported plastic. This news is…very troubling. You have more than paid off your debt, Gnocko, but I'm afraid I must ask a bit more from you. I'm not at liberty to go into details, but believe me when I say this. Without your help many people are going to die."

"Then you can count on our help." The Trofast sat her cup of tea down. Her face was relaxed but her eyes were intense. "Now hold on a minute, Eiodeesh." Gnocko, the Frie Stav, turned to the Sage. "My friend has illusions of being a hero like something from the books. All I want is to gather some advanced tech and head back to my family. I owe it to them to avoid danger. You can understand that, can't you?"

"More than you can realize, Gnocko." The Sage let his head fall back and stared at the ceiling. "Still, I'm asking you, anyway. I would handle this myself, but I have too many obligations. I need to outsource this. It's nothing dangerous. Just keep an eye on Oshu. I know all the fieldbenders in town. He's not local. More importantly, I need to be informed the minute Lord Vyken returns to GardenKeep. Under no circumstances are you to confront Vyken. When he gets here, I'll deal with him."

"But sir," Barnes said. "You promised…"

The Sage glared at Barnes. His servant lowered his eyes and fell silent.

The Sage turned back to Gnocko. "I'm needed up north. Barnes is investigating Lord Vyken's fortress. There is no one else I can trust to watch Oshu."

"As I said, we can do this." Eyes gleaming, Eiodeesh rubbed her hands together. "Explain to us when you can."

"Of course." The Sage motioned to his servant. Barnes set a small purse of gold and silver coins in front of her. "This should pay for your hotel and provisions for the next month. Gnocko, I also have access to advanced Nizarian technology. Things you cannot buy on the market. You can head back home once this is finished. Please let Barnes know if there is anything else you need. Now, if you'll excuse me, I have somewhere else to be."

The Sage stood and left the room. Barnes followed.

"I know what you're going to say, Barnes, so don't bother saying." The Sage bent to put on shoes.

Hands out defensively, Barnes shook his head. "I'm not the one who promised the most powerful fieldbender on the planet…"

"…that's debatable…"

"Oh, please don't split hairs. If Elmontrazar isn't technically the most powerful he's definitely in the top ten. And you promised him you were going to leave Lord Vyken alone."

The Sage hung his head and rubbed his forehead. "How can I do that? You heard Gnocko. Vyken has played us for a fool. All this time, in my city and I didn't see it. Thanks to Gnocko and Eiodeesh, we can prove he's behind the robberies, but we have no clue why he's doing it. And now he knows the Sword of Kassandra escaped the Void. He doesn't know where it is, or DunDegore would already be under attack. It's only a matter of time before he finds it. The only advantage we have is that Lord Vyken isn't aware of our knowledge. He has to be stopped."

Barnes helped clip a military cape around the Sage's shoulders. "I didn't say he shouldn't be stopped. I just said you promised Elmontrazar you wouldn't be the one doing it. Vyken is royalty with ties to the Redgravians. If you kill him…"

"…who said anything about killing? I just said I'd deal with him."

Barnes lowered his head and blinked slowly at the Sage.

"Okay, I *was* planning on killing him." The Sage ran his fingers through his hair and took a deep breath. "Damn. Sometimes I hate that you know me so well. Didn't anyone ever tell you that servants are supposed to obey their employers?"

Barnes smirked. "I must have missed that lesson. Dad always told me you need someone to keep you in check. Don't look at me that way. His words, not mine."

The Sage laughed and wiped a tear from his eye. "I miss him. He would be proud of you. Thank you. You're right. It might be bad if I killed Lord Vyken."

"If by bad you mean start a civil war and have the entire country turn against you, yes. It would be bad. Maybe you should just, I don't know, talk to him."

The Sage rubbed his lips and stared at the ground. His forehead wrinkled as he thought for a moment. "In my experience, men like Lord Vyken cannot be stopped by conversation. I'm heading to DunDegore now. They brought the Sword to the monastery. I'm meeting with Sirion and the others to discuss security protocols. If Vyken knows it's returned, we have to assume others do as well. It's more important than ever to hide its energy signature. After that I'll visit with Elmontrazar at Castle Nizaria. He's better at political chess than I am. Maybe he can think of another way to get Vyken out of the picture."

"Maybe if the royal families of GardenKeep find out what he's involved with, they'll side with you."

"Doubtful," the Sage said. "Experience also tells me family rarely turns on itself for strangers -especially the royal families. Up until now, we've been working under the assumption Lord Vyken is working without their knowledge. If that's not true, we have much bigger problems. Civil war may be inevitable. It may even be the reason for all this. I'll be back by supper. Have you had any luck convincing Pwella to leave her job and come here?"

"Yes, sir." Barnes winked at the Sage. "I can be very persuasive. She gave her notice last night."

The Sage flicked his wrist and a glowing circle of light appeared. "Best news of the day. It's important that you see her tonight as planned. Learn everything else you can about Vyken's fortress even if it means you stop being subtle about it. Things are progressing quickly. The time for secrecy will soon be past."

The Sage stepped into the circle of light and was gone.

Chapter Eighteen

Tadgh collapsed face-first on the bed, exhausted. It was the end of the eighth straight day of walking, and every muscle in his body hated him. His feet, legs and back ached from walking. His arms and legs ached from the training exercises Menphis forced him to do throughout the day. He had learned several basic attack and defense motions with the quarterstaff. Menphis forced him to practice the simple movements for hours as they walked along the highway. His hands grew calloused, the muscles in his forearms numb from the constant exertion.

There was a knock at the door. Knowing it was Shonn, he was slow to answer.

When they had left Flesh Prayer, Menphis had been true to his word: he had bought Tadgh several history books. The only problem was that Tadgh couldn't read them. Whatever magic had taught him to speak and understand the Sirian language did not extend to the written word. He knew he could just wish the ability on himself, but every time the thought came to him, he remembered Instructor Mal's warning.

So instead, Shonn had been coming to his room each night and teaching him how to read. Despite endless pleading from Shonn, it was all they did together. Tadgh could not bring himself to do anything else.

The knock came again. He rose from bed and let Shonn inside.

"I was thinking we could skip the reading tonight."

Shonn's lips lifted ever so slightly.

"Come on! How many times do I have to tell you?"

"Yeah, yeah, whatever." Shonn grabbed Tadgh by the neck and pulled him closer. Before Tadgh could resist, their lips touched.

"No!" Tadgh pushed himself away and walked to the other end of the hotel room. He sat on a plush grey sofa and hung his head in his hands.

"How long has it been now?" Shonn leaned against the wall, arms crossed.

"Since what?" Tadgh could not even look up at Shonn as he spoke.

"Since you claim you brainwashed me. How long has it been?"

Tadgh shook his head. "I don't know."

"Exactly. You don't know because it never happened. You had some sort of power over the soldiers, but it can't last forever. It's been over a week now. I still feel the same way about you. Don't you think your power would have worn off by now?"

Tadgh opened his eyes but did not look at Shonn. "I don't know. And neither do you."

Shonn knelt in front of Tadgh. "I can see you're afraid. You don't want to take advantage of me, which is cute and all, considering I'm older than you. I have feelings for you, Tadgh. Real feelings. We're halfway to GardenKeep now. Let's say we take the night off your reading lessons and just go see the city instead."

Tadgh looked at Shonn now. "Is there anything to see here? It looked pretty dull on the way in."

"Well it's no Flesh Prayer," Shonn said, his voice light with laughter. "Jaxonville is pretty reserved for a city this far south. They have this massive library. They say it's the largest one in all of Shirza. It goes on for blocks and stands ten stories tall."

"Wow," Tadgh said. "You want to take me to the library on a date? Looks like I didn't leave high school after all."

"You've mentioned this high school before. They really force everyone to become educated?"

"Well, they try." Tadgh slumped back, sinking into the cushions of the sofa. "I don't really remember much learning going on, but I suppose something sunk in. You don't have that here?"

Shonn shook his head and sat on the couch beside Tadgh. "Back in Tarkon, most kids stop going to school by the time they're thirteen. They need so many people working in the mill and the shipyards that most can't justify staying in school past then. Normally it's just fieldbenders and the Elmire Ahk that stay in school."

"You seem pretty educated," Tadgh said. "Did you stay in school?"

Shonn groaned. "Yeah. My mother felt I wasn't man enough to work in the mill and I didn't have the strength to work the shipyard. She thought maybe I could make a go of it as a teacher. It would never work, though. I kind of hate children."

"Seriously?" Tadgh frowned. "How can anyone hate children? It's like hating puppies."

"I have no idea what a puppy is."

Tadgh glanced over at Shonn. They held the stare for several seconds too long. Then both broke down into completely irrational laughter.

"Feels good to laugh with you," Shonn said. "Let's get out of here."

Tadgh looked over at the bed. "Yes. Getting out of here is a very good idea."

They spent the next three hours wandering the torch-lit streets of Jaxonville. They stopped for pastry that looked like donuts but tasted like frozen yogurt. Every few blocks the streets broke into open squares filled with sculptured fountains and artists selling oil paintings.

"This almost feels like a vacation," Tadgh said. "I'd give anything for life to be like this all the time."

"You haven't talked much about your life before you got here. Was it really so bad?"

Tadgh licked sugar from his fingers. "Yeah. I'm not sure I want to talk about it, though. I'm having such a good time I don't want to spoil the mood."

"So tell me something good. What do you miss about your world? There must be something? Someone."

'Colin,' Tadgh thought. He shook the thought away. "To be honest, things got so bad there I can't think of anything I miss. Life was so busy, stressful. School was a complete nightmare by the end. If I'd gone back after…"

He stopped. He was about to say 'after I killed those boys,' but he couldn't admit that to Shonn. Tadgh didn't want him to know about that. It would change everything.

"After what?"

"I was attacked," Tadgh said. He hated lying, so he decided to say as much about the truth as he could. "We were leaving school later. My friend was part of the debate team. I waited for him so we could walk home together. He was looking at me, talking about some stupid movie he'd seen on TV the night before. The next thing I knew something slammed into my head. I fell forward and smashed my head against the sidewalk. I screamed and turned to look up at Colin. They smashed a baseball bat against the back of his head. He fell. He never moved again."

Shonn put a hand on Tadgh's shoulder.

Tadgh shook himself free. That touch felt like the ultimate betrayal. "I guess I'm not ready to talk about it yet."

Shonn stared at him, open mouth. "Dear gods. I had no idea. I'm sorry. I foresaw the attack on the monastery. I saw so many people lying in the dirt, blood leaking from them. When my visions come to me, it's like I'm living through it. I feel the heat fading from their bodies, smell the salt of their blood. If you ever do want to talk about, I'm here."

"Thanks." Tadgh stared at the ground. He knew he'd shaped the truth to manipulate Shonn. He felt guilty but also happy he had been able to hide the truth.

They walked back to the hotel and said goodnight.

Chapter Nineteen

They spent the next seven days walking to GardenKeep. Tadgh's training with the quarterstaff intensified. Every day, his muscles grew stronger. When he asked Menphis if training for battle was all the Brothers of Tyche did, Menphis smacked him on the head.

"I'm not training you for battle," Menphis said. "I'm training your body to be strong. Once your body is strong, we'll start training your head. That will be much harder."

Long before they reached the gates of GardenKeep, traffic increased. Most of the travelers were merchants heading into town with carts full of produce destined for port. By the time the city walls came into view, they walked single-file along with hundreds of others. Directly in front of Tadgh was a group of female Elmire Ahk in white robes. Behind Menphis was a cart filled with poultry. The smell and noise made the waiting even more uncomfortable.

"Strange," Menphis said. He glanced at the armed guards pacing on either side of the road.

"It isn't always like this?" Tadgh studied the high walls of the city. Armored guards walked the length of the walls as far as he could see.

Shonn shook his head. "I've never seen it like this. I've been to GardenKeep dozens of times. Hundreds of travelers entered the city every day but I've never seen the line to get into town like this."

"Usually you wait no more than a few minutes." Menphis leaned on his quarterstaff and stretched his legs.

"We've been waiting for more than an hour." Shonn stepped out of line to look towards the front of the line. "Something odd is going on here."

Menphis stared at him. "Are you getting one of your…things?"

Eyes wide, Shonn looked around to see if anyone was listening. "Geesh. No. It's just a statement."

Menphis nodded and turned in a slow circle. "I think you're right. Something strange is going on. But let's focus on why we're here. We get Tadgh to the Sage as quickly as possible, see what he knows, and get out of here. We have enough strangeness in our lives as it is."

"Can I make a request?" Tadgh sat on the ground. "Can we just head to the hotel and see this Sage guy in the morning? I'm exhausted."

Menphis raised his left eyebrow. "I would have thought you'd be in a hurry to meet him? We've traveled two weeks to get here and…"

"Exactly!" Tadgh leaned his head back to look Menphis in the eyes. "We have traveled for two weeks without taking a break. It would be nice to just stop for a bit. Get something to eat and maybe stop moving for five minutes."

Shonn frowned. "We've already stopped moving for five minutes."

Tadgh sighed. "It's a figure of speech. I'm just…"

"Scared?"

Tadgh looked up at Menphis again.

"Look, I get it," Menphis said. "There is a lot riding on what he says to you. He may be able to recover your memories, maybe find a way for you to get home."

"And maybe the wizard will give me a brain too." Tadgh laughed at his own joke, then bit his lower lip. "I probably am a little freaked out. But I'm also tired. Really tired. Can we just put it off until tomorrow?"

Shonn cleared his throat and stared at Menphis.

Menphis grunted and let his shoulders slump. "Fine. We'll head to the hotel and check in. After that, we'll head down to the docks. There's a restaurant there that sells the best fried fish."

"You guys have fried fish!" Tadgh got to his feet. "Finally, some real food!"

***

"What the hell is this?" Tadgh looked at a foot-long brown fish, still covered in scales, on a white plate. It was covered in a thick orange-brown sauce and thinly sliced nuts.

"This is the best fried fish you'll ever have you in your life." Menphis grinned as he cut into the fish on his plate. As he lifted it to his mouth, Tadgh noticed the fish was filled with a white, fluffy substance like potatoes. "I thought you said you had fried fish back home."

"It looks nothing like this." Tadgh tried to ignore the lifeless, beady eyes of the fish's head. "Oh, what the hell. It's hardly the weirdest thing I've eaten since I got here. I guess I should be happy you have utensils."

Tadgh sliced into the fish and took a bite. Both Shonn and Menphis stopped eating to watch his reaction. A moment later the flavor hit his tongue.

"Oh," he said. "Wow. That is…wow."

"You are a master of the language," Shonn said. "Try not to drool so much."

After entering the city, they had checked in to a lower-scale hotel near the edge of the city. Prices were significantly higher here than in the smaller towns, so their choices were more limited. For the first time in their journey, Tadgh had ended up with a room on the ground floor. The hotel had no bar or restaurant and only minimal staff. Still, it had everything they needed.

"Is this local fish?" Tadgh realized he was speaking with his mouth full. However, he did not want to stop eating long enough to talk properly.

"Yes," Menphis said. "Dwarb. It's found all along the east coast of Shirza. So what is fried fish like where you come from?"

"It's skinned, for one thing. And they always cut the head off, because, honestly, that part is just gross. Then they dip it in a mixture of flour and bread before dropping it in a large skillet of boiling fat."

Shonn dropped his fork.

"Dear god," Menphis said. "That sounds…"

"Horrific," Shonn finished.

"No! It's beautiful. You should try it some time. Of course you probably won't, seeing as how, you know, it's on another planet and all."

"Are you sure you want to go home?" Shonn's voice was a little too sharp. Menphis stared at his cousin, his left eye twitching slightly.

Tadgh looked back and forth between Shonn and Menphis. Then he hung his head. "I'm not sure about anything anymore. Maybe it's best I go before I cause any more problems."

Shonn reached out for Tadgh's hand. Tadgh pulled back.

"Can we change the subject?" Tadgh focused back on his fish. They finished the meal in relative silence.

After supper they took the long way back to the hotel. They walked past rows of taverns filled with cheerful and rowdy patrons, many dancing between the tables. Groups of young people in rich clothing sat on the edge of marble fountains. Some held hands; others loudly discussed politics. As they moved away from the docks, the salty air was replaced by heavy scents of restaurants selling flavored meat dishes and their own varieties of fried fish.

When they reached the hotel, Shonn followed Tadgh to his room. Menphis said nothing, but his lips trembled with the effort.

"Whatever happens tomorrow, I need you to know something." Shonn avoided Tadgh's eyes and focused on cleaning the dirt from underneath his nails. "I understand why you have your guard up around me. And I respect you for that. But I need you to know there is no doubt on my part. I don't want you to go home. I want you to stay."

Tadgh stared at the door to his room. Suddenly it was difficult to breathe. "I should get to bed, Shonn."

"Just look at me."

Tadgh took a deep breath and reached for the doorknob. "Good night, Shonn."

Shonn put his hand over Tadgh's, stopping him from opening the door. Tadgh closed his eyes.

"Please," Shonn said. "Please let me come inside."

Tears ran down Tadgh's face. His lower lip quivered as he shook his head. "I can't. How can I? You say you know how you feel, but I don't know *why* you feel that way. How can I let you inside knowing I may be using you?"

"You're being ridiculous."

"No, I'm not. And you know it. Maybe you do have feelings for me. Or maybe I altered your brain and forced you to fall in love with me. I don't know which one is real and I don't want to be that kind of person. I can't be that kind of person. So please, just let me go inside. Alone."

Shonn removed his hand. "Fine. But we'll talk again after you meet with the Sage. Agreed?"

Tadgh nodded but did not open his eyes. He kept them closed as Shonn leaned in and kissed him on his cheek. He left them closed until he heard footsteps fade away. He only opened his eyes when he knew he was alone. Then he headed to bed.

It took him a very long time to get to sleep.

***

James Fitzpatrick has a very public funeral. I watch the graveside service from the branches of a tree at the edge of the cemetery. I can't get closer. Too many police officers patrol the grounds. In the movies, serial killers often show up at funerals. Maybe they come to gloat or relive the thrill of the murder. I'm not sure why I'm here. I should be happy. James is dead. Colin is avenged, at least in part. But what I feel is something else.

The others are here, the two scumbags that beat Colin to death. Vince Downing is the taller of the two. He's dressed in a blue shirt with a black tie. His girlfriend, Sarah, is beside him. She's holding his hand. I can't see his face, but I imagine he's crying. The shorter one is Everet Smith. He's thick and heavy, mostly muscle. Even from this distance I see how red his face is. He stands apart from everyone else and he keeps turning, looking over his shoulder. It feels like he's looking for me instead of listening to the service.

I stay in my hiding spot long after the last guest leaves. I have nowhere else to go.

"Don't tell me you're losing your bloodlust so early?" I look to my left. Bes appears out of nowhere. He's sitting on a nearby branch, a smile on his face like the Cheshire Cat.

"No," I say. I'm amazed at how unfazed I am at him showing up like this. "It's just weird. When I was doing it..."

"You mean when you were killing the boy and eating his soul?"

Bile rises in my throat, coating my mouth. "Yes. Then. When I was doing it, I felt amazing. Happy he was dead, even happier I was the one killing him. But now? Did you see his mother? I watched her during the service. She's devastated. I did that. I made her feel that way."

"Perhaps I chose the wrong avatar," Bes says. The smile fades from his face. I realize cats aren't supposed to smile. It seems more unnatural than his ability to talk. "I can take the power back."

"No!" I scream. My voice is louder than anticipated. "I want this. They need to pay. I'll do it. I'll kill the other two."

"When? It's already been days since your first kill and I can't eat until you're finished. Trust me. I would love a little nibble, but there are rules I have to play by. So act quickly. I'm getting hungry, and when that happens I lose my patience."

"Okay." I glance at Bes and swallow. "I'll kill another one tonight."

Bes nods his head and jumps to the ground. I watch him walk into the graveyard for a bit. Then he disappears. A chill runs through me and, shivering, I jump out of the tree.

Bes is right. I killed James five days ago. I've been watching the other two since then. Plotting. Procrastinating. The problem with waiting is I get to see their lives. I watch Vince through the windows of his house. I listen to him flirt with Sarah. I listen to them make plans for the summer and watch movies. The more I listen, the more human he becomes. It is hard to kill a human. It is much easier to kill an animal. When I think of what he did to Colin, that's all he is: an animal. Now I know people will mourn him when he dies. That complicates things.

It is 5:00 p.m. I know where Vince will be. Every day at this time he goes to the gym. I hop a bus to get there. When the driver asks me for money I touch her hand. She smiles up at me and lets me on for free.

The gym has a security guard on site. Members show ID to get past reception. One of the personal trainers is behind the front desk. She is in her mid-twenties, thin and attractive. She looks a bit like Claire Danes. She smiles at me as I walk up to her. I reach out to shake her hand. On instinct, she grabs my hand back. I squeeze lightly and turn her will to mine.

"Let me in," I say. "Then go for break. A long break."

"Of course," she says. She buzzes me through the gate into the gym. Then she walks out into the cold, right past the security guard.

I clench and unclench my fists as I walk past the free weights and fitness machines. People are starting to look at me. Maybe it's because I'm the only one not dressed in gym clothes. Maybe it's the slow, steady anger in my eyes. I see Vince on one of the treadmills at the back of the gym. His eyes are on the row of TVs. He doesn't see me coming.

"Can I help you?"

I turn my head to the right. I see an Asian man wearing the same uniform as the woman at the front desk. He's older than me with large, well-formed muscles. He smiles, all teeth. He is trying to be helpful.

"No, thank you," I say. I unzip my hoodie and let it drop to the floor. My chest is bare. I look skinny and harmless next to him. "I will help myself."

Before the employee can respond, I start to change. I see it in his eyes. At first they are confused. Then they go wide. After that, he screams and runs away, still watching me over his shoulder. The gym erupts in screams. Weights are dropped loudly to the floor. Machines stop moving, replaced by feet hitting the ground.

I'm now in full form. I stand nearly a foot taller; my muscles bulge beneath a layer of orange fur. The world changes color; everything is in faded shades of blue and green. Saliva drips from the large fangs in my mouth. I howl at the air, my voice no longer human. It sounds monstrous. Demonic. Vince takes out his earphones and, placing his feet on the stationary frame of the treadmill, turns around. Everyone else on the treadmills reacts at the same time. They turn to see me walking slowly towards them, a slow shark against the panicked school of fish. My eyes lock on Vince. He tries to back up, forgetting he's on a treadmill. His feet slip out from underneath him and he falls into the person behind him.

I smile and pick up my pace.

Vince is screaming now. He pushes himself to his feet. I grab him under his arm and pull him up to face me. I rip off his shirt with my claws and place a paw against his sweaty chest. Immediately, the fear on his face is replaced by something very different. He smiles and his eyes grow bright.

"You owe me," I say. "Give me your life."

"Anything," Vince says. Again the rush of energy flows up my arms, filling me, making me stronger. Life fades from his eyes and color fades from his skin. I am overwhelmed by a feeling I cannot name.

Then I snap his neck.

Something in me goes soft, a small voice telling me to stop. Before I can answer it, I hear something behind me. A gunshot. I turn to see the security guard pointing a weapon at me. I look down and see I am uninjured. He missed. I hurl Vince's body at the security guard and head towards the side exit. It is the type of door that can only open from the inside. As soon as I slam through it, an alarm sounds. I run across the parking lot and jump on the roof of the nearby strip mall. By the time the police come I am far away.

***

Tadgh opened his eyes. Instantly, he knew something was wrong.

Chapter Twenty

"Where the hell am I?" A quick look revealed he was naked, lying on a cold stone floor. Tadgh tried to stand, but searing pain shot through his ankle and up his left leg. He looked down at a thick silver manacle around his ankle. It was attached to an even thicker chain embedded in the floor. His eyes darted around the room as he tried to remain calm. It was small, no more than 10' x 10'. There were no windows and only one wooden door. There was no sign of his clothing.

"At least there's no hacksaw around." His tried to laugh, but his voice cracked. He pulled at the chain, then, with a scream, jerked his hand back. It felt like he had touched acid. He looked at his fingers. The flesh was raw and red. He quieted his breath and tried to clear his mind. It took time, but eventually the panic subsided.

"I guess this is why Bes told me to avoid silver. How the hell am I going to get out of this? Shape-shifting is probably a dumb idea. My legs will get bigger. I may end up with this silver chain stuck in muscle. I suppose I could just wish myself out of here, but Instructor Mal told me not to. He said it was dangerous. Still, I think this counts as an emergency."

The door to the cell opened. An overweight man in pale pink robes stepped into the room. His head was shaved bald and he had no discernible eyebrows. He clasped his hands in prayer over his chest, a gesture that was at once effeminate and sinister. For several moments, the man said nothing. He simply glared at Tadgh with wide wet eyes. His lower lip quivered excitedly.

"Where am I?" Tadgh asked.

"You really don't expect me to tell you that, do you?" The stranger took another step closer to Tadgh and knelt down, the better to look him in the eye. "You don't remember me, do you? I guess you were too busy putting

Desdemona in her place to even notice I was there. You are truly fascinating. I've never seen anything quite like you. Your energy field is extremely…unique. So you can imagine how happy I was to see you in GardenKeep last night. I got here right after the disaster at the monastery. Poor Desdemona. She's been in a rage since you bedazzled her."

"Again with the bedazzle?"

"That sounded like you're trying to make a joke. I suggest you take this seriously. Illuminati pride themselves on their strength of will. You made a very dangerous enemy."

"She can join the club. Who are you?"

The man thrust out his chest and stared down at him. "My name is Oshu. And you are Tadgh, a very appropriate name. I'm glad to see I was right about the silver. When you were sleeping I checked several substances against your skin just to be sure. You are not like any demon I've seen before, but you have certain qualities in common. I think if you were exposed to enough silver you may just explode."

Tadgh held his breath.

Eyes wide, Oshu smiled. "I see you understand. As you can imagine, my employer is very interested in you after what you did to Desdemona. He was thrilled when I let him know I'd found you far away from the Elmire Ahks."

"Why am I naked?" Tadgh adjusted his body to best hide his most vulnerable parts.

"Because I don't trust you. Don't worry, boy. We won't be here long. Lord Vyken will arrive in a few hours and we'll go to the fortress outside town. In the meantime, I'm hoping to run a few more tests on you. With luck we can convince you to work with us. Talents such as yours could be very useful to our plans."

"You're kidding, right?" Tadgh angled further away from Oshu. "You honestly think I'll work with you after you kidnap me and…?"

The man lifted a finger and Tadgh's mouth slammed shut. No matter how hard he tried to open it, his muscles would not respond.

"I never kid." The bald man extended his hand and touched Tadgh's forehead. "And trust me. I can be very persuasive."

For a moment nothing happened. Then sharp pain flooded Tadgh's body, like shards of glass flowing through his veins. He screamed until he passed out.

***

When Tadgh woke, he found himself in a different room, strapped to a metal operating table. A single white sheet covered his body. Silver bands were locked over both wrists and his ankles. Another band held his neck in place. He was careful not to lift his head or breathe too deeply. Every touch of silver was like acid eating into his skin.

"Ah, you're awake."

"What are you doing to me?" Tadgh turned his head slightly but could not see Oshu. He knew it was him based on the voice.

"Testing a theory." Oshu came into view. He stood over Tadgh with a dagger in his hands." You see, there has been another, shall we say, phenomenon in this area. I think it may be coming from you. Of course I could be wrong, but after I dig through your aura I'll know one way or another."

Oshu twirled the dagger in his hand the way people would twirl a pencil back in school. His fingers were thin, dainty and flexible. "What are you, exactly? I've met shape-shifters before, creatures capable of changing from human to animal form. There are herds of them, actually, out in the Badlands. The Armies of Dispayre sometimes recruit them for hunting or games in the arena. They're like any wild animal: untamed and hungry. But you are nothing like them. But you are not feral. You are chaos wrapped in a tightly woven illusion of civility. I can feel the Void energy dripping out of your pores like a graunskyeg. Like a demon."

"I'm not a demon." Tadgh lifted his head. Immediately, the silver burned his throat and forced him to back down. "Damn it! You kidnap me and strap me to a table just to experiment on me. As far as I'm concerned, you're the bloody demon. I made a deal with someone. He gave me these powers. "

"A deal? Interesting. And with whom did you make this deal?"

"His name was Bes." Tadgh winced. The pain from the silver burns wasn't fading. "He was a talking cat. That's all I know."

Oshu leaned forward. "A talking cat? Sounds like a demon to me. Desdemona said you were immune to normal weapons. I want to test that." Before Tadgh could react, Oshu stabbed him in the chest. The blade pierced his skin easily. Tadgh screamed. Pain radiated from the wound. A moment later, Oshu pulled the knife out and peered at the wound. "Fascinating. It is already healing. Such an incredible rate, too."

"You'll pay for that."

"Doubtful," the man slowly slit into Tadgh again.

This time he dragged the blade across Tadgh's throat. For a moment his vocal chords filled with blood. Tadgh felt like he was drowning. Then the blood stopped and air rushed back into his lungs.

"Now, that is truly impressive," Oshu said. "If we had an army of creatures like you, the continent would fall even faster than we expect it to."

"What do you mean, the continent would fall? Is that what this is about? You're planning some sort of invasion."

"Why do you keep asking questions you know I'm not going to answer?" Oshu set the dagger down and studied Tadgh. "I need to run the test on your aura. It would be helpful if you were quiet during the procedure. Will you do that for me?"

"Screw you."

The man sighed. "Fine." Then he put his finger on Tadgh's forehead again. The pain was more intense than last time. Tadgh passed out quickly.

When he woke, he was back in his cell. Alone.

"I can't wait any more," he whispered. "I need to get out of here before he gets back. So here goes. I wish my leg was free."

Instantly, the silver shackle snapped. It fell to the stone floor with a clank.

Tadgh looked at the section of his leg burned by the acidic touch of silver. It was red and raw. Unlike the stab wounds from the dagger, it appeared to be healing very slowly.

'Now what?' he thought. 'Do I just wish myself out of here? Where will I go? I don't even know where I am. I guess I could just wish myself back to where Shonn and Menphis are. But what if they're in here too?'

Tadgh shook his head and decided to start small. "I wish I had my clothes back."

With a swirl like smoke solidifying around his body, his Elmire Ahk uniform appeared around his body. Instantly he felt better.

'Let's try the door.' He tried to push the door open, but, unsurprisingly, it was locked. "I wish this door was open." As he said the words, the door clicked open.

The earth rumbled.

'What the hell?' For a moment he lost his balance. He leaned against the doorframe before he fell on his face. 'Did I cause that? Maybe I better be careful with this wish thing after all.'

On the other side of the door was the room with the table to which he'd been strapped. There was no sign of Oshu, but the room wasn't empty. A servant in brown robes washed blood from the operating table with a damp cloth that smelled like bleach.

The servant did not hear the door open.

Tadgh rushed the servant, grabbing him by the forearm. Tadgh had him under his will before the servant could scream.

Tadgh watched the fear fade from the servant's eyes. Only then did he remove his hand.

"Where am I?" he asked.

"Lord Vyken's palace, sir," the servant said. "Has anyone told you how beautiful your eyes are?"

"You are so not my type. What is your name?"

"Fenrick, sir. Is there anything I can do for you?"

"Yes. You can tell me if that creep in the pink robes kidnapped my friends, too."

"Not that I know of, sir. I believe Oshu only wanted you."

"What is he? Some sort of sorcerer?"

"I'm not familiar with that word, sir. Oshu is a fieldbender. He's been in Lord Vyken's service for many years. Would you like me to call him for you?"

"No! Absolutely not. I need to get out of here. Where is the nearest exit?"

"We're in the basement. Just outside that door over there is a hallway that leads to a set of stairs. You can take them up to the guard room. Though, I wouldn't recommend it. Oshu is pretty intent on you staying here until Lord Vyken can see you personally. The guards would try to restrain you."

"Lovely. Is there another way out?"

"We could always go through the servant quarters, sir. Would you mind if I sat down for a bit? My head feels funny."

Tadgh shook his head. "Later. I need you to lead the way. Get me out of here before that sicko gets back."

The servant dropped his wet rag on the table and opened a thick wooden door into a hallway lined with electric lights. Tadgh blinked at how modern and earth-like they appeared, but it was a mystery for another day. He followed Fenrick down the hallway to the first intersection.

From straight ahead he heard voices of several men. Fenrick turned and walked in the opposite direction. In a matter of minutes, they stopped at what looked like a dead end. Then Fenrick pushed a button melded into the wall so well it was nearly invisible. The wall retreated, revealing a staircase up.

"That is totally something out of a Scooby Doo episode," Tadgh said. Then he sniffed the air and spun around to look behind him. "Damn. It's Oshu. I need you to close this door, Fenrick. Do it now."

Unhurriedly, Fenrick smiled at him and pushed another button. The wall slid back into position, cutting off much of the light.

"We have to move quickly," Tadgh said. "He's going to realize I'm gone pretty quickly. I may need you to distract him for me."

"I will give my life for you, sir."

"Wow. That's not disturbing in the slightest. Please don't say that again, okay?"

"Anything for you, sir." Fenrick turned and continued up the stairs.

"How far is it?" Tadgh followed him closely. Sweat dripped from his armpits and dampened his hair. He found it hard to breathe and remain calm, even with Menphis' training.

"We just have to get to the first floor, sir. This leads directly to the kitchens. From there, you should be able to sneak out the back door."

The walls shook.

"What was that?"

Fenrick shrugged. "I'm not sure, sir. Perhaps Mr. Oshu is doing something in his lab."

"That's what I was afraid of. Pick up the pace a bit."

At the end of the first flight of stairs, Fenrick pushed another button. The wall slid open to a kitchen filled with servants dressed in white. Many of them were chopping and peeling vegetables on long rows of stone islands. The smell of cooked meat and spices filled the air. Young men in unbleached cotton tunics unloaded food onto the counters. Tadgh could see the back door. It stood open, leading to a back alleyway. Several people glanced over at Tadgh and Fenrick, but no one stared at them for long. They quickly returned to their work.

"Almost free." Tadgh walked quickly to the back door. Then something slammed into his back, throwing him forward. His face slammed into a stone island. His vision blurred with gray stars. Panic told him to move quickly, but his body responded very slowly. When he lifted his head, another blast slammed into his back. Only this time, he saw the source. Oshu stood at the entrance to the stairwell behind him. Fields of ever-shifting energy like purple amoebas encircled each of his hands.

"You are an impressive beast," Oshu said. "I really need to get you back to the lab and figure out how you got free. This is all pointless. I've seen your aura. I have your scent now. Even if you slipped out that door, you'll never escape me. I am under orders not to kill you. Lord Vyken said nothing about keeping you conscious."

Oshu lifted his hands. Twin beams of purple energy shot towards Tadgh. He ducked. The bolt slammed into the stone island, cracking it. Not waiting for another shot, Tadgh slipped behind the island as the servants scattered.

"You're just prolonging the inevitable," Oshu said. "And you're annoying me. Let me try something else. There is void energy in you, which means you should be sensitive to celestial energy. Enough would kill even the most powerful graunskyeg. Let's see how much you can handle."

Oshu's entire body glowed with warm, yellow light. It poured over the tops of the counters, filling every corner of the room. Slowly, like honey, it dripped onto Tadgh even in his hiding place, but it did not hurt him. In fact, it made him feel wonderful. He looked at the acid burns on his leg. They healed as he watched. By the time the energy retreated, there was not even a hint of a scar.

"You're not screaming." Oshu frowned, eyes darting along the floor as if reading something in his mind. "Well, that's unexpected. It would seem you truly are not a demon after all. Tell me more about this Bes. How did he give you these abilities?"

Tadgh laughed. "And you honestly think I'm going to answer that question?"

Oshu shot another bolt of purple energy over Tadgh's head. Chunks of the ceiling fell on his head. He threw himself to the side before more of the ceiling fell down.

"You!" Oshu pointed at Fenrick. "Go get security!"

"Absolutely not, sir." Fenrick picked up a pot full of hot water and hurled it at Oshu. The fieldbender spat a curse and extended one hand out. The purple amoeba expanded, forming a shield. The pot and water bounced off harmlessly.

"What the hell are you are doing?" Oshu asked.

Fenrick did not answer. Instead, he picked up more and more dishes and hurled them at Oshu.

'Time to make a run for it,' Tadgh thought. He lifted himself into a crouch and made a run for the door. He did not get far before another bolt of energy pounded his side. He slammed to the ground. He heard something in his ribcage crack, and pain shot through his body.

"Stop moving!" Oshu shot another bolt of energy at Fenrick. It hit the servant square in the jaw. He was unconscious before he hit the ground.

"You know what I wish," Tadgh said. "I really wish I could shoot bolts of energy just like that."

The air grew solid, every hint of a breeze stopped. For a moment, there was no sound, no movement. Tadgh saw Oshu's eyes grow wide with understanding. Then, the world came crashing down. The earth trembled again, stronger than before. More cracks appeared in the ceiling. Oshu put a hand to his head. He looked to be in physical pain, as if he'd been hit by a sledge hammer.

"It *was* you," Oshu said. "You're the one who cracked the Void."

Tadgh stretched out his hands towards Oshu. Soon they were covered in purple amoebas, too. Then, there was a pulse. Energy shot out from his hand and hit Oshu before he could erect another shield. It slammed Oshu back through the door and down the stairs.

Tadgh looked down at his hands and smiled. "I could really learn to like this wish thing."

He stood and ran out the back door.

'I need to find the others before Oshu gathers reinforcements.'

Chapter Twenty-One

"Thank you again for this posting, sir," Pwella said. "As much as I enjoyed Lord Vyken's, the workload was very intense. Not that I have anything against hard work, of course. Still, it will be nice to see Barnes more often. Not that I will neglect my duties."

"You can relax, dear," the Sage said. "You already have the job. You do not need to impress me. Why don't you start work immediately? It is a tad early, but I would love some breakfast."

"Yes, sir," Pwella said. She bowed to the Sage and smiled over at Barnes before leaving.

"I see it's not only her thighs that are eager," the Sage said.

Barnes had a slight coughing fit which made the Sage chuckle.

"I'd appreciate it, sir, if you didn't mention I made that comment around Pwella." Barnes cleared his throat and looked over his shoulder to make sure Pwella no longer lingered in the doorway. "You know how women can be about that sort of thing."

"It has been a while, but I seem to remember."

"You never talk about her."

The Sage raised an eyebrow.

Barnes stared at the floor. "I'm no Sage, but you don't have to be a genius to know there was a woman in your past. Dad said he never knew you to be interested in romance. Not once in the whole time he served you. Same for me. There's only one thing that swears a man off love. A broken heart."

The Sage looked over at Barnes, his eyes intent. "It was a very long time ago. I should be over it now, but she's still there. Always in my head. I watched her die right in front of me. The other day I could have sworn.... Never mind. Be careful. Don't move too quickly with Pwella. Love can make you a better person, but if it goes wrong, it can destroy you."

Barnes nodded. "Understood. How did things go in DunDegore yesterday?"

"As expected. Sirion is completely insufferable. He won't listen to any of the recommendations Torch Karehn makes about security. I'm heading back there in a few hours."

The world stopped.

The Sage could not breathe.

Just as quickly as it had begun, the strange sensation ended. The Sage gasped, drawing air hastily into his empty lungs. Feeling returned to his limbs and he slumped forward.

"Sir?" Barnes asked. His face wrinkled with concern as he rushed to kneel before his employer.

"It happened again." The Sage waved him away and jumped to his feet. He looked out over the city.

"What, sir? You mean the thing with the Void?"

The Sage nodded. "Whatever cracked the reality field just happened again. Only this time, it was very close. Somewhere in town. I need you out in the streets. Meet with your people. Someone must have seen something. Go!"

Barnes nodded and ran from the room. As soon as he was alone, the Sage shivered. For the first time in many, many years he was genuinely afraid.

***

Tadgh knocked again, this time more insistently. Moments later, Menphis opened the door wearing only his sleeveless robe. It covered his body from shoulder to knee looking like a nightshirt.

"What is it, Tadgh? We don't wake up this early even at the monastery."

Tadgh looked back over his shoulder. "Let me in. Please. Something happened."

"Is that Tadgh?" Shonn's voice came from deep in the room.

"Yes." Tadgh spoke and pushed inside past Menphis. "Something happened last night. I'm not safe. I don't know if they followed me."

"Who are they?" Shonn said.

"Start from the beginning." Menphis closed the door. "Who followed you?"

Tadgh quickly recounted the story of being kidnapped by Oshu and waking up in the home of Lord Vyken. He told them how he escaped and tried not to see their reactions to his experiences.

"That sounds horrific," Shonn said. "Are you okay now?"

Tadgh nodded. "Weirded out, mostly. But they know me now. I don't feel safe going back to my own room. It's probably not even safe staying here. What should we do?"

Menphis nodded and reached for his leather pants. "We should head for the Sage immediately. We've come all this way. I don't think we should let the actions of these people deter us from our goal. After we meet the Sage we can head back to the monastery. You're probably right, Tadgh. The sooner we are out of GardenKeep the better."

***

"According to the front desk clerk, this is the place," Shonn said. The three of them stood in front of the Sage's house. As predicted, it was easy to find.

"This is…odd," Tadgh said. He glanced at the building and compared it to the other buildings in the neighborhood.

"That's an understatement," Menphis said. "I've never seen anything like this before."

"That's just it," Tadgh said. "I have. I've seen dozens of houses like this back home."

Shonn and Menphis exchanged a look. They shrugged at almost the same time.

"Let's get this over with before your new friends come find us," Menphis said. He walked up the front steps to the stone door and pounded with the heel of his fist. Moments later a young woman dressed as a maid opened the door.

"Can I help you?" She smiled as she spoke. Her cheeks were plump and slightly red and her brown eyes twinkled even in the early morning light. Tadgh felt immediately comfortable around her.

"We're here to see the Sage," Menphis said. "It is a matter of some urgency."

"Oh dear," the woman said. "I'm afraid he's not taking guests at the moment. It is very early."

"It's okay, Pwella," said a voice from within the house. "Have them come in."

The woman at the door blushed and stepped aside as she opened the door further. Menphis smiled and nodded in thanks as he walked past her. Shonn followed suit. Tadgh stopped at the front door.

"Whoa," he said. "Guys, I'm getting a very bad feeling about this."

Menphis looked at Shonn.

"Don't look at me," Shonn said. "I don't feel anything bad here."

Tadgh took a step further inside and scanned the room. "It's just, this whole place looks like an Ikea catalogue."

"I'm going to pretend that means something," Menphis said. "Don't insult our host. We've come a long way to see him. Try not to anger him before he agrees to help us."

"It wasn't meant as an insult," Tadgh said under his breath. "Just an observation. I like Ikea."

A dark-skinned man wearing a white cotton suit appeared at the top of a staircase. He stared down at them for a moment. Then his eyes fixed on Tadgh.

"Good morning, sir," Menphis said. "My name is Menphis Bannmerci. This is my cousin, Shonndira Bannmerci, and our friend, Tadgh Dooley. Instructor Mal of the Brotherhood of Tyche sent us to you asking for help."

The Sage did nothing but stare at Tadgh. Then he took a deep breath and descended the stairs towards them.

"How is Instructor Mal?" The Sage smiled as he talked. The expression in his eyes was very different. "I haven't seen him in years. We worked together on a trade agreement between Norshire and Shirza ten years ago. I have great respect for him. So what can I do for you?"

Nervously, Tadgh licked his lips. The entire time the Sage talked, his eyes focused on Tadgh. It was as if he was seeing something Tadgh was trying to hide.

"Our friend here has an unusual problem," Menphis said. "We were hoping you could help us with it."

"Yes," the Sage said. "I can see that." He reached into his pocket and pulled out a piece of paper and a pencil. After a few seconds of writing, he passed the paper to Tadgh.

"I'm sorry, sir," Tadgh said. "My friend Shonn has been giving me lessons, but I'm not very good at reading."

The Sage smiled. "Try."

Tadgh looked at the paper in his hands. There was one word written on it with a question mark.

American?

His jaw dropped. "This is English!" He stared at the Sage. "How do you know English?"

"Perhaps it would be best if we had this conversation in private," the Sage said. "Menphis, do you mind if I borrow Tadgh for a few moments? Pwella, take our guests to the kitchen? Get them something to eat and drink. We won't be long."

Menphis turned to Tadgh. "Are you okay with this?"

"I think it's okay." Tadgh folded the note and crossed his arms. "Just don't leave without me, okay?"

"Never," Shonn answered.

Tadgh followed the Sage up the stairs and down a white carpeted hallway. He stopped in front of two wide-backed wooden chairs on a balcony and motioned for Tadgh to sit down.

"How do you know English?" Tadgh asked again.

"The same way as you. Practice. I spent many years in America, mostly Chicago and New York. But what you really want to know is how I got here. Strangely, that is the same question I have for you. How did you get here, Tadgh?"

Tadgh shook his head and stared at his hands. "I don't really know. One minute I was home, the next I was at a Shaolin temple."

"We're not going to get very far if you're not honest with me." The Sage leaned forward. "What were you doing before you came to Maghe Sihre? Be exact."

Tadgh glanced up at the Sage and twitched. Suddenly, the dark-skinned man's eyes seemed to burn with an internal flame. "The truth? I don't remember. Seriously. Something has happened to my memory. I remember some of what happened, but not all of it."

"I'm listening."

So Tadgh quickly told him what he could remember. He talked about Colin's death and the visit from Bes in the hospital. He talked about his ability to shape-shift into a feline being and his apparent ability to make his wishes come true. Then, surprising himself, he talked about the murders he committed.

"And the next thing I remember is waking up at the monastery. I think that's why Instructor Mal wanted me to come here. He thought maybe you could tell me how I got here."

The Sage's eyebrows squeezed together. "This planet, Maghe Sihre, has a special relationship with Earth. Space folds strangely in certain areas. Weak spots. People and animals travel back and forth between the planets more often than you think. The Loch Ness monster, for example, is a common freshwater creature here that occasionally slips through. I came here a long time ago through one of these weak spots. They're called foramen. It's possible you used your ability to open a portal between Earth and here, but something doesn't feel right. My instincts tell me there's another force at play."

"What do you mean?"

"Not sure." The Sage shook his head and looked at Tadgh more closely. "By nature the universe is random. I've been around long enough to recognize that when patterns appear there is some intelligence behind them. Your arrival here was a little too…neat."

Tadgh rolled his eyes. "I wouldn't call it neat. I nearly died."

The Sage waved his hand dismissively. "Maghe Sihre is three times the size of Earth. What are the odds you would just so happen to land in a monastery filled with excellent healers? As far as I know, the two of us are currently the only people from Earth on this planet. Don't you find it unlikely you landed within walking distance of my house?"

"Walking distance is debatable."

"You walked here, didn't you? Get serious. Your arrival was not random. Someone planned this. Perhaps it was this being, Bes, but that pattern doesn't fit. You're not the first young man with special powers and amnesia I've met." The Sage scratched his chin for a moment. "Have you ever heard of the Council of Peacocks?"

Tadgh shook his head. "Is that a band?"

The Sage sighed. "Let's do this the quick way. I'm going to touch your head and look through your mind quickly. I need to check something about your parents."

"Um, okay." Tadgh let the Sage touch his forehead. The touch only lasted a moment and the Sage smiled when he took his hand back.

"Well, at least there's some good news here."

Tadgh rubbed his forehead where the Sage had touched him. It tingled. "You said people travel back and forth from Earth all the time. Do you know how to send me home?"

Hand on jaw, the Sage looked Tadgh up and down. "Do I know? Yes. But I'm afraid you can't go home, Tadgh. Earth is going to be very different in the next few months. There will be no place for people like you there."

"I don't understand what you're talking about."

The Sage slumped in his seat. "What I'm about to tell you will sound unbelievable, but it's true. I left Earth hundreds of years ago. I traveled back in time because I wanted to hide. Something is about to happen on Earth that will bring our two planets even closer together. People will look for me, thinking I could help them. I don't want them to find me. I left for a reason, the same reason you can't go back."

The Sage stared at his hands, watching his fingers tremble. "The Earth you know will not exist much longer. You're safer here. And, to be honest, Earth is safer without someone with your abilities there."

"How can you possibly know that?"

The Sage looked up at Tadgh. "I've seen the future."

Tadgh squinted. For a moment, he thought the Sage was crazy. Then, he remembered Shonn could see the future too. "For real? Well, if you know what's going to happen, can't you change it?"

The Sage shook his head. "I tried that before. Knowing what's going to happen is very different than being able to stop it. It's like watching a cup fall off a table. A knife after it's been thrown. All you can do is wait for impact."

"You came here hundreds of years ago?"

The Sage smiled. "I'm older than I look."

"So you're not human."

The Sage shrugged. "Human is a relative term. I would have traveled back further in time, but the time stream is completely unstable before that."

Tadgh thought back to the book Menphis had bought him. "Because of Starfall?"

The Sage raised an eyebrow. "Looks like someone's been doing their homework."

"A little. Like I said, my friend Shonn has been teaching me how to read. Starfall is something about gods fighting. It sounded like Clash of the Titans."

The Sage chuckled. "I suppose it does. But no mechanical owls. I thought by going back far enough, maybe

I could nudge events. I can't stop the knife from being thrown, but hopefully my actions have helped the aim."

Tadgh rubbed the back of his neck. "This is a lot to take in. So, you're saying I'm stuck here?"

"There are worse places to be stuck. Imagine eternity in Toledo."

"Hey! Watch it. I'm from Ohio."

The Sage raised his hands in surrender. "Down, tiger. Hmm. That's actually kind of funny when you think about it."

Tadgh rolled his eyes.

"On a serious note," the Sage said, "I need you to stop using your wish power."

Tadgh stared at the floor. "I know. Instructor Mal told me it was dangerous. But the first few times I used it today I didn't feel anything."

"You used it multiple times today?"

Tadgh flinched and looked away. "Three times." He told the Sage the story of his capture and escape.

"Curious," the Sage said. "I only felt it once. Maybe the damage is relative to the size of the wish. Moving a lock sent small ripples. Gaining advanced fieldbending abilities caused a small earthquake. If you ever wished for something big, you could, in theory, crack the planet. I suppose you felt justified using it to save your life. Let me tell you what your actions have done. Have you learned anything about Lord Dispayre and the Void in your time here?"

"Sort of," Tadgh said. "Shonn said he was like the boogeyman. He supposedly played a part in Starfall, and now he's trapped in some place called the Void."

"Here's the short version. Lord Dispayre began life as a Trofast. He started as a military leader, conquering several small countries up north. He created an empire, even called it the Realms of Dispayre. That should give you an idea of the size of his ego. Unfortunately, the only thing larger than his ego was his power. He became so adept at manipulating the reality field he was essentially a god. Completely immortal. They say his body changed. At the end, he looked like a Behersker and stood 20' tall. And then came Starfall."

"The books are a little vague about how the war started."

The Sage nodded. "That's because no one really knows. Oh, there are theories, but no one knows the truth. Not even me. Maybe it was when the barriers weakened. Reality became more porous. Beings from other realms of existence walked the planet. These are the gods you mentioned. People saw them as gods because of the things they could do. While many people panicked, Lord Dispayre saw a moment of opportunity."

"Right," Tadgh said. "That's the part I'm reading right now. He made allies."

"Yes. He recruited powerful friends and tried to take over the Great Castles. The conflict lasted a decade. In the last days of the war, Dispayre almost won. The other Castles were in ruins, their armies scattered around the continent, fighting battles on many fronts. Then, a powerful fieldbender named Orpthus designed a weapon. Although shaped like a sword, the Sword of Kassandra was something much more than a prosaic weapon. It had the ability to create pocket dimensions within the Void. An ally of Orpthus, a man named Tempertin, used the sword. He banished Dispayre to this dimensional prison. And he paid the price. In order to ensure Dispayre was captured, this warrior, Tempertin, locked himself away in the Void as well."

"I thought you said this was the short version."

The Sage glared at Tadgh.

"Sorry. So what does that have to do with me?"

The Sage crossed his legs and leaned back in his chair. "Unfortunately, everything. Thanks to a series of cracks in the reality field, the prison within the Void has been compromised. Things are starting to escape."

"Again with the riddle-speak. What sort of things?"

"Dispayre's power is virtually unlimited. After hundreds of years in prison, I can only imagine the extent of his rage. The very thing locking Lord Dispayre within the Void, the Sword of Kassandra, is once again on our planet. Each time you use your ability, the crack in the Void widens even more. Unless we can reseal the Void, it is only a matter of time before he escapes."

Tadgh shivered. Suddenly the room felt unnaturally cold. "Do you think I could use my power to close this crack? Maybe I could just wish it closed."

"That's a risk I'm not prepared to take. You have no training and no discipline. By trying to help, you could actually cause more damage. Look around you, Tadgh. This city is my favorite place on the planet. There has not been a war here in hundreds of years. Children grow up without fear. Men die of old age. Each time you use your ability, you are sentencing them to death. Promise me you will not use this ability anymore. I must insist."

For a moment, Tadgh thought about asking the Sage what he would do to stop him. A quick look into the fire of the Sage's eyes showed him exactly what the Sage would do to stop him.

"So what am I supposed to do?" Tadgh whispered. "If I can't go home and I'm being chased by people who want to dissect me, what choice do I have?"

The Sage reached out and put a hand on Tadgh's knee. "You always have choices. Sometimes all the choices you have are bad ones. For now, stay here until we figure out a better plan. My home may not look like much, but it has security features you cannot see. Safeguards against tracking. Alarm systems. Oshu won't find you as long as you stay inside. Long term, it's probably best you disappear. Your face is known here and the monastery will not be safe for you, either. Once it's safe you should take a ship north, as far away from here as possible. Maybe the Nizarians could train you to control your abilities."

Tadgh looked towards the stairs.

The Sage followed his eyes. "Ah, I see. You have made friends here. Believe it or not, I know how tough it can be to leave everything you know and love behind you. Sometimes the most loving thing you can do is leave."

There was a knock on the door downstairs.

"I have to see the people at the door," the Sage said. "Head down to the kitchen with the others? I'll have Pwella fix up rooms for you on the third floor. We can talk more later tonight when I get back."

***

The Sage headed to the front door. He was not surprised to see Gnocko and Eiodeesh standing before him.

"Something weird happened at Lord Vyken's place this morning," an out of breath Eiodeesh said. "We thought you'd want to know immediately."

"I know all about it," the Sage said. "You two should come in. I have some people you need to meet."

Chapter Twenty-Two

Tadgh walked into the kitchen. The maid, Pwella, handed him a plate of dried meat and cheese. Shonn and Menphis drank tea from plastic mugs.

"How did it go?" Menphis asked.

"I'm a little overwhelmed," Tadgh said. "I'll tell you about it later." He glanced at Pwella. "When we're alone."

Pwella lowered her eyes. "If there's nothing else, sirs, I'll take my leave."

Once she was gone, Shonn turned to Tadgh. "Did you ask him about me? About us?"

Tadgh smacked his head. "Damn. With everything else he told me, it slipped my mind." Tadgh told them about his conversation with the Sage. As he finished, Pwella re-entered the kitchen.

"The Sage is requesting you join him in the living room" she said. "There are some people he'd like you to meet."

When Tadgh entered the living room, he couldn't help himself. He squealed. "What are they?" he asked. Two strange beings sat on white couches around a circular glass table. One was 3' tall with orange skin. Thick black goggles covered his eyes. The other was a 7'-tall muscular woman with light mauve skin. Her black hair was tied back in a ponytail. Her facial features were completely alien, almost feline.

"Nice to meet you, too," the orange-skinned man said.

"You need to work on your social skills," the Sage said. "Gnocko is a Frie Stav. His people are from a subterranean country at the far end of the continent. His colleague, Eiodeesh, is a Trofast. From your reaction, I assume they are the first non-Sirians you've met."

Tadgh nodded, his face beet red. "Sorry. That was probably rude."

"I've had worse," Eiodeesh said. "My people aren't very popular in the south. The Sage wanted us to meet because, apparently, you're key to something we've been investigating."

Tadgh told the newcomers about his journey from Earth to Maghe Sihre. He left out the details about the murders he committed. The Sage finished by discussing Tadgh's fod sel-onde ability and its impact on the Void.

"That's quite the tale," Eiodeesh said.

"This is insane," Gnocko said. "This young boy has the power to break the Void, and we're just letting him wander around. Shouldn't we…?"

"Don't finish that sentence." Menphis clenched his fists and leaned forward.

"Easy, now," the Sage said. "We're not at war with each other."

"Gnocko, I'm certain the boy is not a danger to us." Eiodeesh put one hand on Gnocko's shoulder while resting the other on the hilt of her battle axe. "The Sage is a wise and respected man. He thinks the boy is safe."

"The boy has a name," Shonn said. His face flushed red and his eyes narrowed. "His name is Tadgh and you all need to stop talking about him as if he's not right here in the room with us."

"It's okay, Shonn." Tadgh sighed and turned to face the corner of the room. "They have a right to be worried."

"No, they don't," Shonn said. "You are not dangerous. You are beautiful and kind and I will die before I let anyone harm you. I love you."

The silence was sharp. Tadgh looked around the room at the raised eyebrows. Eiodeesh looked back and forth between Shonn and him. Then she took a deep breath and nodded.

"I'm confused," Gnocko said.

"I'll explain later," Eiodeesh said. She took her hand off her axe hilt and turned to face Menphis. "How long have you known what this boy, Tadgh, is?"

"He's only been with us a few weeks." Menphis glanced over at Tadgh, suddenly unable to meet his cousin's eyes. "He is not the smartest man I've met and he can be completely insufferable…but he means well. Many people I care about would be dead if not for him. I am in his debt."

"If you'll excuse me, I have to head north." The Sage stood and smoothed the lapels of his suit. "I believe you all have a few more things to discuss. I'll be back in the morning."

Once the Sage left, Eiodeesh crossed her arms and studied Tadgh. "So what are we going to do about Lord Vyken?"

"What do you mean, 'we'?" Gnocko turned to face her. "You can't seriously want to get involved with this. We came to GardenKeep to have the Sage remove the curse that graunskyeg put on me. We've more than repaid that act."

Eiodeesh simply returned his stare, saying nothing.

"Flaming lip crack. You're insane!" Gnocko jumped off his chair pointed his right index finger at Eiodeesh. "I know you have this fool idea in your head about being a hero, but this is beyond us. Beyond me, at least. I'm a simple man and, unlike the boy – sorry, Tadgh – I don't have world-altering power. How the hell am I going to go up against something like Dispayre? Let the world leaders of the Great Castles deal with this issue."

"I'm inclined to agree," Menphis said. "What does the Sage expect us to do? I can't think of any good we can achieve here. I'm a just a Prelate of the Elmire Ahk. Give me something to hit and I'll hit it. But this? I can't punch an army."

"You won't need to." Eiodeesh leaned forward and stroked her chin. As she spoke, her eyes glazed over as if she was looking at something far away. "We aim small. Reconnaissance. If we can figure out Lord Vyken's next plan, we might be able to slow him down. Gnocko, you heard this fieldbender, Oshu, say the war would be here soon. Aren't you curious what he meant?"

"No." Gnocko looked at the ground; the tone in his voice made the word more a question than a statement. "Anyway, even if I was, Lord Vyken is not coming to town. He's been up in his fortress for days and going there is…"

"A brilliant idea," Eiodeesh said. "I'm so glad you suggested it. See, what I'm thinking is…"

"Now, hold on a minute!" Gnocko said.

"I'm in," Menphis said. "We'll sneak into the fortress and look for invasion plans. I've seen this fortress outside of town. We could be there and back by the time the Sage returns in the morning."

Eiodeesh smiled. "I like you. Your brain works just like mine."

Menphis grinned back at her.

"You're right," Shonn said. "Apparently you're both insane. Didn't you say Lord Vyken is building an army just outside town?"

"Yes," Gnocko said. "We've been watching the place off and on for days now. There are at least 300 soldiers stationed there."

"It's a bit more than that, actually," Pwella said. She entered the room carrying a silver tray covered with several plates of biscuits. She set them down on the coffee table. As she spoke, she walked around the room, offering tea refills to everyone. "I never counted, but there has to be at least double that. I used to work in the kitchens there. I never met Lord Vyken, but I know the layout of that place well. Sneaking in there is really not smart. The guards will slice off your head first and ask questions later."

"God, that's such a stupid saying," Tadgh said. "It's always bugged me. How exactly are they going to ask you questions after you're dead?"

"There are dozens of demstraki there," Pwella said. "They have ways of making the dead talk. Or so I'm told."

"You were told correctly," Gnocko said. "Dem straki use their abilities to create graunskyeg and Umbral Knights.

Forcing a corpse to talk would be child's play to them. So can we drop this insanity now?"

"Actually, the idea seems less insane now," Menphis said. "Pwella, do you think you could draw us a picture of the fortress' layout?"

Eiodeesh slapped her leg and laughed. "I was just about to say that."

Gnocko looked back and forth between Eiodeesh and Menphis. Then he sat back down and hung his head. "We're doomed," he said.

***

Menphis and Eiodeesh sat around a wooden table with Pwella. They asked dozens of questions as she drew the diagrams of the castle. She pointed out entrances and locations she'd seen guards in the past. At the same time, she told them her memories were mostly of her time in the kitchen. Shonn sat nearby, listening to their conversation as he nibbled on cookies.

Gnocko refused to be part of that conversation. He walked to the window and looked out over the city. It was mid-afternoon now, the streets filled with people. He saw several members of the city guards gathering across the street at the bakery. A dark-haired man was being led away in handcuffs. Nearby, two blond children stood, hand in hand, silently crying.

"What's going on?"

Gnocko looked up at Tadgh, who now stood beside him at the window. "Not sure," he said. "Probably a domestic issue. Could be a robbery, of course, but I don't know why someone would rob a bakery."

Tadgh nodded. For several moments the two silently watched the scene across the street. Eventually a body was carried out on a gurney.

"Oh dear," Gnocko said. "I believe I know why those poor children are crying."

"Do you have children?"

Despite himself, Gnocko smiled. "Yes. Two boys and a girl. You?"

Tadgh laughed and stared at the ceiling. "No. I'm not thinking children will be in the cards for me."

Gnocko frowned. He looked up at Tadgh, then over his shoulder at Shonn. His eyes lit up with understanding. "Oh. Well that conversation makes much more sense now."

"Even if that part of me was different, I still have this thing inside me. Can you imagine what my children would be like? Would they have the same abilities as me? The thought is terrifying."

Tadgh watched as a man, hands bound, was pulled from the bakery. He screamed in agony, a look of panic and loss carved on his face. He tried to move towards the children, but city guards held him back. The children cowered and moved further away from him.

Tadgh closed his eyes. "Listen, I need you to do me a favor."

"Go on." Gnocko turned away from the window.

"I know I'm dangerous." Tadgh cleared his throat and scratched his neck. "I did some very bad things before I came here. I'd like to say it wasn't my fault, but I know that's not true. Not fully, anyway. I made very bad choices and people died. I don't want to make bad choices anymore. What I'm saying is, if you see me heading to the dark side I need you to take care of me."

Gnocko held his breath.

Tadgh closed his eyes. "I know what I'm saying and I mean it. If you have to take me out, use silver. It seems I'm pretty much immune to everything else."

"Why are you asking me?"

"Because you're the only one I know that can." Tadgh looked over his shoulder at the others in the room. "These are all good people. They would try to save me, somehow. It's not like I have a death wish, but if you feel I'm a danger to others, stop me."

"Understood." Gnocko looked up at Tadgh and removed his glasses. For a moment he was unable to focus in the bright light, but he wanted to look Tadgh in the eyes. "I'll do my best to keep you in line, Tadgh. Just be careful, and hopefully I won't have to."

Chapter Twenty-Three

"They should be back by now, Tadgh." Shonn bit at his thumbnails as he looked out the living room window. Menphis had left with Eiodeesh and Gnocko six hours ago. They had not returned. "I'm telling you, something's gone wrong."

"We don't know that yet," Tadgh said. "Unless…. Are you having one of your premonitions?"

"No," Shonn said. "Nothing like that. It's just a feeling. But my feelings are normally right. We have to do something."

"Like what? If they've been caught, the dumbest thing for us to do is follow them in. We need to wait for the Sage to get back."

"What if there's not enough time for that?" Shonn stared at Tadgh with red-tinged, teary eyes. "If Menphis is in trouble, I can't just sit here."

"And if we run off after Menphis to save him, what's to say we don't get captured, ourselves?" Tadgh turned his back to the window. "He wouldn't want that and you know it. Try to get some sleep. The Sage should be back in a few hours. If Menphis and the others are still not back by then, we'll head after them. Deal?"

Shonn frowned but nodded. He left the room and headed to his quarters. Tadgh went to his own. He stared at the ceiling until sleep took him.

***

I wake up in the utility shed by the river. Bes stands in front of me, staring at me with glowing eyes. There's a pool of darkness around him that squirms with movement, like tentacles.

"What the hell were you thinking?" Bes takes a step towards me.

"I thought you'd be happy," I say.

"The first one made me happy. It was perfect. Efficient. Quiet. I'm in a great deal of trouble because of your stunt."

"Trouble with whom?" I rub my eyes and pull my knees in to my chest. I feel cold, exposed. "And why should I care?"

Bes takes a few more steps towards me.

"Trouble for me is the last thing you want." The darkness around Bes expands. The unseen things within swirl faster. "There are rules, you stupid human. You are expected to kill them quietly. We don't need the press."

"Who exactly is 'we'?"

Bes snarls. Green saliva drips from his fangs. "That's not important. Finish the last one quietly. Don't push me on this. You will not like the consequences if you make them angry."

The darkness grows around Bes, covering his body. When the darkness fades, Bes is gone. I'm alone.

The shed is cold and damp. I shiver and realize I'm topless. I left my hoodie back at the gym, so I switch into my feline form. The cold affects me less this way. I lean my head against the wall and stare at the ceiling. In my mind I see it again. I watch as James and Vince die before my eyes. Shouldn't the memory make me feel something? Joy? Relief? Horror? I feel nothing. Empty.

I open the door and look into the night. I'm not sure how long I've been sleeping. It is snowing lightly. With my weird feline sight everything sparkles against the crystalline flakes that coat every surface.

"It's beautiful," I say. My voice sounds different in this form. Deeper.

I leap over the fence, the snow cool against my bare feet. I run along the path. Before long, I'm smiling. Everywhere I look, mundane objects are transformed into works of art by the falling snow. I cannot remember the last time I saw so much beauty.

I stop running when I reach W. Superior Ave. The path goes under the road which rises into a bridge over the river.

Greenery turns to pavement. The park is behind me. Ahead is a set of condos along Detroit Ave. Traffic moves slowly through snow-covered streets.

"I should probably get this over with," I say. I know where Everet Smith will be. Home. I have followed him as often as I followed Vince. Everet has no girlfriend and not much of a social life outside of football. He's not far away. He lives with his father in a townhouse on River Rd. across from Ontario Stone Corp. Their place is tiny, at the end of a row of houses. I've watched Everet sit at the window looking out at the street as he smokes. The last one will be the easiest.

I run along deserted sidewalks. Snowflakes melt as they strike my fur. The heat of my breath forms puffs of fog in the air. The only sound is my feet crunching in the new-fallen snow and the panting of my breath. Soon, I'm at a chain-link fence that blocks the road. There's a no trespassing sign. I jump to the other side.

Everet is in the window, but it's not him I'm watching. There are two police cruisers on the street. This is new.

"Guess it's not a secret anymore," I say. Part of me hoped they had not figured out who I was. I realize I've been an idiot. They saw me at the hospital. Two of the three boys that put me in there are dead. Of course they would protect the third.

"I can't go back," I say. Once Everet is dead, Bes will come back and take away my powers. I'll go back to being regular Tadgh Dooley. They'll arrest me. I'll probably go to jail, assuming they don't try to kill me first. I'm a monster, after all. They always kill monsters in the movies. I think I'm okay with that. Colin will be avenged. What more can I expect?

I jump onto the roof of the nearest row of apartments. It must be late. The lights are off in most of the apartments. Everet is smoking at the open window. His fingers tremble. I can smell his blood.

He extinguishes his cigarette and throws the butt out the window. He turns away and I jump. I land on a slab of concrete, a solid awning over the door. I glance down at the police officers. They don't move. They have not heard me.

I reach up and push the window fully open. Everet's no longer in the room. It's an easy jump into his bedroom. It reeks of body odor, cigarette tar and flatulence. Dirty clothes litter the floor. The bed is unmade, making it obvious how thin the mattress is. The doors to the closet have been removed. There is nowhere for me to hide.

'No sense waiting here,' I think. I walk into the hallway.

Something slams into my head. I drop to my knees and my vision blurs. Before I can stand I'm hit again. And again.

"Die you friggin' monster!" Everet smashes an aluminum baseball bat into my head, my back. My legs. "Dad! Get the cops. He's here!"

I hear movement below me and a door opening. I know I have to move quickly before the police officers get here. If not, I could be overwhelmed.

I focus past the pain, moving faster than I ever have before. I grab the baseball bat out of Everet's hand and toss it down the nearby stairs. I see Everet's eyes grow wide. He is about to scream but he never gets the chance. My claws are around his throat. I feel sweat drip from his face onto my hand. It takes longer this time for me to take control of him. He fights harder than the others did. Still, it is only a few seconds before the fear in his eyes is replaced by something else.

"What can I do to make you happy?" He smiles and his eyes light up with joy. All the tension leaves his body. Below me, I hear the front door open. Voices I don't recognize call out to Everet, asking him to get clear.

"Give me your soul," I say. "Then, burn in hell, you murdering bastard."

Everet smiles even more. I feel the rush of energy pour down my arm.

I'm thrown back. It feels like a sledgehammer slamming into my shoulder. As I look down at the bullet hole, three more shots slam into my chest.

"Stop!" Everet says. He jumps in front of me to protect me.

"Get out of the way, son," one of the officers says.

"Don't hurt him." Everet steps towards the officers on the stair.

"What are you doing, Everet?" This is his father. I can't see him but I know he's on the stairs behind the officers. "Get out of the way."

"Attack," I say. Everet throws himself at the officers. I hear gun shots and Everet's father screams.

Then I move. I leap at the officers, slashing claws across their throats. Blood flies everywhere. I throw their bodies at Everet's father. After that, everything is a blur for some time. Eventually, things clear in my mind. There are seven dead bodies around me. The only one still alive is Everet. I walk back to his body where it lies at the top of the stairs. He is bleeding out, the fire in his eyes dimming with each breath. He looks up at me, the adoration still in his eyes.

"What have I done?" I drop to my knees.

The moment he dies, the lights flicker. A blob of darkness drops from the ceiling. When it hits the floor, the darkness becomes Bes.

"Does this look like quiet to you? Do you realize what you've done?"

"I don't care." I glance at Bes for a moment, then stare down at Everet's dead body. "Nothing matters anymore. So just take your power back and leave me alone."

"I can't do that anymore, you idiot. They've told me I can't let you go now."

"Who is 'they'?"

Bes laughs, a very disturbing sound from a cat. "You really should have thought about that before you ignored me. I'm going to take the souls you've gathered, and I'm taking you back with me. You can stand in their presence and explain yourself. I pity you. You have no idea the things they will do to you."

"I'm not going."

Bes is not laughing any more. "You don't have a choice." Bes starts to grow. At first I think it is a trick of the light. Within seconds, Bes is as large as a lion.

I take a step down the stairs. "Stay away from me."

"Where exactly do you think you can run, boy?"

"I'm not going with you." I take another step. "You told me all I had to do was kill them. I did. I'm done. I don't want this power any more. Just take it and leave me alone."

"It's too late for that." Bes is now the size of a pony. The floor groans under his weight. "I'm not allowed to kill you, but that body of yours can take a lot of punishment. I will smash you into puddles of bone."

Then he is on me. Claws the size of butcher knives cut into me. They slash through my chest and my face. In moments, I look like walking hamburger. When he stops I am twitching at the bottom of the stairs.

"Enough?" Bes shrinks back to the size of a house cat. "Or do I have to tear off your arms?"

"No." I get to my feet. "I'm not going anywhere with you. Leave me alone. I want out of here. I wish I was somewhere far away. Somewhere you'll never find me."

Bes' eyes go wide. "What the hell?"

Then, the world around me twirls. Bes fades into shadow. For just a moment, it seems there are two other people in the room. I can't make out their features, but they seem to be talking to each other, pointing at me. After that, the entire room is gone. Cool air is all around me. I'm falling. Something must be wrong with my sight. For a moment it looks like there are two moons in the sky. Then I slam into something. My brain stops working. Everything is darkness.

***

Tadgh woke with a scream. He looked down at his body to confirm he was healed. He almost wished for amnesia again, but stopped himself. The memory of what Bes did to his body and the look of peaceful surrender in Everet's eyes was too much. He lay awake for hours.

Before sunrise, there was a knock at the door. Shonn stepped inside without waiting for a response.

"Gnocko and Eiodeesh are back." Shonn's voice was a trembling whisper. He did not look at Tadgh as he spoke. "Eiodeesh is pretty wounded. The graunskyeg was there. The one from the monastery. It bit her and then it took Menphis. He didn't come back, Tadgh. I don't know what to do. I lost my father. I can't lose him, too."

Tadgh jumped out of bed and embraced Shonn. He held him as Shonn cried into his shoulder.

"It's going to be okay," Tadgh said. He put his hand on the back of Shonn's head, stroking his hair. "We'll get him back. I won't let anything happen to him. I promise."

When Shonn finished crying, he took a step back and wiped his face dry. "The Sage is back, too. He told me to get you. He has a plan."

"See," Tadgh said. "I told you. We'll find Menphis. You're psychic, right? You would know if he was in trouble, right?"

"My abilities don't work that way. I wish they did, but…"

"Be careful what you wish for." The memory of blood and bodies everywhere filled Tadgh's mind for a moment. He pushed the thought away. "Let's go see what this plan is."

When they walked into the room with white chairs, Pwella wrapped a blanket around Gnocko. Eiodeesh sat beside him. It was the first time Tadgh had seen her out of armor. Her arms, throat and one shoulder were covered in bandages. The Sage stood by the window, silently staring into a glass of wine.

"I told them it was a dumb idea," Gnocko said. "Damned girl should have listened to me. She nearly got us killed."

Eiodeesh said nothing. She stared at her trembling fingers.

"No sense dwelling on the past," the Sage said. "You can't change it. Trust me. I know. All we can focus on is the future." He looked up as Shonn and Tadgh sat on the white couch opposite Gnocko and Eiodeesh, nodded, and finished his wine in one gulp. "You know, this all feels very familiar. Many, many years ago I went through something very similar to this. It seems history has a habit of repeating itself. Now, we can't change the past but we can definitely learn from it. I've seen a great deal of what you would call history. I know stuff. That's why people call me the Sage now."

"What did they used to call you?" Tadgh accepted a plate of dried meats and cheese from Pwella. He realized he could not remember the last time he had eaten.

The Sage sighed and looked out the window. "Long story. And my time is limited. There is another matter to the north that demands my attention, and I cannot be in two places at the same time. We need to move quickly. You two will come with me. Gnocko, you and Eiodeesh have seen enough of that place for one day."

"I'm not an invalid," Eiodeesh said. "Let me help."

"Just do what I ask, please." The Sage held out his glass for Pwella, who refilled it. "You're wounded and lost several pints of blood. Also, Lord Vyken has seen you. For my plan to work, I need inconspicuous warriors. Besides, I need your help on another matter."

"Wait," Shonn said. "Look, I'll go with you. Of course I will. I'd do anything to get my cousin back. But I'm not anything close to a warrior. And Tadgh's only had a few weeks of training."

"We both know what Tadgh is capable of." The Sage turned his back to the window. "I've seen his memories. I know what he did before he came to Maghe Sihre and what he did at the monastery. He is exactly the type of warrior I need. As for you, Shonn, you are fod sel-onde. You have abilities you haven't even tapped yet. I can help with that."

"What do you mean?" Shonn sat forward on the couch, suddenly tense.

"In another life, I helped a group of young men and women with powers very similar to yours. The origin of their powers was different, but they were similar to you. Shy. Unsure of themselves. Unaware of how powerful they really were. I taught them to tap into their abilities. I could do the same for you. Unfortunately, like I said, we do not have a lot of time. We'll have to do it the hard way."

"Why is it never the easy way?" Tadgh finished the last piece of cheese and placed the empty plate on a nearby coffee table.

"Does it involve fieldbending?"

"Yes, Shonn. Something like that. I'm going to take control of your body for a few minutes. It will be painful. You will likely thrash around, so I'll paralyze you first. That will also stop you from harming yourself. Using the simplest of terms possible, I will be rewriting the coding of the cells in your body."

"You're manipulating his DNA?"

"They don't use that term on this planet, Tadgh, but yes. Fieldbenders learn how to manipulate reality the same way concert pianists learn to manipulate the piano. Or the way Olympic athletes gain mastery over their bodies. It takes time. Practice. Dedication. Part of the reason they hate fod sel-onde is jealousy. Shonn was born with the ability to do things naturally that take them years to master."

"I thought they hated us because we could destroy the world." Shonn smiled as he spoke, but his voice cracked mid-sentence.

The Sage waved the idea away. "Hardly. True, Tadgh's abilities are dangerous, but there is almost no precedent to fod sel-ondes proving dangerous. Take your power, for example. I can see your memories. They are painful, so out of respect, I'm trying not to dig too far. You dream of events before they happen. Up until now, you've had no control over what you see or don't see. That is an easy fix. When I'm finished, you'll be able to enter a light trance at will. When you're in that trance, you will see visions. Unfortunately, it's a cruel power, knowing the future. You will see things you don't want to see. Many of them you will not be able to change. But at least this way you can turn off the ability when you don't want to know."

"That's wonderful," Tadgh said. "But it still won't make him a warrior."

"Of course. So I'm going to have to tweak him a little more than that. Shonn, your visions were always of events of several hours or several days in the future. Imagine, for a moment, if you could see just a few seconds into the future. See yourself on the battlefield knowing exactly where your enemy will be, where they will strike, moments before they do. This ability will make you the perfect soldier. You could dodge any attack, see every weakness."

"You can do that?" Shonn's mouth dropped open. He looked back at Tadgh as if to verify he'd heard correctly.

The Sage nodded. "Yes. But like I said, it will be painful. I thought it best you know the outcome first. It will make the experience more endurable. Will you submit to the process?"

"Absolutely!" Shonn stood smiling wider than Tadgh had ever seen him before. "Anything for Menphis."

"Good. Tadgh, I need you to go back to your room. No, don't argue with me. We both know how you'd react to seeing Shonn in pain. There is no time for that drama, so just go to your room. We'll come find you when it's over. Shonn, head to the top floor. I'll be up in a moment. You'll see a white sheet on the floor. Lay down. It will feel strange to you because it's Nizarian surgical material. You'll probably want to take your clothes off first. The process is painful. There will be blood. Best not to wear anything you don't want ruined."

"Are you sure about this?" Tadgh looked Shonn in the eye.

Shonn nodded. "If this works I won't be a loser anymore. Don't look at me like that. You know what I mean. Menphis has his training and you have so many amazing abilities. My powers didn't help me at all when the monastery was attacked. I hate feeling powerless."

'I know all too well how that feels,' Tadgh thought. With a sigh, he turned and went back to his room. 'And I know that sometimes the price for strength is too high.'

***

When Shonn and Tadgh left, the Sage turned to Gnocko. His eyes burned with fire.

"Come with me."

Gnocko glanced at Eiodeesh and put a comforting hand on her knee. Then he got off the couch and followed the Sage to an adjoining room.

The Sage closed the door. "I can't believe you were so stupid. When I left the five of you alone last night I expected you to talk, to get to know each other. Not stage a coup. Lord Vyken is of the royal families. He has powerful allies. If Menphis is dead, it is on your shoulders."

Gnocko's shoulders slumped.

"You have power but you don't use it," the Sage said. "That is the worst type of evil. When I came to this planet so many years ago, I did nothing. I wandered for years. It was nice seeing new things. Everything back home was known to me. No secret spots, nothing undiscovered. Eventually I realized I wasn't really wandering. I was running away. I didn't want to face what I'd lost. Who I'd lost. I became another person. I sat by as many bad things happened, things I could have prevented. Learn from my lesson, Gnocko. It is your obligation as a fieldbender. Use the power you have to do good. The next time you see someone you care about doing something stupid, stop them."

"What would you have me do?" Gnocko's voice was heavy and quiet. "They're both adults."

The Sage hit the wall. "They are barely adults, and you know it. I can read your memories too, Gnocko. You're older than you let on. I'd wager you're at least forty. That may not be mature for your people, but it's nearly twice as old as either of those two. You also have more fieldbending tricks up your sleeve than you pretend. You could easily have paralyzed those two, forced them to stay here until I got back."

"And what would have happened after that? Do you think either of them would ever forgive me for attacking them like that?"

"At least they would be alive to hate you." The Sage sighed and leaned back on the couch. "But like I said, focusing on the past is a waste of time. We have another concern. I don't want the others to know about it yet. Not until I'm sure there is reason to be concerned."

The Sage waved his hand slowly through the air. The room became transparent, a completely new scene superimposed upon it. Gnocko saw a group of men and women in uniforms. All wore black metallic armor bearing the same crest: a red mountain behind a black bird. They moved slowly through the streets of GardenKeep. They followed a woman with short red hair and cold, green eyes.

"Who are they?" Gnocko leaned in closer. "Soldiers?"

"Worse." The Sage waved his hand again and the image focused on the woman. She studied people's faces as she moved through the crowd. "I know this woman. Her name is Arem. She's a Kvartermester from Karaj Robat. They're a long way from home. I think I know why they're here. Arem is known for hunting fod sel-onde."

"Are they here for the boy?"

The Sage waived the image away. "That's what I need you to find out. The fieldbenders of Karaj Robat may be following Tadgh. The shielding in this house will hide him.

When we leave, I'll continue to block him, but that doesn't mean they're going to give up easily."

"Why is it so important for you to help Tadgh?"

"They will kill him for what he is. Probably Shonn, too." The Sage scrubbed a hand over his face and shook his head. "I have so much blood on my hands. So many people I tried to protect died on my watch. I can't lose any more. As soon as we head to Lord Vyken's, I need you to track Arem down. Get me whatever information you can."

"Why me? Surely if you know this woman…"

The Sage interrupted. "It's precisely because I know her that I cannot ask her. I'm walking a very tight line here. I'm working on an extremely sensitive issue with the fieldbenders of Karaj Robat. If they know I'm harboring a fod sel-onde it could complicate our relationship. After we leave for Lord Vyken's fortress, Barnes will escort you to a hotel by the docks. That's where they're staying. Search their rooms and listen in on them. But first, I'd like it if you could assist me with my work on the boy."

Gnocko frowned. "I've never attempted anything like what you discussed. I have no idea how to rewrite someone's cellular codes."

"You would only serve as a power source. Let me be concerned about the actual mechanics. Time to get started. Let's give Shonn something to fight back with."

Chapter Twenty-Four

Tadgh knocked on the door lightly with the tips of his fingers. Thirty minutes ago, Shonn had locked himself in the bathroom to clean up. There'd been no word from him since. Tadgh pressed his ear to the wood, hoping to hear a response.

"Give him time." The Sage stood nearby while Barnes helped him into his suit. It was white with cream-colored trim. "It worked, but it wasn't easy on him. Are you sure you know how to use that thing?"

"Not in the slightest." Tadgh glanced at his quarterstaff. "Menphis has been training me for a few weeks, but I'm still basically using it like a long baseball bat. I'm probably better off in feline form. Are you sure they would feel me coming?"

"Positive. Stay in human form unless absolutely necessary. Remember, we're not trying to start a war. Get in, rescue them, get out."

The bathroom door opened with a soft click. Tadgh smiled in relief. The expression turned into worry almost immediately.

"Dear God. You look like hell."

"Is it almost time to go?" Shonn sighed and ran his fingers through his damp hair.

"Are you sure you're okay?" Tadgh reached out for Shonn's arm in support. His friend twitched. A thin streak of blood dripped down Shonn's nose.

"I'm fine." Shonn wiped the blood away with a white hand towel. "The bleeding's stopped…for the most part."

"You're stronger than you look. You've recovered faster than I expected." The Sage pointed Shonn towards another set of leather armor and a short gladius sword. "Barnes will help you into the armor when he's finished with me. How is the pain in your head?"

"It feels like worms are eating my brain from the inside out." Hands trembling, Shonn folded the bloody towel. "Are you sure it worked?"

The Sage drew a stiletto dagger and threw it at Shonn's head.

Shonn moved only a few inches, but the weapon sailed easily past him.

"Are you insane?" Tadgh screamed.

The Sage laughed. "You'd be surprised at how many people have actually asked me that. I'm fairly certain I'm not. All the talking in the world would never convince him of his abilities. He had to see it. Now he has. We should get going. It will be light in a few hours."

***

"How exactly is this a better idea than what the others did?" The three of them rode on horseback from the city towards Vyken's fortress.

"Because Lord Vyken knows me." The Sage wore a simple white suit, while Tadgh and Shonn wore elaborate white leather armor. "He'll want to talk to me, if for no other reason than to find out what I know. I do have a reputation, after all. There's no reason for us to sneak in if we can simply walk through the front door."

"It's the part after we get inside that has me worried." Tadgh tried to stretch his legs and buttocks. It was his first time riding a horse; it was not going well. "What are we going to do if you get captured?"

"Don't worry about me. I can teleport."

The horse shifted beneath him and Tadgh winced in pain. "Teleportation seems like a really handy talent. I wish…"

The Sage smacked him in the arm before he could finish the sentence.

"Geesh," he said. "Sorry. I didn't mean that kind of wish."

"Words have power. Especially for you. Be careful what you say."

It took them half an hour to get to the front gate of the fortress. Guards blocked the entrance. The Sage raised his hand and the horses stopped a few feet from the armed men.

"State your business," one of the guards said.

"I'm here to speak to Lord Vyken. Don't waste my time pretending you don't know who I am. Send a runner if you need approval. I'll wait." He leaned forward to look the guard in the eye. "But I won't wait long."

The guard looked over his shoulder for a moment. Another guard nodded and took off at a run. Moments later the fieldbender Oshu appeared.

"Keep your helmets on," Shonn said. "He doesn't recognize us. Stay calm."

Tadgh swallowed. "How do you know he doesn't recognize us?"

Shonn laughed. "Because he's not attacking us."

"Stay here and keep quiet." The Sage slid off his horse and walked towards Oshu. The two spoke quietly for a moment. They spoke in whispers, so Tadgh could not hear what they were saying. After a moment, Oshu grunted loudly and walked back into the Fortress. The Sage walked alongside him.

"Stay with the horses," the Sage shouted over his shoulder. "I'll be back soon."

With that, the guards parted and let Shonn and Tadgh ride inside. The horses were led to the stable, right off the main entrance. They both jumped to the floor, and servants took the horses.

"That actually worked." Tadgh rubbed his behind. "Although, after half an hour on a horse, I understand why the Brotherhood of Tyche walks everywhere. So, when do we make our move?"

Shonn glanced around. "I'm still not used to how this thing works. I have all these images in my head. I think the guards will lose interest in us in a few minutes, but I can't be sure."

"Trust your instinct. It's really all we have here."

Shonn nodded. Several moments later, he put a hand on Tadgh's forearm and squeezed. Without another word, Shonn walked slowly across the courtyard to a wooden door in the opposite stone wall. Tadgh followed, his heart beating loudly in his chest.

"Calm down," Shonn said over his shoulder. He walked out the only other door in the room and into a hallway. "I don't get why you're so frightened. I've seen you use that quarterstaff in training. Even unarmed, you didn't blink during the attack on the monastery."

"That's because I was basically in Thundercat mode and could use my superpowers. Now I'm just a guy."

"You know, half the words out of your mouth make no sense to me. What is a Thundercat?"

"Never mind. Where are we going?"

Shonn shook his head. "I don't know. I'm just going where my feet take me. It feels like this is the way. Wait. Duck in here for a sec."

They turned into an empty dining room and put their backs against the wall. Tadgh held his breath. A chill ran through his bones. He looked down at the small section of his arms not covered with armor. It was covered in goosebumps. When the sensation faded, he rubbed his arms to heat them.

"What the heck was that?"

"I'm not sure," Shonn said. "I felt it too. It was like the graunskyeg from the monastery, but it can't be."

Tadgh took a step back. "You said graunskyeg can't move around in the day. The Sage said it was important to come now because the graunskyeg will be sleeping somewhere."

"Exactly." Shonn stared at the wall as if tracing the path of something. "Which makes me think it might be an Umbral Knight."

"Do I even want to know what an Umbral Knight is?"

Shonn smiled shyly. "I'm sure there's nothing to panic about. It's gone now. I saw one, years ago. A group of demstraki came into port. One of them was Amir Durgen. He's one of the Quadumvirate who rules Castle Dispayre. There was this thing with him. It was dressed in armor that looked like solid shadows, so I asked my uncle what it was. He told me it was an Umbral Knight. Supposedly, they are completely skinless. All you see is flesh and veins. And blood. The flesh never heals."

"Like the woman in Hellraiser?"

Shonn blinked slowly. "I have no idea what that even means."

"I'm starting to wish the Sage was here. At least he gets my references."

"Anyway, according to my uncle, Umbral Knights are dead bodies given a semblance of life through a mix of Nizarian cybernetics and fieldbending. During the process, the demstraki remove the eyes and tongue of the victim and seal them permanently in darkstone armor. Their empty eye sockets glow with a phosphorus stream of light and they never sleep."

"You realize you're doing a horrible job of keeping me calm, right?"

"Sorry." Shonn pulled Tadgh back into the hallway. "It feels safe to go now. If we're lucky we'll never be that close to one of those again. I feel like there should be a door coming up on the left. If my gut is right it should lead to the basement."

"Is that where your cousin is?"

Shonn rubbed his forehead. "I don't know. I can't see that far ahead. All I know is that we have to go there." They entered a library filled with leather-bound books. "It's in here somewhere. You look over there. I'll take the side closest to the door."

Tadgh headed to the back of the room. His eyes traced the lettering on the book bindings. Some of the characters he recognized from his lessons with Shonn. Most were incomprehensible. Row upon row of 10-foot-tall bookshelves created numerous shadows. Then a scent hit his nostrils. Before he could respond, a firm hand pulled him into an open door. He was about to lash out when he focused on the person's face: a woman with long brown hair. Her skin was more tanned than anyone else he'd seen on this world. And there was something odd about her eyes.

"I know you." Tadgh pulled her hand away and leaned his quarterstaff against the wall. "You were at the monastery, in the woods outside the infirmary. How did you get here?"

"There's no time for that." The woman glanced out the doorway, checking to see if anyone was nearby. "You have to go upstairs."

"Why would I do that? We're here to rescue Menphis. He's in the cellars below."

"He can wait. There's something upstairs you need to see. I'd take you there myself, but it is too risky."

"Risky for whom?" Tadgh stared at her eyes, trying to discern what was wrong with them.

"Me. Lord Vyken's room isn't guarded now. As long as W...I mean the Sage...is in with him it will be easy. But you have to hurry."

Then it hit him. "Your eyes are like mine. They're not all swirly like the people here. Are you from Earth?"

The woman frowned and stared at him.

Tadgh leaned in close to her. "Look, I don't know who you are, so why exactly should I trust you? I don't even know your name."

She clenched her fists and bit her lip. "We've met before." She looked over her shoulder at a section of shadows.

"What are you looking at?" For some reason, Tadgh could not see past the shadows, even with his enhanced nightvision.

"No one. Look, if you need to call me something, call me Andy. We don't have time for this. If you don't do this, Shonn could die just like Colin."

Tadgh went numb. "What do you know about Colin?"

Andy put a hand to his cheek. It was tender and cool. "Because I was there. I'm the woman that stopped the thugs from beating you."

"What?" Tadgh felt numb. "I heard that a woman stopped them. You're telling me that was you? How did you get here?"

"We have very little time," Andy said. "Just know I'm sorry I couldn't have shown up earlier to save Colin, too, but there are limits to what I can do. Now. Please. Go to Lord Vyken's room. You'll understand when you get there. I promise the next time you see me I'll be able to explain more."

Then she turned and walked into the shadows. And was gone.

"I found it."

Tadgh spun away from the shadow at the sound of Shonn's voice. He followed the voice and found Shonn beside a nondescript section of stone wall. Shonn pressed a square brick and a section of the wall slid aside, revealing a stairway leading down into darkness. There was also a flight of stairs heading upwards.

"I am totally having superpower envy." Tadgh headed up the stairs. "Let me go first. I can see better in the dark."

"Where are you going?" Shonn raced after him, his whisper harsh and full of doubt. "I told you we have to get to the basement."

"We have to go upstairs first. Long story short, I just met a woman from Earth. She said there was something important we had to see upstairs first."

"From Earth? Here? Who was she?"

Tadgh stopped and looked behind him. "Not sure. But I think she was telling the truth. The sooner we get up there and back, the better."

"What the hell," Shonn said. "The only thing we have to lose is our lives."

***

They took the stairs to the roof.

Tadgh's palms were sweating. 'This is insane. Look at all these guards.' The scene before them looked like a military field camp the size of a football field. The stairs came out beside six wooden sheds. The stench, like sun-warmed urine and manure, told him they were outhouses. Less than twenty feet away, a block of dark-canvas tents were set up. They had no windows but were thin enough that he could sense movement inside. Past that, a large fabric dome covered hundreds of sleeping bags laid out in neat rows. Everywhere he looked he saw red flags with dragons in the centers.

Tadgh leaned close to Shonn's ear. "Please tell me you guys don't have dragons here."

"What's a dragon?"

Tadgh pointed at the flags and Shonn nodded knowingly. "We call those wypera. I've never seen one, but the Armies of Dispayre use them in aerial raid."

Tadgh's mouth dropped. "You're seriously telling me you really have giant lizards that fly and shoot fire from their mouths?"

Shonn shivered. "Don't remind me. I think it's more of a flammable acid, but all I've heard about them was in stories. My gut tells me that building along the south wall is Lord Vyken's quarters."

Voices came from every direction. Servants moved between tents, carrying food and water. To the south was a stone structure housing private quarters. From the north came a strange scent: wet hay and new leather. It seemed to come from a wooden structure at the edge of the battlements.

Shonn touched his shoulder. "Look."

Tadgh followed Shonn's eyes and saw a strangely-garbed man leave one of the tents. He was bare-chested and barefoot, wearing only baggy red pants tied at the waist by a yellow cord. He was thin to the point of emaciation. His left arm was branded with the letter "D". The raised flesh was pink, but healed enough to show it was not new.

Tadgh shrugged. "What about him?"

"You can use him to find out where Lord Vyken's room is," Shonn said. "Do your thing."

Understanding sank in. He waited until the servant entered another tent. Motioning for Shonn to stay, Tadgh crept forward. He peeked through the opening of the tent and, after ensuring the servant was alone, he entered. When the man turned around, Tadgh put his hand on the man's chest. Energy shot up his arms, a sensation he now realized meant he was draining some of the man's life force. Immediately the servant's eyes glazed over and he looked at Tadgh with affection.

Tadgh took his hand back. "What is your name?"

"Beilaugh," the servant replied. "Who are you? You...you are glowing. Glowing like the gods in the myths. Are you a god?"

"Damn. It's worse than last time. No, I'm not a god, but I need your help. I'm supposed to see something in Lord Vyken's room. Can you tell me where that is?"

Beilaugh nodded, his eyes glistening with tears, pupils near full-dilation. "I can show you the way. His rooms are heavily guarded. Servants aren't allowed inside. No one goes in or out except Lord Vyken and his fieldbenders."

"Fieldbenders, as in more than one? I thought Oshu was his only one."

Beilaugh shook his head. "I believe there are over twenty. I haven't met most of them. They keep to themselves, mostly."

"Fantastic," Tadgh said. "I need to get into his room. How can you help us?"

The servant closed his eyes for a moment, thinking. Then, his eyes flashed open. "I can cause a distraction. It should give you enough time to sneak past the guards. Come with me."

Tadgh waived Shonn over and followed Beilaugh across the roof.

Chapter Twenty-Five

Guards pushed open both sides of the wide double doors, and the Sage walked into the central command center of the fortress. A raised dais at the far end showed this had once been a throne room. Lord Vyken had renovated it. The dais was empty. Long wooden tables covered in maps and books filled the space. Lord Vyken studied maps at one of the tables. Beside him was a Trofast in an elaborate set of darkstone armor.

"Your visitor," Oshu said. He walked past the Sage to whisper something in Vyken's ear.

"Thank you." Lord Vyken spoke without looking up. "Ein, I'll ask you and Oshu to leave us for a moment."

The Trofast, Ein, frowned and focused his full attention on the Sage. "That is not a wise idea."

"Come, now," Vyken said. "Obviously, he intends to talk. If he wanted a fight there would already be bloodshed." Now he looked up and focused on the Sage. "Isn't that right?"

"My reputation precedes me." The Sage nodded at Ein and Oshu as they left the room. Guards closed the doors behind them. Once they were alone, the Sage crossed his arms and focused on Lord Vyken. "You're right. You and I have much to discuss."

"Do you want to talk about the fod sel-onde you are sheltering?"

The Sage waved the question away. "He's not even in the top ten most important things I'm dealing with right now. What I'm curious about is why you set up shop just outside GardenKeep. If you are planning a war, wouldn't it make sense to attack SouthPoint? They have the larger army, of course, but it is the capital of Shirza. So why here?"

Lord Vyken twitched. "You accuse me of treason? That's an interesting way to start a dialogue. While I admit nothing, I'll play your game. Hypothetically speaking, of course, GardenKeep is also a major port city. Capturing it could have several tactical advantages."

"Bull. You're not an idiot. Neither am I. What are you looking for here?"

Lord Vyken smirked. "For a wise man you know very little about politeness."

"I'll be polite when you're not planning on butchering tens of thousands of innocent people. And for what?"

Lord Vyken turned and looked back down at his maps. "You have to know I'm not going to tell you anything. So why are you really here? Is this some sort of rescue mission? Are you hoping to negotiate for the return of the idiots who attacked us last night?"

The Sage unbuttoned his jacket and took a step forward. "Two things: I never negotiate with warmongers. People like you understand one thing only. Violence. Secondly, if you had anyone in your custody I cared about, I would teleport up to Karaj Robat and come back with a full squadron of fieldbenders. The only thing I want from you is answers."

"Ah, the mighty Sage eager for knowledge." Lord Vyken stroked his jaw and was silent for a moment. "And why would I tell you anything? How could that possibly benefit me?"

"I can tell you where the Sword is."

Lord Vyken spun his head quickly.

"Now that I have your attention, can we skip the small talk? Tell me why you're here."

For a moment, Lord Vyken said nothing. Then he waved the Sage over, inviting him to look down at the map beneath his fingertips. "This port has been an important part of Maghe Sihre for centuries. We've discovered there is something beneath the city. The ruins of a Behersker city. It appears to be nearly as big as DunDegore. However, the majority of the site is buried beneath a hundred feet of dirt. Untouched. Can you imagine the riches?"

"Intriguing." The Sage looked down at a map of the city. He recognized all the landmarks, but there was something superimposed on the familiar. Buildings and roadways marked as dotted lines showed an ancient city nearly as large as the modern GardenKeep. "I know nothing about this. It's not in any of the literature I've read. Truly an amazing find. But I still don't see the significance."

Lord Vyken walked away, chuckling. "Significance wasn't part of our agreement. I told you why we're here. Now, tell me where the Sword is."

The Sage only hesitated for a moment. He knew a lie could escalate the situation. He decided on a partial truth. "We couldn't keep it at DunDegore. Too risky. I had it shipped to the Nizarians. Gods know I couldn't trust any of the Castles with it."

"You what?" Lord Vyken punched a fist against the table, shaking the maps. "Who gave you authority to do anything?"

"Funny. I didn't stop to ask for permission. Did you really expect I'd wave down the nearest Wypera rider and send it back to Castle Dispayre? That is who you work for, right?"

Lord Vyken turned his head to the side and cursed. "No matter. We'll get to the Nizarians in time. Now, if there is nothing else, I have work to do."

"Just one more point. The boy."

Lord Vyken looked up and squinted his eyes.

The Sage looked back at the door, then took a deep breath. "Tell your dog Oshu if he so much as breathes in the boy's direction I will hang him by the ankles from the spires of my city. It would also do you well to remember this is my city. You seek to do war with GardenKeep. You may as well have declared personal war against me. If you knew anything about me you would realize what a bad decision that is."

"I know all about you and your relationship with the fieldbenders of Karaj Robat. I'm not concerned about them in the slightest. So why don't you…"

The Sage lifted his hand. Orange fire reached across the distance in the shape of a hand. It grabbed Lord Vyken by the throat and lifted him off the ground several feet. Strangely, it did not burn the flesh, though the heat from the fire filled the room.

"I do not need fieldbenders to fight my wars," he said. "And I doubt very much you know all about me. So let me educate you. I have stood before monsters, beat down gods and made armies tremble. The only reason I'm letting you live is I don't know what you are planning. You're my only link to the truth. If I kill you now it could take me months to find another clue."

A bolt of Akashic energy hit the Sage in the right shoulder.

Unfazed, he looked over his shoulder at the spot of impact. The fabric of his suit smoldered slightly. He looked back at the doorway. Ein stood there, hands and eyes glowing with sickly purple energy.

"Ein, no!" Lord Vyken spoke through clenched jaws.

"Words of wisdom," the Sage said. "Back away before I lose my temper."

"Enough of your posturing, Sirian." Ein took a step further into the room. His hands glowed brightly. "If you hope to leave here with your life, put Lord Vyken down now."

The Sage clenched his fist. A cage of fiery bars appeared around Lord Vyken, who hovered in the air, trapped inside it. The Sage turned and gave his full attention to Ein.

A second bolt of Akashic energy flew through the air. The Sage opened a teleportation field in front of him. It ate the bolt of energy and spat it back at Ein. The Trofast stumbled to erect a mystical shield, but was not fast enough. The bolt hit him in the chest, knocking him back a foot. Before Ein could attack again, the Sage opened a second portal beneath the Trofast's feet. He fell into the portal and disappeared. Alone again, the Sage turned back to the Lord

Vyken. With a flick of his wrist, he dispersed the fiery cage and Lord Vyken fell to the floor with a thud.

"Coming here was a mistake," Lord Vyken said. "I have powerful allies who..."

"Who are not here. Right now, there is just you and me. Think about that before you issue threats. Ein will be fine, assuming he can find his way home."

"Where did you send him?"

The Sage grinned. "The Badlands. It's no more than a five-day march to the nearest port. I'm sure you'll see him again. Someday."

Still smiling, the Sage turned and left the room.

***

Tadgh found it hard to breathe. His eyes wanted to move in every direction at once. Soldiers were all around them, but no one looked in their direction. Tadgh was glad he had his quarterstaff. He used it as a walking stick to steady his knees. Everyone seemed to assume they were servants as well.

They walked past the soldiers' bunk tents to the stone structures to the south.

"Where are we going?" Tadgh put a hand on Beilaugh's shoulder.

Beilaugh put a finger to his lips, motioning for silence. Then he slipped into the first door in the stone structure. Tadgh and Shonn followed. Inside, the room was dimly lit. Streams of light fell on clouds of dust particles hanging in the air. The air smelled of a scent that was nearly – but not quite – sandalwood. A black desk covered in books and glass vials sat in one of the corners. At the back of the room, a single bed stood partially covered by a purple curtain. A sword, like the ones worn by the soldiers, lay at the foot of the bed.

"What are we doing in here?" Tadgh searched under the bed and behind the curtains, making sure they were alone. "Is this Lord Vyken's room?"

Beilaugh went back to the door and locked it before answering. "No, it belongs to Mahwibix. Like most of the fieldbenders, he's on a mission in the sewers beneath the city for a few days. Wait here until I cause the distraction."

Tadgh never got a chance to respond. Outside there was a commotion: swords being pulled from sheaths, people yelling and, even worse, a horrendous shriek filled the air.

"Dear god. What's out there?"

Beilaugh answered. "Something has the wypera worked up, sir. Looks like I don't have to create a distraction after all."

"You mean there are dragons *here*? Now?" Tadgh felt his stomach drop. "Well, crap."

Chapter Twenty-Six

'So much for not fighting.' The Sage ducked as a soldier swung a short gladius sword at him. He opened a teleportation field behind the soldier and pushed him through. 'I need to spend more time with Instructor Mal. I really need to work on my diplomacy. Time to find the others and get out of here before this gets any more out of hand.'

He concentrated on Tadgh's mind. An instant later he had a location.

'What the hell is he doing up there?' Calling up another circle of light, the Sage stepped through and reappeared behind a wooden structure on the roof. A familiar smell hit him and he took a step back. 'How the hell did wypera get this close to the city without me knowing?'

He peered through the gaps in the wood beams at the long-legged quadrupeds. Standing twice as tall a man, their heads brushed the top of the stables. They had leather wings, sky-blue with patches of light gray: perfect camouflage for a flying hunter. Their torsos were thick and strong enough to be mounted by a Trofast. Thick necks ended in elegant horse-like heads.

'Damn.' He clenched his fist and lightly pounded the ground with his foot. 'Wypera here means Lord Vyken has official sanctioning of the Quadumvirate. It also means he's going to make his move soon.'

He peeked around the corner of the stables. Dozens of soldiers marched by. Most were local Sirians, but one stood out. A woman in expensive-looking darkstone armor issued orders, directing soldiers where to go. But it wasn't her armor that impressed him; it was her energy field.

'She's an Illuminati. Vyken has demstraki and wypera and Illuminati in his army? I think I'm too late. This is already out of control. I can't let them continue in secret anymore. I need to alert the city guard.'

Just as an idea sparked in his mind, the Illuminati stopped issuing orders. She turned and looked directly at him.

"And my time for plotting is over." The Sage stood up straight and straightened the lapels of his suit. "Here goes nothing."

He flicked his wrist and the stable holding the wypera erupted in flames.

***

"Let's not waste the opportunity." Shonn walked over and picked up the sword on the bed. "Beilaugh, lead us to Lord Vyken's tent."

Tadgh grabbed Shonn by the shoulders. "You want us to go out there where there are dragons? Have you lost your mind?"

"No, but I have lost my cousin." Shonn pulled away from Tadgh and stared at the sword in his hands. "Staying here is not going to get him back. So stop your whining and let's move."

Tadgh smiled. "You're sexy when you're butch."

Shonn blinked. "Now? You ignore me for weeks and this is the moment you choose to flirt with me? And you have the nerve to say I lost my mind." Shonn flung the door open and motioned for Beilaugh to lead the way.

Tadgh saw smoke rising from the north, where he'd seen the wood structure. Between that fire and him was an ever-increasing sea of soldiers. Fortunately, they were all looking the other way. Keeping low, Beilaugh led them to a nearby door. He knocked and, when there was no answer, opened the door motioning, them to go inside.

When the door closed behind them, Tadgh stood and looked around. A stone table lay in the center of the room, covered in something unexpected: a three-dimensional, translucent map. Seven red flags attached to cities were pinned around the map. Tadgh reached out his hand to touch it, but his fingers passed through it. Then he saw something equally unusual: a diamond-shaped crystal small enough to fit in the palm of his hand. Thin beams of blue light shot out from the crystal towards the map.

"Is this fieldbending?" Shonn asked.

Tadgh studied the crystal. "It looks like a hologram. Something from my world. It's a technology that uses light to create three-dimensional images."

Shonn frowned. "How is that any different than fieldbending?"

"I believe it's Nizarian," Beilaugh said. "One of my cousins lives in the north, not far from Castle Nizaria. This sort of technology is actually fairly common up there."

Tadgh shook his head in wonder. "I think I need to meet these Nizarians. Shonn, do you recognize these places?"

Shonn bit his lip. "Unfortunately, yes. See this point here? That's GardenKeep. You're looking at a map of our country, Shirza. Do you think those red flags mean something?"

A bad feeling settled into Tadgh's gut. Each of the flags had a number. "I used to play a board game when I was a kid, called Risk. The goal is to take over the world. My guess is those numbers refer to units of soldiers."

"That can't be possible," Shonn said. "The one by GardenKeep says 5,000. That's way more than Pwella said was here."

"I hope you're right," Tadgh said. "But I think this is what that woman wanted me to see." He reached down and grabbed the crystal. The map disappeared.

"Found you."

Tadgh spun at the familiar voice. Oshu stood in the doorway. There was no sign of Beilaugh. Oshu lifted his chin, looking down his nose at them.

"You're probably wondering what gave you away, right? The Sage's distraction worked very well. But I told you. I have your scent. I recognized you the minute you rode up to the gates. The only reason I let you inside was to find out what you knew."

Shonn stepped between Oshu and Tadgh, sword in hand.

"Ah, bravery." Smiling, Oshu raised his hand and shot a bolt of Akashic energy. Shonn jerked his body slightly to the side. The attack missed him completely and the smile slid from Oshu's face. "That's not possible. No one can dodge Akashic bolts. How did you do that? Do we have another fod sel-onde?"

"You'll never know." Shonn swung his sword. Oshu threw up a shield of purple light, deflecting the blow. Shonn slammed the sword down again, using it more like a club than a blade. The shield weakened, the light dimming.

From out of nowhere, Oshu produced a knife. He stabbed upwards.

The blade stuck in Shonn's stomach. His face went pale and his eyes fogged over.

"No!"

Rage flowed through Tadgh's body. His eyes flashed red. His body started to change. With inhuman strength, he tore the armor from his chest. Fur covered his body. His teeth and claws grew to razor-sharp weapons. All he saw was blood trickling down the dagger and the pale, pained look on Shonn's face.

Acting on instinct, he threw his hands forward, shooting an Akashic bolt at Oshu. It struck the fieldbender in the shoulder, scorching his robes and making him drop the dagger. Oshu looked up at Tadgh, surprised. Tadgh hit him with another bolt. This one was strong enough to throw Oshu backwards through the closed door and out onto the roof.

He knelt beside Shonn. "Talk to me. Are you okay?"

Shonn coughed; a drop of blood dripped over his lip. "Of course I'm not alright. I've been stabbed! I don't know what that blade is made of, but it cut right through my armor. Help me up. We need to get out of here."

***

The Sage ran from the burning stables as the wypera inside howled. 'The smoke should get the attention of the city guards. Unfortunately, those beasts have flame resistant hides. The fire won't hurt them at all. But the distraction is giving me time to…'

Mid-thought, something struck the Sage in the head. He dropped to his knees. A thin trickle of blood streamed from his forehead. Before he could react, a knee smashed into his face, throwing his head backwards. An armored fist hit him in the chin and he fell the rest of the way to the floor.

The Illuminati stood over him, her eyes cold and focused. "What are you doing here?" Her voice was deep but surprisingly civil. The tone unnerved him.

"You're fast." The Sage wiped blood from his forehead. He opened a light disk beneath him and fell through, landing on his feet a few feet away. "I haven't been hit like that in years. I have a renewed respect for your religion, illuminati."

The woman's face reddened. "My name is Desdemona, not Illuminati. And we are not a religion. We are students of the Lake of Silver, the Wheels of Ziwecarma. Making me angry is not your smartest choice."

"You know, that's exactly something I would say." The Sage raised his hand, but before he could trap her in fire, Desdemona moved. She swung her foot in a roundhouse kick that connected with his hip, driving him to his knees again. She punched at him again. This time he was ready. He deflected her fist with his left hand and called up fire with his right. Before Desdemona could strike again, he threw the fire at her chest. She flew back twenty feet, knocking over a tent. Before she stood, the tent caught fire.

"Hmm." The Sage got to his feet and brushed dirt off his jacket. "I almost enjoyed that."

Then he saw the fifty soldiers closing in around him.

Chapter Twenty-Seven

Tadgh helped Shonn to his feet and supported him as they left Lord Vyken's room. They didn't get far.

"Over here!" Oshu screamed. "Spies!"

Twenty soldiers turned to face them, swords drawn.

"You know, I'm really starting to hate that guy." Shonn pressed his hand against his stab wound and winced in pain. Tadgh noticed his face was starting to pale from blood loss. "I don't think we can outrun them. What are we going to do?"

"First, I'm getting you to safety." Grabbing hold of Shonn, Tadgh jumped. He landed on top of the stone structure housing Lord Vyken's rooms. "Now, stay here. No more heroics from you, okay?"

"I promise nothing." Shonn started to laugh, then winced in pain. "You might want to hurry, though. I'm not feeling so good about the whole being stabbed thing."

Tadgh shifted back to human form for a moment. He put his hand to Shonn's face. "You are not going to die, you hear me? I won't allow it."

Shonn rolled his eyes. "It's not like I want to. So stop fighting me and go fight the bad guys."

"As you wish." Faster than ever before, Tadgh transformed into his feline form. The anger was still there, but it was no longer mindless. For the first time, he felt like he was in control. He jumped off the roof and straight towards the soldiers.

At first, he knocked their swords aside with his quarterstaff. Then, he remembered that as long as the blades weren't silver they couldn't permanently damage him. He felt invulnerable. He alternated between attacking knees with his quarterstaff and using his natural weapons. He slashed claws across the bared face of the nearest soldier, enchanting him in the same breath. He willed the soldier to turn on his comrades. Barely skipping a beat, the soldier turned and started fighting for Tadgh. Another soldier fell in a bloody mess.

The enchanted soldier managed to draw blood on one more soldier before his comrades realized what was happening. They took him out of the fight. Tadgh ignored them, driven by his hunger for revenge. He felt pain as swords sliced at him, but his wounds healed nearly as quickly as they appeared. Once more he clawed a soldier's face and turned him into a puppet. He slashed at another's chest armor. His claws ripped through the leather easily. With each attack he converted more and more soldiers to his will.

As hard as he fought, he was eventually overwhelmed.

All his puppets lay dead or incapacitated as soldiers circled around him. Staying at arm's length, ten soldiers pointed their swords at him. They moved in a comfortable pattern, jabbing him. Although his wounds kept healing, the pain of so many tiny cuts made it hard to think. He was surrounded. It was only a matter of time.

'Time to try something different.' He jumped as high and wide as he could, landing far from the circling soldiers. They turned to rush at him, and he quickly fired Akashic bolts at them. Three were blown to their backs before they were in mêlée distance. He jumped again, this time landing behind them. He fired several more bolts of energy.

When the last soldier fell, he realized he could still hear the sound of fighting. Nearby, the Sage threw streams of flame from his hands. It consumed men and women who screamed as they died slow, painful deaths. Then he heard another strange scream coming from the flame-engulfed wood structure. The roof collapsed and five massive dragons took to the air. They circled above like vultures.

'Well, this is going well,' Tadgh thought. 'On the plus side, it can't get much worse than this.'

"Look out!"

Hearing Shonn's warning, he ducked just in time to dodge a blast of Akashic energy. He turned to face his attacker.

"You do have great reflexes," Oshu said. His pink robes were tattered and bloodied. Once again, his hands glowed with energy. He walked steadily towards Tadgh. "You're going to be a great asset once we break you."

"You're welcome to try," Tadgh said.

Oshu shot another bolt of energy, and Tadgh leapt away. Before he could land, Oshu shot him into the air. Tadgh flew back into the soldiers, knocking them down like dominoes. Reaching over, he touched the faces of several soldiers, asserting his will over them.

"Protect me," he said. As he leapt away, the soldiers rose to their feet and charged Oshu. The fieldbender cursed, but, for the moment, the soldiers kept him busy. Oshu threw up a dome of Akashic energy around his entire body. Their swords bounced harmlessly off the solidified energy.

Tadgh leapt back to where Shonn sat above Lord Vyken's room. "How are you doing?"

"Still here. Still bleeding. Whoa." Shonn pointed back below. "There's something you don't see every day."

Tadgh looked where Shonn pointed. The Sage threw spears of fire at a woman in black armor. She moved incredibly fast, dodging each attack. Then a circle of light appeared below the Sage and he teleported.

"Where did he go?"

Shonn looked around, then pointed again. "Up there. Are you seeing this?"

The Sage was on top of one of the wypera, riding it. He directed the beast back towards the combat field, aimed directly at the woman he'd been fighting. The wypera spat a black-green liquid that struck the stone roof. It erupted into flame upon contact.

"All we need is a few lightsabers and this would be the best fight scene ever." Tadgh looked back at Oshu. The fieldbender's hands were up against the protective dome. He shot bolts of Akashic energy through the shield, attacking the soldiers under Tadgh's control.

Tadgh jumped off the roof and headed towards the woman the Sage fought. When he got close enough, he realized it was the woman from the monastery. Desdemona. She was distracted, her entire focus on the Sage and the wypera. Tadgh studied the way she dodged each fiery assault. Then he jumped. Momentarily caught off guard, Desdemona was unprepared for the new line of attack. Tadgh touched her face.

"Stop moving."

Her face went lax and Tadgh jumped out of the way. Wypera spit struck her armor and she erupted in flames.

A circle of light appeared beside Tadgh and the Sage stepped through it. "I think it's high time we get out of here. Where are the others?"

"We haven't seen Menphis yet, but Shonn feels he's in the dungeons below." Tadgh looked at Desdemona's body burning a few feet away and shivered. Suddenly he felt nauseous. "Shonn's nearby. We have to move quickly. He's injured."

"You're going nowhere."

Tadgh and the Sage turned towards the voice. Three figures walked towards them.

"I know one of them," the Sage said. "The Sirian is Lord Vyken."

"I couldn't care less about him," Tadgh said. He focused on the third person. If it could be called a person. Tadgh stared at a six-foot tall nightmarish creature. Much of its body was covered in strange black body armor. It seemed to swirl in the light, almost like flowing liquid, rather than static metal. The parts of it that were uncovered were more disturbing. "Is that what I think it is?"

"Yes," the Sage said. "That's an Umbral Knight."

Tadgh could see now why they frightened Shonn so much. The creature had no skin. Raw flesh covered in still-wet blood stood in its place. He could see every muscle, every tendon. The veins pulsed with a luminescent fluid that was definitely not blood. It had no eyes, no ears, no mouth and only a vague nose. Sick green and purple light flowed from every hole in its head. It wielded a massive sword that looked too big for any man to lift, let alone use.

Lord Vyken scratched his jaw as if having a casual conversation and studied Tadgh. "What kind of creature are you, exactly?"

The Sage placed a hand on Tadgh's shoulder. "I'll tell you what he is. He's the man who just helped me take out a hundred of your soldiers. You might want to think twice about your little invasion."

Vyken shrugged. "I can afford to lose a hundred."

"Really?" The Sage raised an eyebrow. "How many more do you have?"

Tadgh cleared his throat and leaned closer to the Sage. "About another 4,900." He removed the crystal from his pocket and laid it on his open palm. The holographic map of Shirza hovered in the air before them.

The Sage's eyes went wide. "Oh. Well, that changes things."

The Umbral Knight stepped forward, sword raised. He walked slowly towards them, his lipless mouth open in something approximating a smile. Cold, like a physical manifestation of evil, swept over Tadgh. He held his breath, waiting for his grasp on reality to snap, for the urge to run to overtake his sanity, and...

Nothing happened.

"Huh." Tadgh relaxed and squinted at the Umbral Knight. "I'm supposed to be afraid of you, aren't I?"

The Umbral Knight stopped.

"I get it," Tadgh said. "You're about as big and scary as a monster can get. And you know what I feel when I look at you? I feel pretty safe. You guys aren't going to harm me, not even a little bit, because you need me. You all strut up here like you're strong and powerful, but somehow I'm still talking. So tell me, seriously, why haven't you attacked me yet?"

The smile was completely gone from the Umbral Knight. The creature started walking towards Tadgh again, eyes glowing brightly.

Lord Vyken raised a hand. The Umbral Knight stopped. "Perhaps we should talk. Come with me."

Tadgh laughed. "Are you on crack?"

Vyken's face wrinkled in confusion.

"Wrong world," the Sage said.

"Oh," Tadgh said. "Sorry. That means I'm not going anywhere with you because, well, because I'm not insane. We came here today because you captured a friend of mine. And I think you're going to give him back."

Lord Vyken smiled. "Perhaps you are the one who is, as you say, 'on crack.' You do not seem to understand that you are not negotiating from a position of strength. You know how many men I have at my disposal. I have a graunskyeg sleeping in the basement and an Umbral Knight close enough to dismember you. Perhaps the Sage can tell you more about Umbral Knights. It may give you a proper level of respect."

A fire raged inside Tadgh. "No. I'm fairly certain it is you who does not have proper respect for me. With one wish, one simple sentence, I could end you and your entire army."

"Tadgh…" The Sage tightened his grip on Tadgh's shoulder.

"Let me finish. I'm not going to do it. I could, but I won't." Shaking free of the Sage, he walked several steps forward until he was only a foot away from Lord Vyken. "Unless you give me no choice."

The Umbral Knight raised his sword.

Tadgh did not turn to face it. He focused his full attention on Lord Vyken. "Please. Give me a reason. We are going to leave now. The Sage is going to transport us to the dungeons so we can rescue our friend, Menphis. You know what I think? Based on that map, you're not really in charge here, are you? Someone else is calling the shots, someone you have to answer to. You're not attacking because you're not sure what your boss will do if you hurt me. I think what I should do is break the reality field one more time. Destroy all your armies positioned in the 7 cities around Shirza but leave you alive. You and only you. Then you can explain to your leader how this whole screwup is your fault."

Lord Vyken muttered something in a language Tadgh didn't recognize. The Umbral Knight lowered his sword. Then Lord Vyken took a deep breath and leaned forward. "Whatever you think you understand, you are actually completely clueless. You're right. I'm not supposed to kill you, and I do work for someone else. Her name is Myan. The Sage knows her. That's why he's being smart and keeping his mouth shut. But I don't have to hurt you to get you to cooperate. I don't even have to touch you."

"Tadgh!"

Tadgh turned at the sound of Shonn's voice.

Oshu stood on the roof, a dagger to Shonn's throat.

Tadgh held his breath and turned back to Lord Vyken. "What do you want with me?"

Lord Vyken smiled. "That's better. What I want is simple. Oshu tells me you are the one who cracked the Void. Keep doing whatever you've been doing. It's time for Lord Dispayre to come back to the world. Do it now or the boy dies."

Tadgh looked over at the Sage.

"You can't, Tadgh." Shoulders slumped, the Sage covered his mouth and kept his eyes on the ground. "If you open the Void, thousands of people will die. Would Shonn want that?"

"I don't care." Tadgh looked back at the pained expression on Shonn's face. "I can't lose another person I love. I just can't." He wiped a tear from his eye and then set his shoulders. "Fine, Lord Vyken. I'll do it. I'll use my ability again. But if there's one thing I've learned, it's this. Be careful what you wish for."

Understanding hit Lord Vyken's eyes. It was too late.

Tadgh closed his eyes. "I wish Lord Vyken and his armies were dust."

Chapter Twenty-Eight

For a split second, a very small section of the planet stopped spinning. No one and nothing moved. When Tadgh opened his eyes, he saw Lord Vyken's body transform. What once was flesh and blood slowly collapsed into a pile of dirt. The Umbral Knight turned to dust and blew away in the wind. Tadgh spun to look for Shonn in time to see Oshu fade away.

Then the planet's reality field rushed to catch up. The result was catastrophic. The ground for miles around roared in anger. Farmers' fields cracked, spouting steam from underground lakes. Just as suddenly, a massive thunderstorm formed. Torrential rain and strong winds pelted them. Thunder cracked above them. And the fortress began to collapse.

"Gods blast it!" The Sage grabbed Tadgh by the shoulders. "Do you have any idea what you've done?"

Tadgh screamed over the rumbling of the earthquake. "I did what I had to do! If someone you loved was in jeopardy do you expect me to believe you would do any different? Wouldn't you do everything in your power to save them?"

The Sage punched the air and grunted in anger. "We don't have time for this. The building is collapsing beneath us. It will be faster if you can get Shonn out of here yourself. I'll head below and look for Menphis." He opened a teleportation field and was gone.

Tadgh ran towards Shonn, who had fallen to his knees on the roof of Lord Vyken's room. The stone building beneath him cracked, collapsing as quickly as the fortress around them. Tadgh jumped on the roof, collected Shonn in his arms and jumped again. It was just in time. When he looked back the entire stone structure was gone.

"Did you do this?" Shonn held a hand over his wound as he looked around at the destruction.

Tadgh grimaced. "Yeah. I think the Sage wants to kill me. Let's wait until we're somewhere less natural-disaster-like to talk, okay?"

Tadgh and Shonn looked over the side of the building.

"Can you jump?" Shonn asked.

Tadgh looked at the blood on Shonn's torso. "If I was alone I'd chance it. But hitting the ground from this height would be too risky with you in this condition." He turned and headed for the stairs. "Hold on. This is going to be close."

The entire fortress was collapsing. Everything shook, and the air filled with piercing screams. Lord Vyken's army was now dust, but the servants were still very much alive. As Tadgh and Shonn headed for the ground floor, panicked men and women rushed past them, looking for escape. Tadgh moved as quickly as he dared; the stairs kept shifting beneath him.

"We're not going to make it!" Shonn shouted into his ear.

"Not helping, Shonn!" Tadgh sped up a little as they reached the main floor. Chunks of ceiling fell all around them. One servant, a young man, was trapped under a large section of stone. Three others tried to pull him free. Nothing they did seemed to be working.

"You have to help them," Shonn said.

"I have to get you out of here. That's more important."

"No, it's not." Shonn clutched at Tadgh's armor. "They can't lift that stone off him. He'll die in here. And it's all because of what you did for me. You have to help him. I'll never be able to live with myself if you don't."

Tadgh grunted and set Shonn down. "Fine. But if we die I'm never going to forgive you."

He approached the servants, but when they saw him they screamed, frightened by his feline form.

"Relax," he said. Tadgh bent over and grabbed the stone slab. "I'm here to help. Be ready to move him." With his amped-up strength, he easily lifted the stone off the trapped man. The others dragged him free and raced towards the exit. Tadgh lowered the stone again.

"Thanks," Shonn said.

"Can we go now, or is there anyone else you want to save?" When Shonn shook his head, Tadgh lifted him up and ran towards the main gate. Rats were everywhere, running between the legs of the escaping servants and the horses from the stables.

Up ahead, in the fields beyond the fortress, a pool of light flashed. Tadgh ran towards it. The Sage and Menphis stood beside a teleportation portal, waiting for them. They were guiding frightened men and women through it to escape the destruction.

Shonn smiled at the sight of his cousin. "Are you okay?"

Menphis was pale and his eyes twitched. "Better than you, by the looks of it." His voice was not as confident as his words.

"Family reunion later," the Sage said. "Get to safety first. This portal leads to the main square in town. We have to get away from here. The whole area is unstable."

"I had no idea it would be this bad," Tadgh said.

The Sage lowered his voice. "Actions have consequences, Tadgh. You hacked into the reality field of an entire country. Do you have any concept of how many people you just killed? But this is not the time to discuss that. We'll talk about this later."

Tadgh looked back at the fortress. All the towers had collapsed, the walls caved in. The fields surrounding the fortress were cracked and uneven.

'What have I done?' Tadgh shook his head and stepped through the portal.

***

Hours later, Tadgh sat in the Sage's living room with the others. Eiodeesh kept touching the bandages on her face and arms. She spoke quietly with Gnocko while Tadgh sat in silence. Shonn and Menphis, both wearing bandages as well, sat in a corner speaking quietly with each other. With shaky hands, Pwella served tea and biscuits. Her eyes darted over to Barnes, who stood at the window looking out over the city. Everyone was waiting for the Sage to return.

"He should be back by now," Barnes said.

"You said he was speaking with the city leaders," Tadgh said. "If politicians here are anything like they are back home, that could take hours."

"It's already been hours." Barnes took a deep breath and exhaled slowly. "I've never seen destruction on this scale before. No one around here has. Hundreds of homes in the city are in ruins. Boats in the harbor capsized. People are agitated. There are no reports of fatalities, which is a miracle, but the hospitals are full."

Tadgh felt his throat constrict. "I didn't know it would be this bad. I thought I was doing the right thing."

"That's just it, Tadgh." Barnes crossed his arms and stared at the floor. "I think you did. By destroying that army you prevented a war. Thousands of people would have died, most of them innocents. The damage would have been much worse. That war could have lasted generations. Those people out there might never truly understand what you did for them today, but we do. I do. So thank you. Thank you for stopping them."

Tadgh blushed and closed his eyes. Hot tears formed behind his lids. He could no longer speak.

A circle of light appeared in the living room. The Sage stepped through, wearing the same blood-stained and dirty clothes he had fought in. "And that is exactly why I never wanted to rule the world. Seriously. Dealing with politicians all day has to be the worst job in existence."

"How did it go?" Barnes came forward and helped the Sage take off his ruined jacket.

"As well as could be expected." The Sage rolled up the sleeves of his shirt and sat down on a chair opposite Tadgh. "They believed the story we came up with. I told them Lord

Vyken captured a volatile fod sel-onde and was using him to crack open the Void. Something went wrong. The fod sel-onde died, causing massive destruction. Thankfully, I was there speaking with Vyken and found the Nizarian mapping system. It's lucky for us you found it. That went a long way towards proving the story."

"I still don't understand why you had to tell them I died?"

The Sage looked over at Gnocko. "Tell him."

Gnocko took the dark glasses off his face and looked Tadgh in the eyes. "You were being tracked, son. A full squadron of soldiers from Karaj Robat was in town looking for you."

"What?" Eyes wide, Tadgh looked back and forth between Gnocko and the Sage. "By whom? How?"

"I warned you," the Sage said. "Aside from the destruction, each time you use your abilities you send out ripples. The effects can be felt far away. God knows how many people felt the effects when you destroyed Lord Vyken's army. They probably felt it around the world."

"Or further," Gnocko said. "Whatever you did, I felt it. It hit me so hard I nearly blacked out. I was spying on the people following you when the earthquake started. They knew you were near, but the fieldbenders with them were having trouble pinpointing you."

The Sage nodded. "As long as you were in my home the tracking spell was blocked. My guess is Vyken had similar protections around his fortress. Gnocko studied the tracking spell they placed on you and disengaged it. But there would be no hiding you after this. They need to think you're dead. You need to stay that way."

Shonn leaned forward on the couch. "What does that mean? What are you going to do to him?"

"Relax, Shonn," Tadgh said. "I think I understand. As long as I never use my wish ability again they'll continue thinking I'm dead."

"Exactly." The Sage lowered his head and stared pointedly at Tadgh. "If you so much as wish it would stop raining the trackers will be on you again faster than you can blink. My lies were able to save you this time. Don't expect me to be there if you mess up again. Now, I think we need to discuss our next step."

Menphis exchanged a long look with the Sage before continuing. Then he turned to Shonn. "Cousin, you're not going to like what I'm about to say. You're going to want to interrupt me, but please do me a favor. Let me finish. The Sage and I both agree you should head to Castle Nizaria. They have people there, Neurotechs, who can help you gain control of your abilities. Now that the Sage has amplified them up, you need training. More importantly, you are Tadgh's biggest weakness."

"Wait a minute!" Shonn jumped up. The sudden movement nearly reopened his wound. Wincing in pain, he placed a hand over the bandages on his torso.

"No," the Sage said. "We're serious. Tadgh nearly leveled the city to protect you. You need to learn to protect yourself. I can see this is not easy for you, Shonn, but I'm afraid I must insist. If you want me to keep Tadgh's secret, to keep telling everyone he died in Lord Vyken's fortress, prove to me he'll never have to break the planet for you again."

Tadgh turned away. "I think he's right, Shonn."

"You want me to go away?"

"Don't be stupid." Tadgh patted his eyes dry. "I don't want you to go anywhere. But it's the right thing to do. It will also give us some time to get clear on things. I know you're sure your feelings for me are real. I'm not. This will give you a chance to prove it. If you still have feelings for me in a year, maybe it's real."

"I don't need to wait a year to tell you my feelings are real." Shonn stared at the ground. "But I'll leave if you want me to."

"Fine," the Sage said. "A Pharocai is scheduled to be here tomorrow afternoon. A young Nizarian woman named Kisma has been assigned to be your tutor."

"What about Tadgh?" Gnocko asked. "You can't just let him wander around. He needs to be secured."

"He's not a prisoner," the Sage said. "Making him one would only make matters worse. He needs training. Discipline. So I'm sending him back to the monastery. Now that Lord Vyken's armies have been destroyed, he should be safe there. They were the only ones who could tie him to that place." The Sage leaned forward and put a hand on Tadgh's knee. "You're not a prisoner, but I strongly discourage you from leaving the monastery for the time being. We both know you could use the discipline. Maybe with the training of the Brotherhood of Tyche you'll be less likely to use your wish power to get out of every situation."

Tadgh closed his eyes. "Instructor Mal said my path ended at the monastery. Maybe he was right. I know it was wrong to use my power like that. Even after seeing all the destruction it still feels like I made the right call. Maybe a year or two of training is exactly what I need."

"I'm glad you agree." The Sage stood and clapped his hands. "I'll have Pwella make us a meal. Shonn, you'll have one last night to say goodbye to your cousin and Tadgh. Now that everything's settled, Tadgh, perhaps you can tell me what the hell you were thinking heading up to Lord Vyken's room in the first place?"

Tadgh blushed. "Sorry. It wasn't my idea. Really. I met a woman at the fortress. She told me I had to see something up there."

The Sage frowned. "What woman?"

Tadgh shrugged. "I don't know much about her. She was waiting for us in the library. She just told me I had to go upstairs to Lord Vyken's room. I saw her at the monastery a few weeks ago. I don't know how she got here or who she came with. But I noticed something about her. Her eyes..."

"What about them?" The Sage knelt down beside Tadgh.

"They were normal. I mean normal for Earth. She said her name was Andy. She had brown hair and..."

"No." The Sage shook his head repeatedly. "That can't be. It's not possible. I saw her die."

Tadgh leaned back. "Wait. Do you know her?"

"I need to see what you saw." The Sage grabbed Tadgh. Both of his hands clenched around Tadgh's head. "Show me her face!"

Pain like razor blades cut across Tadgh's brain. Seconds later, the Sage released him and fell backwards to the floor. Tears fell down his face and his lips quivered.

"It's not possible. How?" The air grew very hot and the Sage's eyes flashed with fire. Then he pounded his fists against the floor .The house shook. He opened a portal and left without another word.

"What. The. Hell?" Menphis stared back and forth between Tadgh and the spot where the Sage's portal had been. "Is anyone else here completely confused?"

"I think we all are," Gnocko said. "Obviously the Sage knows something we don't."

Chapter Twenty-Nine

Shonn lay in bed, his bandages recently cleaned and changed.

"That should do for now." Menphis took his hands off Shonn's stomach and exhaled slowly. "I've healed you as best as I can. I've stopped the bleeding, but don't push yourself too hard. You could reopen the wound."

"I'll be fine," Shonn said. "Besides, I'm heading to Castle Nizaria. They have the best healers on the planet."

Menphis smiled. "That's debatable." He stood and walked to Tadgh, who stood in the doorway. "I know you want to say your goodbyes. Please make it quick. My cousin needs his sleep."

Tadgh nodded and Menphis left the two of them alone. "Does it hurt?"

Shonn looked at his wound. "It's better now, after Menphis did his thing." Shonn shook his head and sat up in bed. For a moment he said nothing. He kept his eyes focused on his hands and took slow breaths. Tadgh could tell he was on the verge of saying something, but didn't want to press it. Finally, Shonn sighed and ran his fingers through his hair. "I don't know what to do, Tadgh. The last few days have been terrifying. I'm supposed to head to Castle Nizaria and just pretend none of this happened? Every night for the rest of my life I'm going to look outside and wonder if there's a graunskyeg or Umbral Knight hiding out there in the dark. How do I live with that?"

Tadgh shook his head. "Sometimes, when you see the darkness for what it really is, when you find yourself thrown into it, sometimes you can't go back to your old life. I'm going to do what the Sage said. Head back to the monastery and train. I came here looking for a way home. I realize now that's not going to happen. I did very bad things, Shonn. Unforgivable things. All because bad things were done to me. My amnesia was a way for me to hide from the truth. I was frightened by what I'd become. But I can't spend the rest of my life running away. Face your fears. Fear isn't a reason to run away from reality."

"Perhaps you should take your own advice." Shonn looked up from his hands, eyes fixed on Tadgh. "Stop running away from me."

Tadgh turned away. "I should get back to my room."

"Stay." Holding a hand to his bandages, Shonn got out of bed and walked over to Tadgh. "Sleep beside me for one night. Gods know if I'll ever see you again."

Tadgh hung his head. "How about a compromise? I'll sleep on the floor. Deal?"

Shonn groaned and ruffled Tadgh's hair. "You are the most ridiculous man I've ever met, Tadgh Dooley. Suit yourself. But when I come back from Castle Nizaria don't expect me to be so accommodating."

Smiling, Tadgh sat on the floor and leaned against the wall. He watched as Shonn slipped beneath the covers and closed his eyes.

***

Menphis stood at the window to his room, watching the lights of GardenKeep. Repeatedly, he touched the bite marks on his neck. Although he'd already used his abilities to close the wounds, tiny scars remained that refused to heal.

'The house is quiet,' he thought. 'Everyone else must be asleep. Tyche's curse. I don't know how I'm ever going to sleep again.'

"Ah, where is your bravery now?"

Menphis spun around, fists clenched. The voice, horribly familiar, sounded as if it was right in his ear, yet no one was around. He searched the shadows in the corners of the room and ducked to look beneath the bed. His nose wrinkled as a scent filled the air: cinnamon and burnt bark.

"Leave me alone, Teric." Menphis thought of running to the door but decided to stand his ground.

"Or what?" Teric's voice grew stronger, as did the stench. "You'll turn me away with the power of your faith? Pretty boy is tasty but not very bright. You have no power over me now, no matter how strong your faith. I'm only here in your mind. Where is your god now?"

"What do you want, unclean monster?" Menphis found courage in the fact that the graunskyeg was not truly in his room.

"Ah. Better. There's the bravery I tasted in your blood. I told you last night what I want. I want to play. That's the reason you're still alive." An image appeared, hovering in the middle of the room. It was Teric's disembodied face: pale skin, sharp fangs, and red-tinged eyes.

"You're not real." Menphis' mouth dropped open in surprise. "You can't hurt me in here."

"I'm real enough. However, if I wanted you dead it would have been much simpler to kill you at the fortress. I could have drained the blood from your delicious meat, but good toys are hard to find. It was in my best interest to keep you alive. I would strongly recommend that you tell no one about our relationship, however. I would hate to have to kill your friends. Your family back in Tarkon. Your cousin. Don't pretend for a second he'll be safe from me amongst the Nizarians."

Menphis took a step forward. "I will destroy you."

Teric chuckled. "Perhaps you will. That's why this is so much fun." Teric's face faded away, but the voice remained. "Go wherever you want, pretty meat. I will find you. Our game is just beginning."

Chapter Thirty

"You look preoccupied."

The Sage turned to look at Latimer, who sat beside him at the marble table in Karaj Robat. Unlike the last time the Sage was here, the room was nearly empty. Only a few fieldbenders were present.

The Sage closed his eyes. "I found out something impossible last night. I'd rather not get into it now. It's a personal issue." When he opened his eyes, he found Latimer staring at him intently. "Who are we waiting for?"

Latimer's eye twitched and he hung his head. "You're not going to like it."

The Sage furrowed his eyebrows. He looked up at the sound of footsteps approaching. Sirion and Eschandel walked into the room. Between them was a third man with a long, dark gray ponytail and sharp birdlike features. He was barefoot and topless, wearing only loose raw-hide pants. Scars covered his chest. Strangest of all, his left forearm was a different color than the rest of his skin. It was pale white like new-fallen snow. The left hand ended in long, thin fingers completely unlike those on the man's right hand.

The Sage jumped to his feet. "What the hell is he doing here?" The Sage stared at those long fingers, specifically the one adorned with a gold ring.

"Nice to see you again, too," Defksquar said. "I understand your animosity towards me, but I think you'll agree matters have progressed past the point when we can afford personal vendettas. Time to put the past behind us."

"In your case it's not the past I'm concerned about." The Sage unbuttoned his jacket and, placing his clenched fists on the table top, leaned forward.

"Do tell." Defksquar grinned. "Every time I've seen you I hear you say things like that. As far as I know, we've only met once on your homeworld. A short meeting interrupted by your father. I have no idea why you hate me so much. You know something, don't you? Something about the future."

Fire flashed in the Sage's eyes. "I know what you're planning to do, Defksquar. I know how many people on Earth are going to die because of it." The Sage turned to Latimer. "I warned you. I told you if he was involved I was out."

"Please." Latimer stood and put a comforting hand on the Sage's shoulder. "I've never understood the source of your anger, but I respect it. Still, we don't have time for this. Lives are at stake on this world as well. Defksquar has information that will help us. Put your anger aside for twenty minutes."

"Anger like this cannot be set aside." The Sage returned to his seat. "Speak your piece, Defksquar. Then get out of my sight. Don't make me kill you."

Defksquar sat at the table. "If I'm correct, you won't be able to kill me. Not yet anyway. Somehow, I think you are from my future. Killing me would create something of a paradox. Now, if we're through with posturing, how about we get on to important issues?"

"Yes," Sirion said. "Now that we're all here, perhaps the Sage can tell us what the hell happened in GardenKeep? It felt like the world folded in on itself."

"It did." The Sage reached into his pocket and retrieved the Nizarian crystal. He placed it on the table before him and the map appeared in the air above the table. "At least for a bit. Lord Vyken was working with the Quadumvirate. What you're looking at is a war map recovered from his fortress just outside GardenKeep. He was building an army. You can see from the numbers it was sizable and in several locations. He also had a powerful fod sel-onde in custody, one capable of complete control over the reality field."

Latimer scratched his chin. "You mean a wish power?"

The Sage nodded. "Yes. That was the source of the disturbances that cracked the Void. What you felt was the fod sel-onde losing control. Lord Vyken pushed him too far.

The fod sel-onde retaliated and wished Vyken's armies were dust."

"They're all dead?" Eschandel wiped sweat from his forehead. "All the soldiers represented here are dead? Dear gods. That kind of power is terrifying."

"My sources say yes," Defksquar said. "We have witnesses that saw thousands of people turn to dust. Which is fortunate. That many soldiers hidden in Shirza would be catastrophic. The fod sel-onde did us a favor. But the cost was high. Unfortunately, it also widened the hole in the Void. Other things have fallen through. There have been reports of Hermadurs all across the southern continent."

Everyone at the table held their breath. The room grew suddenly quiet.

"Heavens," Latimer said. "Where is this fod sel-onde now?"

"Dead." The Sage folded his hands and placed them on the table. "The exertion was too much for him. He died before the fortress collapsed. I'm sure you're aware of the devastation. We're lucky there were no fatalities."

Eschandel frowned. "Yes. Lucky."

The Sage looked up. The same expression appeared on everyone's face. "Hmm. You think there's another force at work here?"

Latimer turned in his seat to face the Sage. "It is unrealistic to think a disaster that powerful would leave no casualties. Not a single death reported outside the soldiers. It beggars belief. Are you sure this fod sel-onde is dead?"

"Yes, he's dead." The Sage took the Nizarian crystal off the table, the map disappearing. "But I think you may be right. There are definitely other forces at work here. This situation is completely out of control. We have no idea what the Quadumvirate are planning. Don't we have agents inside Castle Dispayre?"

"Of course," Latimer said. "They've given us nothing useful. We know Amir Durgen has teams searching for something in Té Vark. But we're currently blind to anything else Myan and the other two are doing. That's unusual in and of itself."

"They're planning something big," Sirion said. "But what's the connection between GardenKeep and Té Vark? And what does it have to do with these reports we have of strange activity near the copper mines of Surransin and troop movements near Castle Falls?"

Eschandel opened a manila folder and placed it on the table in front of him. It was filled with lengthy documents and photographs. "These reports are from the Nizarians. GardenKeep and Té Vark have one thing in common. They were both once locations of Beherskers' cities."

"That's what Lord Vyken said." The Sage leaned back in his chair and ran his index finger along his lower lip. "He showed me a map of the ruins beneath GardenKeep. He had also systematically been stealing from the royals and council members of the city. Behersker relics. What the hell are they looking for?"

"I believe I know." Defksquar waved his fingers and an illusion appeared above the table, hovering in the same place the map had occupied. To the Sage it looked like a three-foot-long spark plug. It was gold, covered with gems: diamonds, rubies, sapphires, and emeralds. "What you're looking at is a very rare Behersker artifact. The Verdenstab. Its name translates roughly to World Staff or Power Rod. It is part of a device the Beherskers used to control land masses and weather patterns. The same device could also, in theory, rewrite the cellular codes of entire species or create entirely new species."

"You're talking about the terraforming machine." The Sage jumped to his feet again, fist clenched. "The same thing you're trying to transport to Earth. You bastard. This is all because of you."

"What are you talking about?" Eschandel rose to his feet and looked the Sage in the eyes. "Do you know about the Verdenstab?"

"Yes." The Sage buttoned his jacket and turned away from Eschandel. "I told you not to trust this man. Defksquar plans to take this device and activate it on my homeworld. When he does it will destroy Earth and turn it into something else. Millions of people will die because of this device."

Defksquar waved his hands again and the illusion disappeared. "Can you imagine how many will die if it is activated here? Maghe Sihre has a population ten times that of Earth. Over 60 billion people. Think about how many people here will die if the Quadumvirate gets their hands on the Verdenstab and then try to paint me as the villain. Hate me all you want. I care about my world and will do anything to protect it. It's time to pick a side. Which world are you going to protect?"

The Sage turned to look at Latimer. "I'll say it again. If he's in, I'm out. You cannot trust him. And if you can, I can no longer trust you."

Latimer hung his head and took several deep breaths. "I'm sorry, Sage. He's our best lead."

The Sage looked around the faces at the table. No one would return his glance. "Fine. I wish you all good luck, then. You're going to need it."

The Sage walked out of the room. As soon as he was clear of everyone's watchful eyes, he opened a portal and returned to GardenKeep.

Chapter Thirty-One

"Here comes another one." From the patio on the third floor of the Sage's house, Shonn looked up at an approaching Pharocai. Hands clasped, he leaned his forearms against the railing and watched the sky. "Do you think that's the one coming to get me?"

"Too early." Menphis, standing beside him, shook his head. "The Sage said it wouldn't be here for another hour. Now, can you please stop all the pacing? You're driving me crazy. Why don't you go back inside with Tadgh and the others?"

Shonn shook his head. "It's better I don't. Tadgh has barely looked at me this morning. And all Eiodeesh and Gnocko talk about is some sort of deal they worked out with the Sage."

"Yeah. It sounds like they signed up for some sort of reconnaissance mission for him. They're heading up to Té Vark for some reason."

"That's on the other side of the planet."

Menphis bit his lip and turned away. "When we were younger, Castle Nizaria seemed like it was on the other side of the planet. And now you're going there." He turned back to briefly look at Shonn. "You've changed, you know. Something in the way you stand or the curve of your eyes."

"Changed how?"

Menphis shrugged. "Stronger. More confident, I guess. Also a little dangerous. You shouldn't have let the Sage do that thing to you. It was stupid."

"No. Running off with people you don't know to spy on an army, *that* was stupid. I took an educated risk to save your butt. And it worked." Shonn sighed and ran his fingers through his hair. "Let's not fight. You'll be leaving soon, heading back to the monastery with Tadgh. I'll be miles away surrounded by strangers. Who knows how long it will be before we see each other again. I don't want my last memory of you to be a fight."

Menphis gave his cousin a hug. "Like I said. You've changed. But maybe that's a good thing. Come on. Let's go inside. Tadgh and I should get going. I'm going to miss you."

Shonn pulled away from the hug and punched his cousin playfully in the arm. "I'll miss you too."

***

"Is it really going to be that bad?" Tadgh stood in the corner of the kitchen, hands in his pockets.

"Worse." The Sage stood nearby, staring at the ground. "In a few months, that device will be activated. I can't stop it. The way my powers work, I can't be in two places on the same planet at the same time. That means I can't go back to Earth until after I left."

Tadgh shook his head. "Maybe I'm a nerd, but that actually made sense."

The Sage laughed. "Afterwards, the entire world will change. That's why I left. If I stayed, more people like me would be created. That would be bad. Now imagine more people like you. Think about the consequences of dozens of people with your abilities. Going back home is not an option for you. The best thing to do is head to the monastery. Does Shonn know what you did before you arrived here?"

Tadgh shook his head. "No. I don't know how to tell him. I was a monster."

"Correct. Past tense. You did bad things. Make up for them. You're a strong man, Tadgh. Play your cards right and one day people may even call you a hero."

Tadgh laughed and turned away. "I think that's a bit of a stretch."

"Names have power." The Sage walked up to Tadgh and placed a hand on his shoulder. "That's why no one knows my real name. I chose the Sage because I wanted to be known as a wise man, a man of knowledge, not a man of war. Your name means something. Dooley comes from the

Celtic Duhlaoich meaning 'dark hero'. I think that's appropriate."

Tadgh looked confused. "If you say so."

Menphis walked into the kitchen. "It's time, Tadgh."

"Of course." Tadgh extended his hand towards the Sage. "Thanks for everything."

The Sage shook his hand. "Same to you. Take care at the monastery. And remember…"

"I know, I know. No powers, or else." He put his hands behind his back and stared at the ground. "You can trust me. I never want to do that again."

All three of them walked back to the balcony off the living room. All conversation stopped when they arrived. Pwella and Barnes stood arm-in-arm by the railing. Eiodeesh and Gnocko stood opposite Shonn.

The Sage cleared his voice. "My home hasn't seen this much adventure in years. You're all leaving, heading to very different parts of the world. Be careful out there. We stopped Lord Vyken, but don't think for a moment this is over. The world is about to become much more dangerous. Once I had powerful allies. Now, the people in this room are the only ones I can trust. With any luck I can stop this thing on my own. But if things change I may need to call on you again."

"Of course." Menphis bowed slightly. "We are in your debt."

The Sage looked out over the city as the others shook hands and said their goodbyes. He searched the streets for the familiar face of the woman he had thought was dead. Now that he knew she was back, he would never stop looking for her.

***

Inside the bakery across the street from the Sage's house, two figures watched Tadgh and the others through the window. One was the woman who had called herself Andy. The other was a man with pale skin and snow-white hair. He was dressed in black robes. A sheath was attached to his waist, but there was no sword in sight.

"How much longer do I have to do this?" The woman put her hand on the glass and slowly traced the outline of the Sage.

"Not much longer," the man said. "I know you want to go to him, but the time isn't right."

She sighed and turned her back to the window. "When will it be the right time?"

"Wisdom, or the Sage as he calls himself here, still has a part to play." The man cleared his throat. "When that part is over we need to remove him from the playing field. In his heart, he's a hero. He won't want to leave when things get rough for the others. So we need motivation. You are the love his of life, Andromeda."

"You know I hate that name."

"Then why did you tell the boy your name was Andy?"

"Well, I couldn't very well tell him my real name, could I? Wisdom believes I'm dead. He can't know I'm here. I still think you're wrong about him. I don't think he's going to give it all up for me. He's lived without me on this planet for centuries."

The man's eyes grew distant. "Love like yours never dies. We should go before he senses us. Take a last look. You won't be seeing him again for a while."

The woman, whose real name was Echo, pulled her hand off the window. A tear rolled gently down her cheek. She didn't bother to wipe it away. Then she turned and, with the flick of her wrist, opened a square of darkness. The man stepped into the shadow door and disappeared.

"Bye, my love." Echo looked over her shoulder one last time at Wisdom. She bit her lip, stepped into shadow, and closed the door.

Epilogue

Deep in a hell dimension far from Maghe Sihre, a group of demons held court. Thousands of twisted shapes stood in rows: horned humanoids with red, reptilian skin, intangible shadows, one-eyed titans, eight-armed blue creatures and monstrous imps. All faced seven grotesque giants sitting on seven identical thrones. The crowd murmured in anticipation as a solitary figure moved towards the thrones.

Bes approached the lords of hell.

"You've kept us waiting," one of the giants said. "You continue to try our patience."

Bes, the size of a large lion, bowed, head near the ground. "Apologies, lords and ladies, but I had to be sure of my facts before I presented them. The force we all felt shake the worlds was in fact the boy. We've found Tadgh Dooley."

Once of the giants crossed his legs and leaned back against the throne. "You've left that boy out in the world long enough, Bes. Power like that should not be in the hands of mortals. Tell me, does he understand where his power comes from?"

Bes raised his head. "Of course not, my lord. I told him nothing. He has no reason to believe we were monitoring him before he wished for vengeance. He has no idea what he truly is. If you give me leave, I'll head for this planet, Maghe Sihre, and retrieve him."

"Fine," a female giant said. "Bring him back to us. You did well forcing those boys to attack Tadgh. Like you predicted, killing his friend was the right impetus to turn him into the monster we need. Then you let him slip away. Failing us again would be a mistake."

"Understood," Bes said. "I will not fail again. I will search the entire planet if I have to. One way or another, I will drag Tadgh Dooley down to hell."

Coming in Sept 2014 – Demons of DunDegore

What's Next – The Worlds of Maghe Sihre and Earth
Have you ever read a book that changed the way you think about fiction? For me it was actually two books, *Desperation* by Stephen King and *The Regulators* by his pseudonym Richard Bachman. The amazing thing about these books is they are versions of the same events told simultaneously in two different worlds. *Desperation* is a literary horror novel; *The Regulators* is more pulp fiction. That gave me an idea.

Two worlds. Similar problems. Shared characters. Different genres.

Council of Peacocks
If you're interested in the origins of the Sage/Wisdom and how he gained his powers, check out *Council of Peacocks*. It is the first in the Activation Series. On that world, he is known as Wisdom. He trains a group of half-demon young adults to fight a group of evil sorcerers, the Council of Peacocks. The Council plans to use the Verdenstab to take over the planet.

That book also has the first encounter between Defksquar and the Sage/Wisdom. If you want to know why the Sage/Wisdom was convinced Echo/Andy was dead, *Council of Peacocks* also has that backstory.

UPCOMING WORKS BY M. JOSEPH MURPHY

Beyond the Black Sea
As for how the Sage/Wisdom ended up on the planet of Maghe Sihre, put Book Two in the Activation Series, *Beyond the Black Sea*, on your to-read list. (June 2014.)

Demons of DunDegore
For the continued story of Tadgh and his companions, be sure to check out Book Two in the Sword of Kassandra series. Bes tracks down Tadgh and sends an army of graunskyeg, led by Teric, after him. The Quadumvirate finds the Sword of Kassandra. And the war begins. *Rise of the Graunskyegs* (Sept 2014).

Joseph Murphy was born and raised in Ontario, Canada. He earned his geekdom at an early age. He read X-Men comics from at the age of 8 and it only went downhill from there.

As a teenager he wrote short stories and wanted to be the next Stephen King. Instead of horror, however, he kept writing fantasy stories. After surviving high school as a goth with a purple mohawk, he studied English and Creative Writing at the University of Windsor.

When not writing, Joseph works as Lead Accounting instructor at Everest College. He also lectures to other businesses on outside-the-box marketing. He lives in Windsor, ON (right across the stream from Detroit, Michigan) with his husband, two cats, and shy-but-friendly ghost.

www.ingramcontent.com/pod-product-compliance
Lightning Source LLC
Chambersburg PA
CBHW060629260626
47161CB00008B/2841